Bowl of Red

Sarah A. Hoyt

Goldport Press

Contents

1

IT HAD BEEN A dry winter in Colorado, following an exceptionally dry summer and fall. Now at the tail end of December, a dry but freezing wind, carrying particles of ice like an excoriating whip, flung through the streets of the town, making the Christmas decorations dance.

It was almost dark at three pm. Which was good, because in his room, in his parents' house, in one of the old suburbs of the small mountain town of Goldport Colorado, Rafiel Trall, Officer of the Serious Crime Unit of the Goldport Police Department, lay in uneasy sleep.

It had been busy all through Christmas, mostly make-work as the new Police Chief insisted on "organizing" the force.

He needed a nap. Desperately. He was supposed to be Tom's best man at Tom and Kyrie's wedding. He had to be awake and alert.

The howling wind poured into his dreams, turning into baying in his darkly-dreamed night.

In the dark forest, Rafiel, in his lion form, stood in a dark clearing in an impenetrable forest, while around him the snow blew and bit, and thoughts not-his echoed in his mind.

He was vaguely aware of his human body, on his bed, in his cozy book-lined bedroom. But the lion in the dark forest didn't know it. The lion was all alone, terrified. At any minute, a claw would come from the darkness and flail him. He could feel death and hatred in the darkness he couldn't see through.

Out of his fear, he decided he had to make a stand. He set all four feet firmly on the spongy, shifting ground. Throwing back his head, he opened his mouth and roared his defiance.

The thin cold air came in through his mouth. Particles of ice penetrated his flesh.

Round about things that weren't lights, but more like light reflected upon unblinking eyes, ten, a dozen, a thousand, came on, and from the darkness around him, carried round and round by the whipping wind, came the sound of mocking laughter, and words, spoken in a high and thin singsong voice, as if by a deranged child, "Kitty, Kitty, Kitty. Come and be killed."

The lion jumped and made a yelp-like sound. A claw reached for him– tearing, slicing–

Rafiel woke, up a strangled scream in his throat. He was covered in sweat, and his heart raced, as though he'd run a long time.

There was a knock at the door, and his fiancé, Bea, asked, "Raf? Are you all right?"

"I'm fine. Just a nightmare." His eyes, adjusting to the scant light in the bedroom, fell on his tux over the chair in the corner. Tom's wedding–

He looked at the alarm clock on the bedside. An hour. "I'll shower and get dressed," he shouted back.

But he felt slow, stupid, and as though that horrible dream meant something terrible would happen. On Tom's wedding day.

Rafiel shook his head. No. Nothing bad would happen. Rafiel would not let it.

Atop one of the highest mountains of the world, there lived a dragon. And the dragon was the most powerful beast in the world, able to listen to – and control – all of the magical animals everywhere.

And the dragon looked nervous as he said to his bride, "Are you sure it will be all right? Closing the diner for a whole hour? The week between Christmas and New Year?"

Kyrie Smith, the dragon shifter's bride, a panther shifter, and co-owner with the dragon – her very beloved and permanently worried fiancé, Tom Ormson – of *The George Diner* in downtown Goldport, Colorado smiled while shaking her head, and pulled back a strand of dark curls that had worked free from Tom's ponytail. "It will be fine, love. It's just an hour, after lunch hour and before the dinner rush."

Tom still looked worried. Tom always looked somewhat worried. It was part of what was so endearing about him. But Kyrie had worked hard at blocking the time from three to four pm so that they could get married with a modicum of privacy. The right kind of privacy. Though every table was occupied, it was occupied by their friends – a lot of them from the police department, others, regulars at the diner – and people who mattered to them, not whatever rando might wander in from Fairfax Avenue.

Rafiel Trall, one of Goldport's finest, and a lion shifter, patted Tom on the shoulder, "Come on. You'll be fine."

Rafiel wore a tux, which looked odd to anyone used to seeing him in Hawaiian shirts and white pants or jeans. He was nominally Tom's best man, not that anyone was getting that formal about it. "It's actually impossible for the diner to go under in the time it takes Anthony to pronounce you man and wife."

Tom looked doubtful, and Rafiel smiled. Tom mumbled, "That's what you say."

Anthony, server extraordinaire – he'd taught both Kyrie and Tom the trade of table service – stood nervously between the salad station and the corner booth, wearing a dark suit. His wife, Cecily, carrying their son in her arms, periodically ran out to adjust the hang of his coat or dust imaginary hair from his shoulders. The bridal cake, four layers – created by Laura Miller, The George's baker, who had waved away any attempts at payment – was topped with a plastic couple, created by another diner regular – by bashing gaming figures– and didn't look particularly like Tom and Kyrie, except for hair color, but were both attired in aprons that read, "The George," over their bridal clothes.

Kyrie thought that, all in all, it was a very fitting setup. And more than she could ever have hoped for growing up as an orphan without a family or a steady environment.

Conan Lung, dragon shifter, former enemy turned friend, sat at one of the small booths by the window, dressed in the western wear he'd adopted when his country and western singing career had started showing signs of life. He looked a little lost between the ten-gallon hat and the cowboy boots, but no one had the courage to tell him that, and at any rate, his fiancé Rya liked him that way, so what did it matter?

Kyrie herself had just switched her normal jeans, T-shirt, and apron for a short formal dress in ivory. This had been done because everyone else said she should have a wedding dress. It was just that wedding dresses rarely came in maternity sizes, and she was due in two months. Which meant her belly was huge, and sometimes you could see the imprint of a foot as the kid kicked out at the world.

Tom had proposed months ago, but it had taken this long to organize the wedding. And for Kyrie to get over her jitters.

Which was silly, honestly. After all, she and Tom owned a business together and were having a baby together. At this point, marriage was an afterthought, and just a way to make sure everything was legal, should anything happen to one of them. It was just that Kyrie had been alone so long – basically her whole life before Tom – that much as she longed for a family, she was also used to having sole control over her life and hated the idea of relinquishing any of it.

But Bea, the dragon shifter who was dating Rafiel, had come to spend Christmas with his family. And the loose friend group who called the diner their home away from home had come together and told them to get married already.

So. Kyrie took a deep breath, smiling at the crowd around them. So. They were getting married.

Rya and Bea had pinned a short veil over her multicolor-dyed hair. She thought it looked slightly silly, to be honest, but it also seemed strangely formal and traditional. At that moment, she'd stopped being just Kyrie and was now that strange, symbolic creature, "the bride."

Honestly, she should just have had Tom and his friends kidnap her and call it a wedding. And yes, that idea had been brought up by the trio – Tom, Rafiel, and Conan – and heartily endorsed by Cas, Nick, Jason, and all the other miscreants. They'd probably have done it, except that no one could figure out how to kidnap Kyrie from her home and bring her to Tom's when they lived together.

Kyrie grinned, remembering the suggestion that they should kidnap her and run around the block three times before bringing her back. In her mind, they were a massed multitude of their shifted forms, dragons and lions and bears, running around carrying a very pregnant woman.

That would surely have given the various cryptozoologists and collectors of weird news something to write about.

Tom gave her an odd look, and she realized her smile must be very strange. She shook her head at him and smiled.

He gave her a dubious once-over as though wondering if she had some secret plan but never said anything because just then, Rafiel came up.

"Come on, bridegroom," he told Tom. "I don't want to have to marry your woman. Bea would burn my feet off."

Tom laughed, and Rafiel pulled Tom towards the front, near Anthony.

Kyrie shook her head again. Bea – probably already dreaming of her own wedding – had choreographed this whole thing. According to the script, Kyrie moved way back to stand near the cash register. Tom's dad, the only parent in attendance, came up from where he'd been waiting at the door to the annex and gave Kyrie his arm.

Kyrie swallowed a lump in her throat.

She didn't know who her parents were. She'd been found, newborn, at the door to St. Anne's Catholic Church, in Charlotte, NC, on Christmas Eve and been raised in the foster system. Tom's dad had agreed to do the honors.

She couldn't say Edward Ormson had matured much since the time when he'd been a lawyer working for the triads in New York City, but he'd ... grown in different directions.

Tom said that his father was trying very hard to be a good father and prospective grandfather. It was just that he had never really learned how to be an adult, so he mostly got very excited about the idea of being a father or grandfather but really had no idea what that meant. He was already planning the grandkid's first car but would be shocked if asked to change diapers.

Still, he was the best they had, and it was nice to have a parent with them. Weddings were things that called for family, and mostly their family was of choice, not of blood. Except for Edward. All told, Edward wore a very handsome tuxedo, and with streaks of silver on either side of his head, he looked the part.

Even better, Kyrie thought, he'd stopped showering them with the weirdest baby gifts ever, from little squeaky mouse toys to little nets, which he thought would be necessary since he was quite convinced that Kyrie and Tom's babies would be born as "kitten-dragons" with wings. Kyrie hoped she had finally got it through his head that the ultrasounds showed a human baby, male variety.

But she'd rather not make any bets. He'd probably give them a sand-box to use as a baby potty. The best way to look at it was to be amused by the man's insanity and touched by his joy in their relationship. Oth-erwise, she'd live angry. And he meant well, so it wouldn't even be fair.

Conan, looking solemn and strangely nervous, struck up the bridal march on the acoustic guitar.

Edward offered her his arm, and she took it. At the last minute, someone – she thought Cas's ditsy fiancé, ran up and put a bouquet in Kyrie's free hand.

It was white roses, in a tight, circular arrangement, with a wrapping of lace. Looked homemade but very lovely, and Kyrie felt tears come to her eyes. Heaven only knew where Dyce had found white roses in December. She walked on Edward Ormson's arm, slowly and solemnly up to the salad station.

Tom turned. He still looked slightly worried but beamed at Kyrie, his blue eyes filling with appreciation.

A ray of sun came out and gleamed off the polished surface of the very expensive fryer that they were still paying for, and which Tom was perpetually worried would explode.

It was going to be all right, Kyrie thought.

She realized her mistake immediately afterward when there was a bang behind her, and a flash of light reflected from the polished metal surface of the salad station.

Tom had just thought that Kyrie was the most beautiful bride in the world.

His throat tightened when looking at her, and he wasn't sure how he'd gotten this lucky. If someone had told the confused youth he used to be that someday he'd own a diner, be the center of a group of devoted friends and marry a gorgeous woman, he'd have thought they were nuts. He was still nervous about the whole baby thing and unsure how to be a father, but as long as he had Kyrie at his side, he would be fine.

And then, as he was looking at his amazing bride making her way from the register to the salad station, something exploded at the door to the diner.

There was a loud bang, a flash of light in his peripheral vision, and, looking up and at the door, a cloud of smoke.

And Tom said words he never thought he'd say on his wedding day. The words were perhaps shocking to the people around them, or at least to those who didn't know that Tom was a dragon shifter and not the only one in the world, but part of a complex hierarchy of dragon-kind.

The words that reluctantly tore from Tom's lips were: "Oh, no! Enter the dragon."

To the other shifters, they were all too understandable, evoking nervous laughter from Rafiel and Bea, while Conan played a sour note and stood up, pale and trembling, obviously reliving the trauma of his previous life when he'd been handed over to the dragon organization – who in the modern world operated as a triad – and treated as disposable chattel until Tom had ransomed him.

On the other side of the scarred glass-and-aluminum door of The George, under a light swirl of snow, stood a dignified Chinese gentleman of apparent late middle age wearing a traditional red silk gown embroidered in a fantastical riot of gold and silver. To either side of him stood two young women similarly attired, and behind him were four younger Chinese men. All of them were in red, and the women wore elaborate red headdresses and even more elaborate makeup.

They stood like someone waiting politely for a doorman to open the door. Tom groaned. This was all he needed. He hadn't told them. They weren't family. Okay, so the Great Sky Dragon might be his many-times ancestor, but they weren't family.

They were enemies, or perhaps friends, adversaries who sometimes allied.

And then the four men behind the lead man ... er, dragon, threw what had to be very large red paper balls at the ground, and there were bright lights and big bangs.

"Did you forget to invite the evil fairy to the wedding?" Rafiel asked Tom *sotto voce*, leaning forward.

This was perhaps unfair since the gentleman at the door, while a legend, was in no way a fairy or spirit, evil or otherwise. In fact, by his lights –

his own very peculiar and Neolithic-informed lights – he wasn't evil at all. He was the patriarch of the dragon clan, the Great Sky Dragon, practically a god, and in fact, until recently, the most powerful shifter in existence. Recently....

Tom didn't know if the Great Sky Dragon understood that this power – the command over every shifter on Earth – had been ripped from him, nor if he knew Tom held it. What Tom did know is that he, personally, wasn't about to mention it. The very thought of it made him clench with fear of the results.

What he also did know – for absolute sure – was that he hadn't told anyone in the dragon clan when his wedding was supposed to be. And yet, here the dragons were.

Damn it. He'd been trying to keep it simple. And normal. And human.

He took a deep breath, nodded, and said with as much dignity as he could, "Conan, would you open the door?"

Conan stood and shook, and the guitar plinked forlornly. Rya patted him on the shoulder and headed to the door, and Tom called himself several kinds of names. Of course, Conan still lived in fear of the dragon triad. He'd once been a slave of the Great Sky Dragon with almost no self-will. Tom shouldn't have required him to do anything like go close to the old horror.

Rya opened the door and pulled it all the way back because it seemed indicated. The Chinese procession came in as a procession.

Behind them scurried three women. That was the only way to describe it. They also wore all red but did not have elaborate headdresses. And they were like ninja dressers and decorators or something. Tom blinked, and they'd tied something red and drapey around Kyrie's waist over the baby bulge and put a red sash around Tom's bewildered father's middle, over the tux, and draped red cloth on tables and booths on either side of the makeshift aisle that Kyrie was walking.

Tom growled softly as he realized that he, too, now wore a red sash and that they'd draped a sort of red curtain around Anthony's shoulders. Rafiel patted Tom on the shoulder in a way that meant it was probably not worth it to eat anyone over this.

Anthony's open mouth gave witness to his shock if at the emergence of red everywhere or at the speed of it, Tom didn't know.

A few of the guests, now blocked from the aisle by red fabric, giggled nervously. He was vaguely aware that there were more Chinese people streaming into the annex. Someone must have opened the back door in what had once been a large, enclosed porch when this building was a home. It was sort of an overflow area, furnished with plastic picnic tables and chairs. He had no idea what all those people were doing there. And he was afraid to find out.

He felt annoyed, but over it all was a bubbling amusement at how nonsensical it all was. Seriously, being descended from the Great Sky Dragon at probably a hundred removes should not cause this sort of disruption to one's life. What the heck? Most people didn't even know who their hundred times great-great-grand was. No, make that no one who wasn't a shifter knew. And Tom would be quite happy never to have known.

He managed to meet Kyrie's eyes, relieved to note they looked amused rather than appalled. It could go either way, and he was glad she wasn't letting it ruin her wedding day.

The Great Sky Dragon smiled, bowed, and Tom swore that a thin streak of grey smoke curled from the man's lips, as though to show Tom he still had a few tricks to learn. Tom fought hard not to roll his eyes.

And then–

He saw Kyrie lean and say something to Rya, who whispered in Conan's ear.

A shaky rendition of the bridal march started, and Kyrie and his father resumed walking towards him. And Tom forgot the Chinese contingent and all the insanity surrounding them.

Tom never thought he would get married. Not since he was sixteen and realized he could change into a dragon. And did. Often without meaning to. Heck, for the longest time, he'd been afraid that he'd never be able to have a relationship or even sex. After all, who knew what might happen if he shifted in the heat of passion?

Yet, here he was at twenty-four, about to get married to the world's most beautiful woman with whom he co-owned a diner, and about to be a father. Take that, odds. He was winning.

If this required him to have a gaggle of nominally ancestral, vaguely criminal, definitely half-crazy Chinese invade his wedding, so be it. He smiled at Kyrie.

Kyrie had never thought she'd get married. First, because she'd thought she was hideously insane, since she kept having these weird dreams of turning into a panther and roaming the night. Second because after she became aware she really was turning into a panther, she had been afraid of doing something terrible to the prospective groom.

But her groom was well able to look after himself. Even if he worried obsessively about the fryer exploding, no matter how many times they told him that was actually impossible. And even if who and what he was meant that his wedding would get crashed by a supposedly mythical entity and the alleged mythical entity's crazy relatives.

Nothing mattered but that Tom was smiling again. She allowed Edward Ormson to walk her up to Tom, right there by the refrigerated salad bins, with the bowls on a shelf overhead, and then Tom took her hand.

Anthony cleared his throat, "Who gives this woman to be married to this man?"

"I do," Edward Ormson said, all very proper.

And then there was the Great Sky Dragon standing by Tom's side, edging Rafiel aside and almost into the corner booth and declaring full voice, "And I give this man."

There was a scattering of titters, and a dull thud, that Kyrie could see out the corner of her eye was Conan dropping his head with force onto the scarred Formica table.

After that, nothing much mattered. Not even that Anthony wore what appeared to be a red bedspread, elaborately embroidered with silver and gold dragons, which he held with his left hand as a shawl, while he asked the crucial questions that would bind them for life.

There was a flurry at the time of the rings. There had been a dispute about the rings, before. She and Tom had agreed they would get silicon rings, because they couldn't really afford nice gold ones, and anyway, since they worked with their hands, silicon rings which stretched and could be washed with soap were obviously better. Also, they wouldn't be a big loss when they broke and fell off at shifting. You could buy them in bundles.

Then Tom's dad had heard about it, and presented them with traditional wedding rings in gold, and said he didn't want to hear any protests. "For the ceremony and to keep for special occasions when you're not going to shift," Edward had said. "You can wear silicon day to day."

And now....

As Rafiel reached for the rings, one of the elaborately-dressed-with-headdress females was there, staying his arm, bowing and whispering.

She handed Tom an open small red box, and bowed and smiled a closed-lipped, formal smile.

Tom hesitated, then cleared his throat, bowed awkwardly back, and took one of the rings from the box. His voice was scratchy-hoarse as he said, "With this ring, I thee wed, with all my worldly goods I thee endow, in the name of the Father, and the Son and the Holy Spirit," the formula they'd agreed on, because Tom was Catholic and she, despite the place she'd been found was not. So this, as everything else, was negotiated.

It wasn't until the Chinese lady bowed and presented the box to her that Kyrie realized the rings were elaborate filigree, cut in phoenix and dragon shapes. Kyrie slid it onto Tom's finger, saying the traditional oath, and then they held each other's hand, Tom's hand reassuring and warm clasping hers, while Anthony said, "Then by the power vested in me by the State of Colorado, thanks to the mail-in-church ordination, I pronounce you man and wife. You may kiss the bride."

Tom reached for her, grinning, and enveloped her in his arms as he kissed her.

It was the best day of Kyrie's life.

It was after that that things got strange.

Caught between laughter and a growl at how insanely everything had got disrupted, after all their planning and choreographing, Rafiel had found his way to Bea's side.

"I couldn't even give him the rings," he told his fiancé. "And, you know, that's the only function of the best man.

Bea laughed. "That and marrying the bride if the groom is a no-show."

"Yeah, but if I married Kyrie, you'd burn my feet off."

Bea grinned at him, her eyes soft. "If you were lucky. I might roast you whole."

She was a dragon shifter, who had flown from Atlanta for the occasion, and arrived chilled and complaining at his family home the evening before Christmas, to be fussed over by Rafiel's mom, who didn't bat an eye when Bea said that the worst part of flying at night was the cold and the bugs in your teeth.

Of course, Rafiel's mom knew that Bea was a dragon shifter. And was so happy her lion-shifter son had a girlfriend that she didn't care. She might care a little if Bea roasted Rafiel's feet off. At least till they grew back, which was the nifty part of being a shifter. Or maybe she wouldn't even care about that.

The day before, Rafiel had found the two women clucking and talking over his baby pictures, and felt a bit left out at the comradery and secret communication between them. As though they had something that went back to the dawn of time, a power and organization older than civilization and maybe older than words. Probably older than the Great Sky Dragon's organization.

It scared him a little. It probably had always scared men a little. Which might explain a lot about human history.

Bea's smile at him was wholehearted, though, and she reached out to grab his hand when he got near and whispered, in between the vows, "You don't have some great old ancestor who will descend on you when— you know?"

The "you know" was delicate because though he'd asked her to marry and they were engaged, she was only twenty and hadn't finished her art degree. Which she was doing in Atlanta, Georgia, near her parents. They would get married. They both knew it. When, though, would remain open for another year or so.

Rafiel smiled at her, "Not that I know. If the lion tribe has a patriarch, he hasn't revealed himself to me. Of course, maybe I'm the black sheep or something."

"You're not even a black lion," she said. And he laughed and kissed her.

And then the wedding was done, and somehow there were a lot of the Chinese people around, and the Chinese people were pushing Kyrie and Tom while surrounding them. The real wedding guests were somewhere behind. Rafiel caught the eye of the definitely-not-shifter girlfriend of Cas, one of his officers, who looked bewildered and smiled, "Restauranteurs mutual support association," he said, reassuringly. "The owner of the Three Luck Dragon is the president."

He heard her whisper the explanation to someone, which was good, because what the Chinese had done in the annex...

Not only was there red cloth draped on every wall, and red paper lanterns – with candles inside – hung from the ceiling, their light visible in the failing light of late afternoon in winter as the snow increased outside, but the tables had been forced together in the middle, draped in red, and covered in various delicacies. He could see a Chinese hot pot in bronze, with dragons carved around the sides, and there were tower-plates with things he didn't even have the name for, a lot of them either painted red or wrapped in what he suspected was red rice paper.

Aimee Morgan, in shifter form a secretary bird, in human form a sweet, motherly woman, and – as a volunteer at the zoo – the peacemaker of the zoo shifters, went around fixing the way the rice paper hung, and arranging the plates more aesthetically. Which made perfect sense, because she was a born mom.

Through the throng, Tom's plaintive voice came, "But we have to open. It's already been almost an hour."

And the rumble of the Great Sky Dragon's voice, which always seemed to have an echo of thunder behind it, "No. Some things are important. Each of your weddings should be important."

Each of Tom's weddings.... Oh, that was going over like a lead balloon.
He didn't understand why the GSD – as they'd come to call him among
themselves – was counting on Tom having multiple weddings. Shifters
lived very long lives, but Kyrie was a shifter too. Then again, it was entirely
possible that Tom inhered some extra power from head dragonhood. Who
knew? Or maybe the GSD believed in concubinage.

Tom and Kyrie didn't. If Tom tried, Kyrie would get downright testy.
Not that he saw Tom trying.

Rafiel swallowed a chuckle at the look the bridal couple turned on the
GSD. Who, fortunately, was not the kind to catch fire, obviously, and who
smiled inscrutably in return.

And then everyone was talking and eating, and the strangest groups
formed, including a young Chinese lady, not one of the headdress ones –
Rafiel suspected the headdress ones were the GSD's wives or concubines or
something – talking at Tom's dad. She was young and beautiful, and Edward Ormson smiled with a slightly dazed look. And two elderly Chinese
men were talking to Anthony, who kept bobbing awkward bows as if he
felt this was necessary because they were Chinese. It was all fog-shrouded
mountain peaks and bows, as far as Anthony's mind could see.

Tom and Kyrie were handed bowls of food and looked awkward but very
happy.

Outside, several of the Great Sky Dragon's people set off multiple fire-
crackers, and passersby were starting to gather, as well as what looked like
a group of bewildered customers by the door.

Laura Miller said, "Coming through!" And she and Rya carried the cake
to the big Chinese banquet table.

After that, it became even more of a whirlwind.

Tom watched as the GSD, smiling, carved two Chinese characters –
or rather, one character, twice – on the wall with a fingernail. Which
shouldn't be possible, of course, but it happened anyway, and it left behind
glowing, smoldering tracks in the paint. Tom sighed. He would have to

find out what those characters meant. Because as far as he was concerned, it could be anything, from "hot and sour soup" to "a curse upon this house."

But when he caught the GSD's eye, the older man smiled as though he'd done something nice for them, so Tom smiled back, probably a bit nervously.

Then the older man bowed. And as guests started to disperse, and Kyrie went to the storeroom to change into her normal work outfit, the Great Sky Dragon moved closer to Tom. "I will be back for the naming," he said. He handed Tom a red silk envelope and seemed to be waiting for something.

As Tom looked at him, the old Dragon sighed. "I don't know how to tell you this, but there will be a ... problem. There is something headed your way. With the Others. Keep your wife safe. And the son she carries. The future is always the most important thing. Without it, we live in vain."

Tom had absolutely no idea what that was about. It sounded like something from the I-Ching, which, now he thought about it, the Old Sky Bastard might very well have written, or at least inspired.

But he also didn't understand why the Great Sky Dragon was so against Kyrie marrying him before, and now had swung about to support their marriage. But then again, he never really understood the affairs of dragons. Even if he was one, and nominally their head. Maybe.

At any rate, none of that mattered, as he needed to go change for work. Because he'd be damned if he was going to man the fryer in formal clothing. The fryer would sense that this was a rented tux and explode all over him. Even if he survived, he'd never get the oil out of the tux. And between the cleaning charges and the new fryer, he'd be ruined and have to close the diner. And then how would he feed his kid? No way was he going to risk that.

Going into the storeroom, he almost bumped into Kyrie coming out. She smelled of cake and candy and leaned down and brushed his lips with hers, warm and soft and full of promise, and he still had a maniacal smile on his lips ten minutes later as he exited the storeroom, with a red scarf tied around his head, pirate style, to keep hair from falling on the grill, and his apron firmly in place over jeans and much-washed light blue T-shirt.

There was a plethora of orders on the counter, the diner was full of regulars, and people attracted by the commotion. There was a line down the block, people talking and laughing, and waiting as if this were some big premiere of a well-advertised movie, or a mega-bestseller.

And there was a slight extra bounce to Kyrie's hips, as she delivered another order to the counter, as Tom swung into action, throwing burgers on the grill. "An order of souvlaki and Greek salad, husband," she said, her voice on the edge of song.

He looked over his shoulder and grinned at her. "I'll get that started right away, Mrs. Ormson."

They shared a smile he knew was probably daft, until Tom's dad came to the counter. He'd put an apron over his tux, and Tom wasn't even really surprised. Rafiel was out there too, checking on tables. Dad didn't normally help with serving, but he'd done it before. As for staining his tux, Tom happened to know the man owned three tuxes and had a new one made for the wedding because "the others are out of style" so even if this one got ruined, he could afford a new one. And heck, he could afford the cleaning bills, too.

"Sandra says that what the GSD carved on the wall is *double happiness,* both the symbol for a wedding and a wish for good fortune," his dad said.

"Good. I mean, *won ton soup* would be okay too, but *double happiness* is more appropriate," Tom said as his father laid another order slip on the counter. "And who the heck is Sandra?"

"Sandra Li, the young lady I was talking to. I think she's like a hundredth cousin. She's also descended from the Great Sky Dragon. Not that we count hundredth cousins, which is good because apparently, your mother is, too."

"Ew. I don't want to know how inbred the dragon clan is," Tom said, and read the order, and started eggs frying. He'd called his mother, actually, and informed her of the wedding. She'd congratulated him but said she couldn't come. Not that he expected otherwise. She lived in Florida with her husband and had a bunch of kids, and Tom thought she'd quite forgotten her first marriage and her first son. Or at least she'd like to.

After a few orders had been filled, Rafiel came up. "Hey, what did the GSD give you in that envelope?"

"Um, I left it in the tux pocket in the storeroom. Probably a dire warning. I mean, he also gave me a verbal warning. Something about some big bad heading for us and keeping my wife and the future safe."

"Lovely."

"Yep. So I'll read it tomorrow. Not on my wedding day."

Rafiel tilted his head to the side.

"What?" Tom asked.

"Well ... I mean, it might be...." Rafiel said but trailed off as Kyrie sashayed back once more, hips swinging. "Anthony says he'll stay and help with the tables, but I should come back here and help you, because one person alone can't keep up on the grill and fryer. And that it doesn't matter if we're really cozy behind here. Being married and all."

Tom smiled. "I'd like to be cozy with you," he said.

And they were, even though they worked so fast that sometimes it seemed like they'd grown extra arms, as they bumped and sashayed their way around the grill and fryer.

As the rush subsided and the orders became more spaced, Rafiel came up to the counter on the way to the coffee pot for warmups. "Hey, if you guys want to take off, Anthony says he'll take the shift till tomorrow morning. A couple of other people are offering. And you should have at least a twelve-hour honeymoon." He blushed. "I mean, you know, it's decent."

Tom was touched. "Sure. We'll leave at eight, okay? Let us finish the dinner rush."

Just then, a group came in and Tom felt as though all his senses were pulled toward them.

He frowned at a mixed-race family of six. Part of it, he thought, was that every member of the family that came in looked tense. He followed the group of what looked like a black grandfather, a black Mom, a blond bespectacled Dad, and three teen daughters to a large table in the annex.

He couldn't say why they disturbed him. They shouldn't have. After all, this was a downtown diner, and though Goldport was not big on crime and people were more likely to fight with credit cards than knives, he knew they had hosted gang members in the diner. Worse, they had had members of rival criminal gangs in the restaurant at the same time. And he really hadn't been apprehensive or cared much. Because they might start something as soon as they left, but given the police presence that was more-or-less constant in The George, no one was going to start anything here. And people who had seen weird things and weird animals in the back parking lot were double cautious.

So, there was no reason for this family group to ping his alarms. But they did. Lots of three or four-generation family groups came to The George because the neighborhood had been populated by immigrants. Mostly Greek and Italian, then Latin immigrants. All of which ran both to big families and tight family ties.

Not that this family was local. Their clothes, and the way they moved, proclaimed them from out of town and way better off than the locals.

Tom knew the family being mixed race didn't bother him, because... because it didn't. They'd never been able to figure out what race Kyrie was. She got discounts from Greek suppliers, Middle Eastern suppliers, Spanish suppliers, Italian suppliers, and all ethnicities, who assumed she was one of them.

Second, Tom was descended from the GSD despite his blue eyes and pale skin, which he took to mean that humanity was humanity and equal parts curious and insane so that they copulated with anything that moved and had babies with anything that was genetically not too dissimilar.

But third, because he remembered the morning the eighteen-member – not counting babies –three-generation family had come in composed of middle-aged suburban-looking white parents, with three sons, one of which had married a blonde woman, one an Indian woman, and one a black woman. He had felt oddly reassured by the teen kids coming in as a big group, talking and laughing and bickering like family, and by the babies getting passed around and loved on by everyone regardless of external appearances. That family and the way they interacted remained one of Tom's favorite memories, his touchstone against the idea that the world was going to hell. It was as though he'd been vouchsafed reassurance it wasn't, and people were mostly decent.

No, the race mix wasn't what bothered him.

They sat down and Anthony approached to take their order when the old man waggled a finger at Anthony and talked in an obviously angry way.

It seemed a strangely aggressive way to treat a server who hadn't even said hi yet.

Um ... yeah. Maybe he and Kyrie should take the night off.

2

As things slowed down, Kyrie turned around and cast a look over the place, trying to figure out who was on shift and who on what tables. Normally this was well established, but right then things were in a bit of flux, because–

For instance, Anthony wasn't supposed to be on duty. Still, after he and Laura took the remaining cake into the storeroom, and cleared away the banquet table, including a large plate of leftover food brought by the Great Sky Dragon's people, he'd come back out, gone into the men's bathroom, and come out again in jeans, T-shirt, and apron, and carrying his tux, which he put in one of the storerooms. And he was now offering to work twelve hours, so she and Tom could have a "honeymoon."

Conan had also changed, before coming to sign in – officially – to work. Rya was helping him and said she'd stay twelve hours, though she was only part-time help usually.

The Great Sky Dragon's people left – except for one who was talking to Tom's father – Kyrie guessed she should learn to think of him as her father-in-law – but at least half the other guests, including most of Goldport's Finest, sat down at booths, and ordered food, as though they hadn't just demolished a fantastical amount of Chinese food. Kyrie made a face remembering what people said about Chinese food disappearing from your stomach. It had never been her experience, but whatever.

In addition, every booth and table was taken, including the annex, from what she could see. Yeah, they were going to need more servers. She caught sight of James Stephens in the crowd and gave him a nod. He looked surprised but came to sign in as a server.

Food orders were getting delivered; Tom was at the fryer and grill. And she supposed, God was in his Heaven, and all was right with the world, but she felt weirdly unsettled, as though something tugged at her consciousness. Something pulled at her, as though there were something major, she should have done and had forgotten.

She felt the baby move, which was the strangest of feelings, like ... like there was a little person inside her, and he was changing position. More and more like a real person, now they could see a protruding foot or hand, as though he were saying "let me out." She grinned at the thought and patted her stomach. Of course, he was a real person. Maybe a shifter, but definitely human.

But she wasn't used to the idea. Like she wasn't used to the idea that she couldn't shift, which seemed to be part of pregnancy, but was highly annoying.

Of course, if she could shift, the way she felt right now, all jumpy and expectant, she might very well shift and *eat* someone.

Which was her clue to realizing she was hungry. It would have to wait. Maybe after she got through this batch of orders, she could go and have some cake or something.

Instead, she took her position next to Tom, plating food as soon as it was done.

"We should set up an electronic system for the orders and payment," Tom said.

And she didn't even say it wouldn't happen. At this point, she was used to Tom coming up with one more improvement for the diner. At least it wasn't a machine that made doughnuts in the shape of fingers for Halloween. And, hey, maybe an electronic system would be useful.

She had just finished plating a couple of burgers and fries, by rote, when Anthony came back to drop off a batch of orders and looked at her with a frown.

"There's a customer who wants to have a talk with you. He's very insistent."

She frowned at Anthony. "To me? Who?"

"No one I know. That table, in the annex. The one in the middle. He asked for you. He seems pissed, for some inexplicable reason. He said you owed him coming and talking to him."

He pointed at a table where six people sat. It appeared to be a middle-aged couple, three teen girls ranging in age from twelve or so to sixteen or so, and an elderly man. The elderly man and the woman were of definite African origin, he darker than she. From the features, he was probably her dad. The younger man was blond and blue-eyed, and the three girls were obviously the children of the couple. The oldest and youngest looked no particular race, kind of like Kyrie herself; the middle one looked like she had a good portion of ancestry from Africa, but if she straightened her dark hair would pass either way.

The thing that arrested Kyrie's eyes was how angry the older man looked. He was glaring imperiously at her, like he expected her to obey his summons, right then, and no talking back.

She frowned back at him. She felt – There was a weird sense like he was trying to dig into her mind, which was probably her imagination.

A warm hand touched her shoulder and she jumped. Then realized it was Tom.

"Anything wrong?" Tom asked.

It wasn't like Tom could ever say precisely what caused him to turn away from the fryer – risking a potential explosion, whatever other people said – to look at Kyrie.

When he did, she looked tense and Anthony, standing by the counter, looked even tenser.

Tom gave the timer on the fryer a look. He had five minutes before the timer ran out and something – potentially – exploded. Or the fries burned. Whichever came first. He turned back to Kyrie and asked what was wrong.

The weird thing was that she jumped like he'd startled her. Like she'd expected an attack from someone. Which didn't even make any sense.

When she told him what was going on, or at least what Anthony had told her, he remembered the GSD telling him to keep his wife safe. He put his hand on Kyrie's shoulder. "Wait," he said. "I had a really bad feeling when they came in. And I didn't know why."

She narrowed her eyes at him, not as though upset, but more like trying to figure out what he was thinking, then she sighed, "I feel as though the older gentleman was trying to feel my mind. Probably my imagination."

But Tom had lived with crazy shifter politics too long to dismiss such a thing. He extended a probe towards the glaring gentleman. And yelped.

Kyrie had seen Tom make that gesture, but never in human form. He usually made it in dragon form when he'd smelled something particularly unpleasant and his paw went up reflexively and he rubbed at his nose with the back of it. Now he rubbed his nose with the back of his hand. "Don't go near that table," he said, "under any circumstances."

Kyrie raised an eyebrow.

He smiled sheepishly at her, "Not an order, but I had a warning." He told her what the Great Sky Dragon had told him and added, "That old man is a shifter. Actually, I think they're all shifters, though the two younger girls probably have never shifted. But– He's a shifter. And he feels ancient. Maybe as old as the GSD. He slapped away my probe."

"He what?" Kyrie asked. "I thought you could feel the mind of every shifter."

"Yeah, so did I. Anyway, I think I can feel enough. He's dangerous. Don't go." He saw her open her mouth as though to protest, but she closed it. Tom told Anthony, "tell him no. Tell him we're actually going home, and anything he has to say to Kyrie he can give you a note. We'll deal with it later."

Kyrie had been about to protest that she could take care of herself when several things occurred to her: that she wasn't in fact just taking care of herself, but of herself and a child, who was Tom's child too.

Tom understood what she hadn't said, of course, as he always did, which was the most amazing thing. It wasn't telepathy, but close enough. He told her about some vague warning from the GSD, and then–

Something was really wrong with that man if he was a shifter and Tom couldn't sense what he was thinking or probe his mind.

As she looked, an argument seemed to erupt at the table. The older girl must have said something, because the old man stood, yelling at her. She couldn't hear what they were saying, but the girl didn't back down, putting her hands on her hips and yelling back.

The old man threw his napkin down and stormed out, shoving between a group of people getting in. The blond man who was almost for sure the girl's father reached across and put his hand on the girl's shoulder. After a while, she sat down.

"That was interesting," Kyrie said, taking a deep breath. "Tell you what. I'll go to the storage area and grab some cake. I'm starving."

He grinned at her. "If I say you're eating for two, will you hit me?"

"Not hit you," she said, kissing his nose in passing. "Hit on you maybe."

"Yeah," he said. "That's how we got in this mess." He gave her a peck on the lips. "Go on. I'll join you as soon as Anthony comes to take over the grill. Leave me a little bit of cake, yes?" He was only half joking. Yes, he knew there was more than half of the huge cake left, but in the last month, Kyrie seemed to have lost all sense of proportion when it came to eating.

"Maybe. A very little."
*****

Tom didn't know how long it took for him to get worried. Even though the flurry of orders had slowed down, there was still enough to keep him occupied. The dinner hour was extending a little past eight, perhaps because so many of the regulars had heard it was their wedding day. And Anthony didn't come within shouting distance except when Tom was busy talking to customers.

He felt both happy and a little embarrassed at the number of people who dropped by the counter and handed him an envelope, saying, "Something for you and Kyrie, as you guys start out."

The envelopes usually didn't contain much. fifty dollars here and twenty there with the very occasional hundred now and then. But they were the gifts of people who, themselves, by and large didn't have much. So he got tearful and thanked them very sincerely and didn't want to interrupt them to tell Anthony to take over.

And then one of them asked, "Kyrie went home?"

Which was when Tom realized, looking at the clock, that it was nine pm. Kyrie had gone to eat cake at ... seven thirty? How long could it take? Even if she tried to eat the whole cake?

She said she'd wait for him. Maybe she'd fallen asleep. Falling asleep was, after all, something that came over her with disturbing frequency and ease these days. Like ... a new superpower. Yesterday he'd watched her standing in their tiny kitchen, drinking a cup of tea as her eyes slowly closed and her head nodded, while the tea trickled onto her T-shirt.

Afterward, they'd joked that fortunately, the kitchen was too small to allow her to fall, but really, it was almost disturbing. He was starting to suspect that being pregnant was much like being a shifter, a condition that was completely different from normal humanity, and which couldn't ever be fully understood by anyone who had never done it.

He caught Anthony's eyes across the room, and when Anthony came near, he said, "Okay, can you take over? I need to go see what happened to Kyrie. She said she was going to the storeroom to eat cake. I think she might have fallen asleep in there."

Anthony grinned and his eyes had a reminiscent look. "Oh, yeah, the sleeps. Cecily had those the first six months of her pregnancy. I couldn't let her drive because she was quite likely to fall asleep behind the wheel."

Tom took off his apron, wrote his hours in the schedule, wrote Kyrie's hours in the schedule because she'd forgotten, and headed for the storage room, where they kept clothes to change into when shifting ruined them, as well as anything that didn't need refrigeration, from plasticware and paper plates, to vats of sugar and flour. He was thinking that it was important to keep track of their hours because Kyrie said it was. Which was a bit silly, actually, since when it came to being paid, he and Kyrie always took their pay last, as it was more important to keep the employees happy and working. If someone got shorted, it was them. But then–

But then Kyrie had told him it was important to track their sunk costs, too, because they were, in a way, expenses. And their goal was to bring the diner to where income exceeded expenses, including their expenses in time and effort.

Which was why she counted as hours the time spent doing the accounting, too. Very organized and professional. Really, how had he got that lucky in marrying the hottest of women, who was also a genius?

He opened the door to the storage area and stared stupidly, blinking his eyes.

The storage room was empty. Not empty exactly, but empty where it counted. There was no Kyrie. There were the massive, industrial shelves crammed with things, of course. There were bins of flour and rice and other supplies. And there was a table with the cake and other stuff that didn't need to be refrigerated, including a huge bowl of fortune cookies.

But no Kyrie.

It took him a moment to register there was a slice of cake on the floor, amid the shards of a broken plate. And a plastic fork. As if she'd been eating and dropped the plate.

What the heck? Sure, that could have happened if she fell asleep, but then she'd be here, asleep.

His heart speeding, his breath catching, he wandered out of the storage area. Maybe she'd gone to the car? Though he couldn't imagine that Kyrie would just go out and not pick up the plate and the cake and clean up, unless if she'd suddenly become nauseated or whatever.

But she wasn't always acting rationally while pregnant. And everyone told him that was normal.

He stepped out of the diner into the Colorado winter night. The chill air bit at his exposed arms, and fine snow swirled, stinging his eyes. "Kyrie?" he asked the empty night, but there was no sound in return.

The parking lot was still completely visible with the lights on.

Their car was there, parked between the two panel vans they used for supply runs. It was a tiny, dorky car, and technically it was Kyrie's, even if she had endowed him with half of her worldly goods. He looked at it, trying to discern if there was someone sitting in it, but it was obviously empty, so he looked around.

Between the door and the car, there was something – he thought it was a wrapped gyro that had fallen and been walked on, but – approaching – it looked both familiar and weird on the pavement. It was Kyrie's little tapestry purse: yellow and brown, embroidered in an abstract pattern. Rya had made it and given it to Kyrie for Christmas last year. It lay open on the asphalt, spilling its contents: Kyrie's wallet, comb, lip balm, and a battered paperback book.

He bent to pick it up, then thought that he shouldn't because it might be evidence. And then he bent down and picked it up, anyway. It couldn't be evidence of anything because nothing had happened to Kyrie. Absolutely nothing. Nothing could have happened to her while Tom was in the diner, talking to people. He would have felt it. He had to have felt it.

He was telling himself that, and bending to pick up the purse, when he saw it, on the other side of the car – visible between the front and back wheels.

There was a human shape on the ground, in the shadow of the supply van nearest the secondary dumpster. In fact, the shadow was so deep between the two things that though he was absolutely sure it was a human body – he realized he could smell blood in the air – he couldn't really see anything of it except the vague shape of a shoulder, and blue cloth.

Where do one's fears come from?

Things crisscrossed in Tom's mind, paralyzing him. The Great Sky Dragon talking to him about his "weddings – plural – and the warnings about something bad, and–

He had to force himself to walk around the car and the van step by step. It was like he'd either forgotten to walk, or like his feet weighed a million pounds apiece.

But long before he reached the body, he knew it wasn't Kyrie. There was a leg extended, with a male shoe on the foot.

And there was a pool of blood under the body.

He took a deep breath. Which was a bad, bad idea, because the scent of blood came with it and to the dragon blood meant a fresh kill. It meant food. Which was always a danger.

That he knew, Tom had never eaten a human. But there were times he wasn't too sure what the dragon had been up to. And he always feared he had, or he would.

He gritted his teeth and told himself he couldn't shift. No shifting allowed. It just wasn't going to happen. No way no how.

He had to find Kyrie. And if Kyrie was in trouble–

He was now close enough to see the person on the ground. He couldn't tell who he was at all, save that he was large, tall, and male, wearing a pair of jeans and a polo shirt. Nothing else could be told, because from the neck up there was nothing. Except for a whole lot of blood. The head was entirely missing.

He thought of something really bad to say. And then he heard it said, loudly, right behind him, and turned around to see Rafiel maybe two steps behind him.

As he looked, Rafiel took his phone out and called, "Murder victim – looks like – behind The George. I need a team to come and process the scene. Tom?" The last was said after he hung up. "Can you go in and make sure no one leaves The George?"

Tom turned, thinking of yet another string of bad words. He wanted to go find Kyrie. And at some point, having bodies found in or around The George was going to destroy his business.

And he had a son to feed. Or at least he hoped he still did. His heart seemed to contract to a pinpoint at the idea he might not.

Rafiel had seen Kyrie leave, and assumed, if he thought about it at all, that she had fallen asleep in the storage room. He remembered they had a very comfortable chair in there, since they'd had to use it to stash people who were traumatized and tired from having just shifted.

But then he saw Tom starting to look worried, and leaving and–

He'd followed. Tom and Kyrie were family, if not by blood, by everything else that made a family. Understanding, shared experiences, and mutual support. He'd started towards the hallway when he saw Tom wander to the back lot. And Tom didn't look .... right.

Opening the storage area, Rafiel frowned at the cake and broken plate. He rushed out after Tom. Which was when the smell of blood hit him, and he followed his nose to find–

Damn it. What kind of an omen was it to have a murder on a wedding day? He was going to have words with the author of his life, he was.

He called support on the phone. Before he hung up, he knew it was going to be interesting, possibly in the Chinese curse sense. Right now, half of the police force was still hanging around The George, on their fifth order of souvlaki and fries. By half of the police force, in this case, Rafiel meant Cas and Nick, who were cousins but looked like twins, and who were also both wolf shifters.

They'd show almost immediately. Others would be slower. Particularly because most of the others were part-timers. There were the brand-new lab-van and the science people, who probably would take a while to get things together, this being nighttime. Or not. Sometimes he thought the geeks never slept.

He heard his pager go off with an all-hands-on-deck. So, the message had got through. At least they had the brand-new lab van, bought just a few months ago because the city fathers had realized there were a lot of crimes, and the van could help. Because before that they were relying on the coroner's lab and whatever they did there, while now they could process more stuff on the scene.

Unfortunately, with the lab van a Chief of Police had been hired for the serious crimes. While before they had all been more or less equal, at least the senior officers, now they had a chief.

To an extent it was understandable. Faced with an unprecedented wave of murders, the city wanted someone to be the "face" and "voice" of the police department. So, statutes had been reviewed and dusted off and the mayor had appointed an old buddy from Police Department in Los Angeles – where the mayor had lived before moving to Colorado – as Chief of Police.

Rafiel chewed the inside of his cheek thinking about it. The pain matched the pain that Chief Milagros – "Just Call Me Mark" – had already been and was likely to be. It wasn't just that Rafiel had an almost allergic reaction to anyone using the words "trust the process" or trying to impose artificial boundaries and deadlines on police work. It was also that Mark Milagros, poor bastard, wasn't an actual shifter. And while there were a few people in the department who weren't shifters, most of those were part-timers.

While Chief Milagros strutted and posed, and tried to keep the paperwork in strict order, Rafiel was going to have his work cut out for him. Not only figuring out murders, most of which in Goldport involved shifters, but also – heaven help him – to keep Mark Milagros from ending up eaten. Because it had taken Rafiel himself all his self-control not to shift and take a bite, when Chief Milagros said for the tenth time in any given day, "The way we did it in LA–" And from the expressions on Cas and Nick's faces, they were even closer to chowing down on the Chief.

They might as well nickname him Not-Dinner, like Tom and Kyrie's cat. Chief Not Dinner. Rafiel wondered if he'd dress up and come out and enlighten them on crime scene investigation the LA way.

He heard Cas behind him– presumably – talking to Cas's fiancé, Dyce. "Just take E. home. I'm going to be late."

He heard Nick's footsteps. He heard him mumble at his fiancé, Ben, to, "Go with them. I'll pick you up."

Tom was holding Kyrie's bag as he stared at the corpse. Normally, if both of them were normal people, he'd assume Tom was in shock. Or just very worried about Kyrie. Which he probably was, both in shock and very worried.

But they weren't normal people, not by any means. And he could see the tension in the lines of Tom's body and face and how Tom's face seemed slightly elongated. Somehow the whole posture of Tom's shoulders and legs seemed ... *lizardy*, for lack of a better word.

"Tom," he said. "Can you go inside and secure the diner, and make sure no one leaves?"

Tom turned, and his movements were still *lizardy*. Nick grabbed Tom's arm and stepped in front of him. "No. You're all dragon. You can't go in like that," he said. "Control it."

Which gave Rafiel time to rethink sending Tom inside and to go and grab his friend's other shoulder, "Tom. Why are you holding Kyrie's bag?"

Tom turned around. There was a set of under-lids visible beneath his normal eyelids, and his voice hissed slightly as he said, "It ... it was on the ground. I can't find Kyrie."

Which suddenly made sense of everything to Rafiel. Neither he nor Tom were inexperienced shifters, and Tom might have more power than just about any shifter in the world – or maybe out of it, which Rafiel guessed they'd find out sooner or later – and he had the control that went with the power. So it wasn't like just smelling blood should send Tom down a shifting mode with no recourse.

But if Kyrie was missing and he was out of his mind with worry and *then* he smelled blood... the saurian just might win?

He patted Tom's shoulder. "Right," he said. "Right. I see." He didn't actually see much of anything. He was – all of them were, he supposed –

socially inexperienced. When you started shifting in your early teens and worried about scaring – or eating – your play friends, you tended not to have friends. He'd been very lonely till he met Kyrie and Tom. He still didn't know how to express the bolus of worry, affection, confusion, and yet his need to be a policeman, to Tom. Particularly not to Tom.

Clearing his throat, he patted Tom's shoulder again, then said, "Nick, go secure the diner. I'm going to talk to Tom for a moment."

He grabbed Tom's forearm and dragged him across the parking lot to the alley. It was pretty much deserted, though about a block away a guy was slumped on the ground against the wall. Fortunately, Rafiel could see he held a bottle. So probably not a murder victim, except perhaps slow self-murder. He couldn't arrest people for that. Besides, Chief Milagros had issues with bothering "the unhoused." Apparently not what you did in LA either.

"Tom, how long has Kyrie been missing? Can't you sense her?"

Tom turned to him. He blinked again. He had got his face under control, and now just looked lost in the way he hadn't looked in years, not since getting together with Kyrie. Lost in a way that Rafiel had never thought his friend could look.

He only remembered that expression from when Tom was just another of the many rotating servers at The George. Before it was The George.

Back when it was a dive that drifters rotated through as servers.

Tom shook his head to clear it. He hadn't thought of sensing for Kyrie. He just hadn't thought of it. How could he not have thought of it?

Perhaps because it wasn't part of his normal thought. He'd gone most of his life unable to reach people with his mind.

He took his hand to his forehead, rubbing. There was a pressure, not quite a headache, yet, behind his eyes. "I never thought of it. I–" He swallowed hard. If Kyrie were alive and conscious, wouldn't she have reached for him? Wouldn't he have sensed her distress? "It's not like a telephone, you know? It's really– It's hard to reach for the right mind, unless you have line of sight to the person, and even then ... I don't think I control it very well, at the best of times."

But even as he spoke, he was feeling around with his mind, trying to find Kyrie. It was a bit like reaching through fog so dense that he couldn't tell what he was reaching. Periodically his mind touch would find a mind, but he wasn't precisely sure what the mind was until he poked around a bit.

He ran through minds nearby, looking for the feel/touch of Kyrie's mind. There was someone named Aurelia, who was fretting over her daughter. Um ... that must be her husband, Peter, who was also fretting over his daughter, though both had an undertone of relief.

No. He ignored the diner, which for good and sufficient reason had an unusual number of shifters at any time, and particularly now, and quested into the distance, desperately, calling out mentally, "Kyrie?"

He got an impression of dark, of rushing wind, and then.... Nothing.

Which is when the Great Sky Dragon touched Tom's mind. *The Queen of the North is awake. She is here. You are needed.*

Darkness and rushing wind. Kyrie woke up throwing up and became conscious of being high up in the sky. Something uncomfortably tight held her middle, like a belt. But a really tight, strong belt. The baby didn't like it and kicked like crazy. At least he was still alive, she thought, groggily.

And she was.... She blinked as the lights of Goldport swam beneath her. No. As she was carried above it. She threw up again and felt the child move in her. He felt like he was trying to run away.

She reached down and found talons around her middle. A familiar shape. Dragon?

"Tom?" she yelled, her words taken by the wind.

But at that moment she felt his mind-touch, and it wasn't coming from that close. So this wasn't Tom, couldn't be Tom?

And then.... Something interposed between her and Tom, and her mind beat in vain against the barrier of what felt like impenetrable ice.

The police had set up a field headquarters in a corner of the annex, and Tom couldn't believe the speed with which it had gone from his wedding banquet to a crime investigation. And he'd lost his bride. What kind of an idiot lost his bride on his wedding day?

At least it wasn't Kyrie dead in the parking lot, but still he couldn't figure out what had happened or why he couldn't reach Kyrie's mind. And he wanted her back. He desperately wanted her back. She was like half of him, chopped away.

He felt weirdly numb and detached. He needed to do something, to go through the motions, or he was going to go dragon. All he needed was to go full dragon in the diner.

They'd left him for last, after "processing" everyone else. There were police officers–probably police part-timers and volunteers, because there simply weren't that many police officers in Goldport – standing around in the diner, glaring at everyone so they wouldn't talk to each other. Which was good, Tom thought, since his father was looking at him with the kind of look that if it could talk would sound somewhat like a maniac toddler, "Why? What's going on? Why? Where has Kyrie gone? Why? Where is my grandson? Wanna, wanna, wanna, grandson," and possibly, "Kitty dragons now, now, now!"

The rest of the people were nervous, standing alone, or in silent groups, because any attempt at talking was stopped.

Tom turned the fryer off, and cleaned the entire area, as it was usually cleaned during the lull in the night, when the diner was mostly empty. And then there was nothing more to do.

And the whole diner was quiet, and his questing mind could not find Kyrie, no matter how he looked for her.

Tom couldn't stand it. He had to do something. He went to the refrigerated storeroom and got baklava, warmed it up, and started slicing it. Filled the coffee maker, started making coffee, and announced, "Free coffee and baklava for everyone", as he lined the plates and cups side by side on the counter. Anthony came to help him, pouring the coffee, and setting out creamer, sugar, and stirrers in a sort of station so people could help themselves.

Weirdly, Tom noted by the corner of his eye, that most people taking either coffee or baklava or both left a close enough estimation of the cost on the counter, next to the lineup of food and drink. After a while someone – maybe Bea? – got a big glass bowl and put it on the counter for the bills.

It looked more natural, Tom thought, as he came to the end of the baklava and went to get pie, announced the change, and started cutting it.

Most people kept getting coffee and some came back two or three times for the sweets. Part of him wanted to start on the wedding cake, but that seemed wrong. It was his wedding cake. He was supposed to save some to eat on his anniversary with Kyrie.

Tom thought it was because it gave them something to occupy their hand mouths, without speaking. It was unnatural to have that many people crammed into a place, not talking.

From the corner of the annex came a murmur of voices, too low to be understood.

Outside, lookers-in were gathering, and trying to see in. He wondered what they'd make of the groups of silent people eating pastries and desserts.

At least with the head missing, it should be obvious the murder wasn't a poisoning and that it wasn't us who poisoned him.

He wondered who "he" was, and what had killed him.

After a while there was a break in the pattern, as the middle-aged couple who had sat with their three daughters and almost certainly the mom's father was escorted through to the back lot, looking worried. Cas and Nick escorted them, and had their "policeman" face on, so impassive they hardly looked human.

A few minutes later they were escorted back in. The man had his arm around the woman's shoulder, and she was crying. Uh. Oh. He had wondered, though details were hard to discern in the parking lot, and of course, the corpse's head was missing, whether the dead man had been the older gentleman who tore from the table in a huff.

Had Kyrie been back there when the murder took place? Had she gone out back because she'd heard a scream from the back? The man had seemed to want to talk to her. Had he tried to harm her? Had Kyrie? He shut the thought down forcibly.

Behind that were squirrely thoughts, that they might have to figure out a scapegoat if Kyrie had killed a man for cause.

It was implicit in what he did, as leader of local – perhaps all – shifters, that he protected them when their crime was justified but couldn't be explained to normal people.

Except implicit didn't mean everyone agreed. First, Rafiel would kick a right fuss if Tom did something to protect Kyrie that involved dodging the law. Second… Tom didn't want to become the Great Sky Dragon, who shielded his own and punished those against them.

How far was it from there to ordering crimes committed and covering those up, for the right of the clan, and the good of the dragons? Tom didn't know and he wasn't sure he wanted to know.

He felt like he was walking in circles in his mind. Or rather, he felt like he was walking around and around a circle in his mind, round and round and round, as though expecting to reach a different place by following that route.

Would the Great Sky Dragon know what was going on? And, more importantly, would he tell? And if he told, would it be the truth? Because the GSD had a disturbing habit of speaking like an old Chinese oracle. Tom fully expected to hear him say things like, "The disturbance is great. The superior dragon goes forth. No blame."

Thinking about it, he decided the Old Sky Bastard definitely had invented the oracle books, written them in the original, to keep the monkey brains occupied and not interfering with him and his. File that under things that wouldn't surprise Tom one little bit.

And now, even though Tom had slammed his mind's door on it, the Great Sky Dragon was nattering somewhere in the back of Tom's brain about the Queen of the North. Some rivalry between dragons, which couldn't interest Tom less at the moment.

After a while, a police officer – a young woman who very much looked like she was one of the new and part-time recruits – stood at the door to the diner. People who had been interviewed were called one by one to read the transcript of the interview – on a tablet – sign it and leave their contact info. They were then allowed to leave.

Finally, all that remained in the diner were Tom, the waitstaff, and the family whose mom had been crying. They sat at the table they'd been at, and Tom would judge that was police instruction, since they didn't look in the least like they were enjoying themselves.

And looking at them, Tom realized what had been disturbing him so much about the older girl. She looked like Kyrie.

3

I T WAS A MESS. It was a perfect mess. It couldn't be more of a perfect mess if it had been ordered as a mess from Perfect R Us.

Rafiel's head had started throbbing with a headache. Not that he was surprised. Frankly, he was surprised he still had a head, as such. It should have exploded long ago.

He hated this case. To be fair he hated all murder cases, but this case was—

The diner had had fifty-seven people. None of them, except perhaps the man's immediate family, had any reason to be upset at the murdered man.

And frankly, the man's immediate family didn't have much reason, either. After all, not wanting to go to the Natural History Museum was no reason for his family to murder him. Not even the teen daughter who wanted to be a paleontologist could be said to be a good suspect. Besides, none of them had left the table after the argument. Rafiel had interviewed dozens of people who had said that. They'd sat there, talking, trying to calm the teen down.

If the old man –

He had smelled like a shifter. But the area around there was saturated with a different shifter smell. And even if he were a shifter, Rafiel couldn't exactly put that in his notes. "Look into shifter politics, and which shifter might have been mad at him." Because he was fairly sure that was not how it was done in LA.

But worst of all, through the interviews, the careful, by-the-book interviews, Rafiel felt.... something.

It was the feeling of a mind-compulsion seeking to get hold of him. He'd experienced that before when an old shifter had controlled him into having sex with her. His mind froze in horror.

He shuddered, a body-long shudder, which made Cas give him a weird look. "You okay? You coming down with something?"

"I'm fine," Rafiel said. But of course, he wasn't. He was–

He'd been working with a shifter-psychiatrist who'd convinced him that he'd been raped and had made him read all sorts of books on surviving rape. But he still had moments he had trouble not reacting. And the mental – psychic? – scrabbling and scratching, trying to get hold of his mind and make him do things. He shuddered again, then exhaled slowly and turned his mind to the case. File it under things you also couldn't tell the Chief, or anyone in the force: *I was raped by a prehistoric shifter who took hold of my mind.* Yeah, that would go over well. He'd be on a psychiatric hold before he could say, "boo."

No. Let's think of other things.

Where was Kyrie? If they hadn't found this body, Kyrie's disappearance would be consuming all of their work and worry.

He still worried.

He felt a hand on his shoulder. Looking across the table, he caught Cas's eye, but those eyes said, "Rafiel, I know you said you didn't want to be bothered, but I'll be damned if I'm standing between you and your fiancé."

So, Rafiel knew before he turned that it would be Bea standing there, her hand warm and reassuring on his shoulder. He inhaled deeply and let his breath out, slowly.

Bea smelled of fresh-cut apples and clean.

Bea was not an ancient shifter who had mind-controlled him into having sex. Who had –raped him. Though he didn't like the word. He was not going to shrug her hand away. She was trying to give him comfort and support. But with his senses spun up, it was hard to endure touch. Any form of touch, while he could feel something sniffing and clawing around his mind, trying to get in.

With extreme control, he reached up and put his hand over hers. He felt like his body was a puppet which he was operating remotely and with extreme difficulty. His hand must be very cold, because hers felt like it was burning. He inhaled and exhaled again, slowly.

"What happened? Who killed– you know?"

Cas snickered. "We don't solve things like that. It's not that easy. This is not a TV show."

Rafiel bit his tongue, so he wouldn't yell at the werewolf. There was no point. He and Nick might occasionally be juvenile, but they were decent officers and law-abiding shifters. It might be a thing of wolves to be slightly .... juvenile.

Bea's eyes got huge, in that look she had when she was sure she'd offended him, and said, "But were they ... you know ... was he one of ours?"

Rafiel nodded and sighed. "I think so. He was the father of that family, and they all smell shifter."

Tom wasn't ready. That was the foremost thought in his mind. He wasn't ready. Though if you asked him what he was ready for, or wasn't ready for, he wouldn't be able to answer. Mostly because he didn't feel ready for anything.

He'd given his deposition to Nick, clearly, succinctly. There wasn't much to tell. He'd gone to look for Kyrie, and he'd found the room, and he'd gone out and–

It was a mark of how close he was to losing control that Nick had said, "Tom. Your eyes."

And Tom had understood his eyes were going dragon. He'd taken deep breaths and pushed the dragon to the back of his mind by force.

And the screaming from the Great Sky Dragon demanding he come and lead the battle – battle? – now wasn't helping.

Tom's dad had tried to say something about being really sorry, but Tom couldn't process why he thought he was sorry. Or what he'd thought he'd done. None of it made much sense.

It took him a moment to understand his father thought Kyrie had left Tom. Something about, "Sometimes a wedding makes it too real."

And Tom wanted to laugh, because he and Kyrie were married in all but law, had been almost since they'd met. And he couldn't explain that to his father. His father's relationships were different and had taught him different things.

Normally Tom would have been offended. Not now. He just felt– odd.

He felt like his physical body was a very important part of him, one he needed to remember to move around. Meanwhile, his mind was going lightning-fast.

And the things it jumped to and from were not pleasant things.

Like, he wondered if Kyrie could have killed the old shifter. Not that he could figure out why she would, but the older girl looked like her. Was she Kyrie's sister? But still, why would Kyrie be mad at the old man? And what had the man wanted to tell her? Why had he seemed angry? And by what power had he slapped Tom's probe?

And how would Kyrie have killed him? Kyrie was a small woman, and pregnant, and while the man looked like early sixties or so, that didn't mean he was weak, right? And Kyrie couldn't shift. Not unless she'd given birth. But people didn't give birth in storerooms, and he was almost sure there would be blood left behind if she had. And a baby.

Some animals ate their babies. He shuddered. Kyrie was not an animal, any more than Tom was an animal. And she wouldn't eat their baby, any more than she would eat their cat, Not-Dinner. Neither of them ate Not Dinner. Not Dinner was never in danger.

"Tom." The voice seemed to come from very far away, but Rafiel's hand grabbed Tom's forearm. "Tom, are you okay? You're going lizardy again."

The words were spoken in a whisper, since there were still police officers around who weren't shifters.

Tom swallowed hard. He felt the ache in his face, as his bones tried to contort into the dragon's elongated muzzle. And he became aware that though he'd shut the metaphorical door on it, the Great Sky Dragon's ... consciousness? ... was still beating on his mind and demanding that Tom come, as he was needed.

Since the GSD hadn't told him where he was needed, Tom would continue ignoring him. Besides, finding Kyrie was way more important. But–

"Tom, come sit down. We need to talk to you," Rafiel said. Since Cas stood behind him, Tom assumed this was official. Perhaps Nick had found something worrisome in the pre-interview.

It was official and it wasn't. Rafiel sighed. Interviewing Tom was done in a far corner of the annex, with Cas taking notes, but after about two minutes, Cas leaned in and said, "Two copies of notes. One for us only, one official?" and Rafiel nodded, without speaking.

They weren't completely insane. And if they put in the official report stuff like, "I felt for the mind of the old shifter, and he ... slapped me mentally," or, "the GSD told me there was something bad headed for us, probably related to the Others," Rafiel's superiors, let alone any lawyers who had to deal with this mess in the courts, would have a field day. And there might end up being a psychological evaluation for the whole department.

As it was, Rafiel was treading a fine line, because, since his run in with the saber tooth tiger, and the... rape through mind control, he'd had moments of blanking and nights when he could not sleep, and anger issues that had caused people in the department to say he should have counseling.

If they had the slightest notion of what was causing it, or even what could have given him PTSD, they'd already have forced the issue. And he couldn't tell them he was seeing Dr. Nik for it. Nikhil Rao was a child psychologist. He was also a bear shifter, and the terror of poachers in the Colorado mountains. But that was something else that couldn't be talked about.

Dr. Nik had helped. Truly. Even if most of what he did was give Rafiel stuff to read, like a deranged literature professor. It was pertinent stuff. And it helped.

He said it was a problem of control, and that Rafiel needed to reestablish his boundaries and convince himself he had control over his life and his body.

Which was easier said than done, when stuff like this kept happening. Shifters.

Not just his being a shifter, but all the shifters around him. He kept finding his duty as a policeman getting obscured or tainted by his loyalty to other shifters, and his desire not to get run out of town by people with torches and pitchforks.

He took a deep breath, as his head ached. He still felt like someone or something was reaching for his mind, trying to control it.

"So, no one saw Kyrie leave?" he said.

Tom shook his head. He looked tired and dejected. "I don't think it can be her who ... who killed the man. But–"

Rafiel shook his head. "No," he said. "His head was sliced off. By a saber, they think. Unless Kyrie was carrying a saber around, or you had one in the storeroom–"

"What?" Tom said and was echoed by Cas.

"His head was sliced clean off. I don't think Kyrie has the upper body strength, much less getting the guy to stay still while– The text came while we were interviewing his family. Kyrie can't have done that. She can't even shift. And this guy was a shifter. He'd not be defenseless."

"She could if she'd given birth."

Rafiel frowned. He was about to point out that when people gave birth there was pain and blood and stuff, and also that there would be a baby somewhere, but he could very well tell what Tom was thinking: Stuff out of all the dark fairytales. And they'd lived through so much stuff that came from the dark fairytales in recent years, that he couldn't even tell Tom it was impossible.

But he was almost sure it was. Even if the armies of madness were marching behind Tom's eyes, and if Rafiel was almost sure that something was hammering on his consciousness seeking to get in and make him a meat puppet, one thing he was sure of: Kyrie was good. Good all through. And people who were good all through didn't eat their own babies or attack older men in parking lots.

"Panthers are really bad at holding sabers. No thumbs. And anyway Tom, I'm sure–"

He didn't know what he would have said, or if anything could convince Tom, but he never said it, because Edward Ormson, Tom's father, had come in.

"Damn it, I've been trying to tell someone, and I'm tired of being shushed."

He spoke a little too loud so, of course, Rafiel, Cas, and Tom shushed him.

Edward glared. He looked mulish. He pulled a chair back from the table, jerkily, which made him seem like he was twelve years old at most and about to throw a snit fit. He sat on the chair backward, too, glaring at them. "Look, Sandra said she saw Kyrie walk out of the storeroom. She said she thought it was weird, because she was walking like all her limbs were rigid. Like she was impersonating a robot."

"What?" Tom said. "Who is Sandra?"

"Sandra Li," Edward said. "I told you."

Rafiel took a deep breath. "Please tell us again."

Tom stared at his father. Surely if this were true, he'd have said it earlier. And could this Sandra Li be trusted? She was one of the GSD's people, after all.

Edward threw his shoulders back. "She said that Kyrie was walking like she didn't want to. She says the Great Sky Bastard..." He hissed out a breath. "She says sometimes he does that to them. Or at least to some of them. When they're not behaving. I guess your friend Conan would know that, right?"

Tom bit the inside of his cheek hard, to keep himself quiet. He actually had some idea of all the things Conan could tell them, and none of them were good. It wasn't an accident that the man turned pale and shook at the very mention of the Great Sky Dragon. Taking over your mind and walking you was the least of it.

"Anyway, Sandra said it looked like she was being controlled. And then someone opened the door from the parking lot and Kyrie walked out."

"Who? Who opened the door from the parking lot?" Tom asked.

Edward shrugged. "She doesn't know. She had an impression of someone big and blond out there, but that's all."

Big and blond meant it wasn't the guy who was found dead, right? It might have been one of the Great Sky Dragon's people, though. Tom was living proof that not all of them looked Chinese.

He controlled the dragon by extreme willpower, refusing to let the shift happen, but he could feel a rolling ball of anger mounting. Could the Great Sky Dragon have been controlling Kyrie? To what end? And why? To get Tom to come and fight in some great battle?

And why hadn't Tom felt it?

Rafiel looked as puzzled as Tom felt. And also weirdly twitchy, like he, too, was keeping something at bay by sheer willpower. "Look," he said, "the best guess we have is that Kyrie saw the crime happen. And someone took her so she couldn't talk. But in the meantime, I'm going to have a word with this Sandra Li." Rafiel looked at Cas, "Don't tell me she was allowed to leave."

"That's okay," Tom's dad said. "She gave me her number."

Rafiel was extending his hand for Tom's father's phone, and the Great Sky Dragon sent a new imperative straight into Tom's brain: *We must man the watches. You should be in charge.*

Whatever that meant. Tom screamed incoherently back that he wasn't going to do anything till he found Kyrie, but he doubted the Great Sky Dragon heard. What he was receiving had the feel of a public announcement, a widely disseminated message that went everywhere.

Kyrie was cold. Cold and cramped in very specific ways. Being cramped – and cramps, usually on one's legs – seemed to go with being pregnant. She'd reached the point in the pregnancy where there wasn't really a comfortable way to sleep. Most of the time, she settled for sleeping half-sitting up against some pillows, while the kid jogged in place or whatever it was he did in there that felt like he was playing soccer with her bladder and bumping his head against her diaphragm.

But this was a different kind of cramped. Her right arm and shoulder and leg hurt with a combination of lack of circulation and cold. Like she was lying down on stone.

She moved to relieve the pain, smacked her lips together, tasted bile in her mouth, and felt with her hand under herself. Damn it, she was lying on stone. Rough, uneven stone.

Opening her eyes didn't help much. It was dark as the bottom of a sack. And there was a smell of must and disuse.

From somewhere, outside wherever she was, there was the sound of language that struck her ear like two pieces of wood banging together. She heard one of the words as Fafnir, but she was almost sure that wasn't true. At any rate, no one was breaking up into opera. Hopefully. All this needed was opera.

She sat up and blinked again.

The kid kicked her bladder and she whimpered, then sighed in relief. At least he was alive. Dead babies don't play soccer with mommy's organs. Probably.

She had disjointed memories that made no sense.

She'd been about to take a bite of the cake when something had …. grabbed her. In her mind, it felt like something had grabbed the back of her neck and made her walk.

Walk out to the parking lot.

No. Not something. Someone. In her mind she saw the old man, who'd sat at the table with his daughter's family. He was waiting for her in the parking lot, radiating fury.

She couldn't remember what he'd said. She just had a feeling he'd called her disobedient and good-for-nothing. And how she should be dead.

Disobedient to whom? And why?

Then there had been a tall blond guy in nothing much...

Her next memory was of flying, with someone holding on to her midriff. But there was a ... memory of the smell of blood?

She blinked again.

The darkness was resolving itself, if not into vision, at least into a sense of walls around her. She got a feeling she was in some kind of round chamber. And at one end, there was – she'd almost swear there was a gate barring an entrance.

Somewhere deep inside, she heard water running, which combined with the kid kicking her bladder to make her very uncomfortable.

She reached with her mind and called, "Tom?"

For just a second, a glorious second, she felt his presence, his mental
.... being, reaching for her, and she heard, as clear as day, his voice, very
relieved, "Oh, Kyrie, thank heavens."

And then it felt as though a sheet of ice descended between them.

She remembered this had happened before. She growled in frustration.

"Oh, you're awake," said a heavily accented voice just outside the gates.

****

Tom had stayed at the diner. People – and by *people* one should understand his father and Anthony – had tried to convince him to go home. But
the thing was that Tom was probably better off staying awake and working
through the long night.

Going home meant confronting the fact that Kyrie was really missing.
Worse, she was missing during the crucial twelve hours that were supposed
to be their honeymoon. They were a stupid twelve hours, when compared
to people who went overseas for their honeymoon, but they were supposed
to be theirs, some time to spend together as a married couple. To be
themselves. To.... Even if they didn't do anything more than hold each
other, to be together.

In a month, they'd have a son. But today they were supposed to rejoice
in being married at last. And in having twelve hours when the diner and
running the diner didn't intrude on their happiness.

So....

So, the house without Kyrie would be bad. It would be proof he'd failed
her. And the Great Sky Dragon, too. He'd said to keep an eye on her, but
Tom had let her go like a fool, all in the name of doing a little more work.

At that moment, he'd have traded the diner, the fryer, and all for a used
stick of chewing gum and then spit it out.

And yet he stayed behind the counter, cooking, plating, nudging the
servers towards refilling drinks or attending to new tables.

It was a peculiarity of the diner, because most of the clientele were
shifters, or at least a lot of them were, that a murder in the parking lot
increased the crowd, as they sat around and talked about what must have
really happened and why.

Tom tried to pretend he didn't see all the servers and not a few of the
customers gave him worried looks.

"Tom, I'll go by the house and feed Not Dinner, okay?" That was his
father, and Tom was surprised, briefly. Mostly because his father rarely

thought of doing something that needed to be done. But no. That wasn't right. His father had been trying. It was more that his father didn't often remember little things like cats.

He pulled the key from his pocket and handed it to his father. And that's when it came. Kyrie's mind-voice, clear in his mind, reaching out, calling his name, and the impression of stone walls and a locked gate, and that Kyrie was tired and cold. And alive. Kyrie was alive. And the baby was alive.

"Oh, Kyrie, thank heavens," Tom said and realized he'd said it aloud, as his father's face came alive.

"Kyrie? You heard from Kyrie?"

And then something like a sheet of ice fell between them, deadly and cold and obliterating.

Tom screamed. And every eye in the diner turned to him.

In Rafiel's car, not even the department's, Cas turned the heat full-on and aimed both vents at Rafiel. Rafiel frowned distractedly.

From the back seat came the sound of Nick smacking his hands together and grumbling about the cold, and how if he knew how fast it would get cold, he'd have worn mittens.

Rafiel realized it was indeed very cold. Much colder than it had been when he'd left home. Not that this was strange. Colorado was Colorado, and the temperature could change in minutes. Besides, he'd been so busy with Bea's visit and preparing for the wedding.

What a ridiculous way for the day to go. He had an unsolved crime; Kyrie was missing. All he'd managed was a kiss to Bea while telling her to go to his parents and tell them what was happening. And stay there, where she would be safe.

"I couldn't allow Bea to come with us to see the Old Sky Bastard," he said. "She has a history." He thought about it a moment. "And I thought it was better not to tell Tom either. The last time he got crosswise of the Great Sky Dragon, he ended up dead. Okay, only for three days, but who knows? This time the old bastard might bite Tom's head off."

Like that, the missing head came back to his mind. Oh. Someone knew the guy was a shifter and wanted to make sure he stayed dead.

"Yeah," Cas said. "Though you know, I'm not absolutely sure the old Chinese gentleman is involved in any of this."

"Oh yeah? Then explain why the forensics geeks found a very large green-blue scale, like from some kind of snake, in the parking lot near the corpse."

"I don't know. Could be Tom's last time he shifted. Heck, the entire parking lot might be peppered with scales."

Rafiel gave Cas a serious side look. "It's been my experience that when something goes wrong in this town, the GSD either knows what is wrong or is involved in it right up to his little shiny fangs."

"His fangs aren't little," Nick said from the back seat. "But if it comes to that, I thought Tom had close to the same power he has, or more."

"I don't know," Rafiel said. "I thought so, too, but Tom acts like it's something you have to learn to use."

"Makes sense," Cas said. "No one gets anything for free. If you suddenly grew a tail, you'd have to learn to use it."

"As it happens," Rafiel said, drily, "we all periodically grow tails, and I don't remember any lessons."

"Yeah, but that's different, right? There's instinct. And frankly the first few times, it was very disorienting."

Rafiel frowned. It was still disorienting. He'd thought he'd come to a point where the lion and himself were one, and he could control the lion, *be* the lion while keeping his rational mind and his human purpose.

And then – and then someone else had controlled the lion. And since then, Rafiel didn't know what was happening. It was like the lion thought his own thoughts and did his own things. Rafiel had no more than a vague inkling of what had happened then. He remembered what looked like a basic itinerary: the lion walked this way, looked here, did that.

It always worried him. What if the lion decided to start eating people? After all, as a policeman, he was sworn to protect the people of Goldport. What if the lion started harming them? What would he, as a policeman, have to do?

"Rafiel?"

"What?"

"One, you are starting to look lion-like. Two, we just passed the Three Luck Dragon. And there was something weird in the parking lot."

Kyrie didn't answer the person asking if she was awake. She didn't react when the gate opened.

She almost reacted when the guy came in. Had someone slipped her funny tobacco?

He was blonder than Rafiel and built like the proverbial brick shithouse. And yeah, he was blond to the point one rarely saw in real life. Hair the color of spun ice, she thought. His eyes were icy too, a very pale, reflective blue.

But what was really weird about him was that he was dressed like an opera Viking, horned helmet and all.

She continued ignoring him. Having grown up in large cities all over, it wasn't as if she hadn't seen some pretty weird people. She had. Dressing in furs and homespun clothes, with a helmet that had a nose-covering thing attached, was only relatively weird. She'd seen crazier when ComiCon was in town. Or the Renaissance Fair was in session. But the problem was ... it looked so *authentic.*

He stared at her. She stared back. He cleared his throat. It seemed to her that his hair moved with a mind of its own, waving about even though there wasn't a hint of wind.

"The Queen wants you," he said, sullenly. It sounded more like *vants.*

She raised her eyebrows at him.

He growled at her. It wasn't an entirely human growl. No surprise there. Kyrie had learned to smell shifters, and he stank of shifter more than the diner on Saturday night.

He planted his feet and crossed his arm. "I don't think you heard me," he said. "Up you. The Queen wants you."

Kyrie felt an incredible amount of "no" building in the back of her mind. She wasn't in the mood for this game. Whatever it was. She bent one knee and put her hands on it, trying to assume a position of relaxation, though it was pretty hard with the belly in the middle. The kid kicked her bladder, but she pretended she couldn't feel it. She also pretended she hadn't been dying to go to the bathroom for a long time.

"Right now," she said. "The only throne I'm interested in is a toilet."

He looked confused and blinked several times at her. "Toilet? Washing? Combing? Making yourself fit to see the Queen?"

Okay, good, then. "Peeing."

He opened his mouth and closed it. Suddenly, six-foot-something of guy seemed to melt, as though he'd become about two years old. "But–" he said. He kind of shrunk into himself as if confusion were so great, he didn't know what to do. "But the queen wants you."

"What queen? I'm American. We don't have queens."

This time his mouth hung open for real. Like she'd just told him that the moon was made of cheese and a rat was about to eat it.

A sound came out, like he thought he'd argue with her. But then he snapped his mouth shut, so suddenly and forcefully that it echoed.

And then he left. He left her alone, sitting in the dark.

"Thor," she said. "That's just dandy, but I still need a bathroom, or I'm going to pee on your shoes."

Rafiel's dad used to make a joke when Rafiel was very young. Something about driving his car in reverse, so as not to put extra mileage on it.

A responsible driver, of the sort of the police department liked – of the sort Mark Milagros had supervised "back in LA" – would have driven ahead on the road, then turned around and come back to investigate the parking lot.

But it was the middle of the night, on a little-traveled road on the outskirts of Goldport. The Three Luck Dragon was in a mini-mall with a jewelry store, and some other non-descript shop that seemed to change between liquor stores, tobacconists, and dubious small press and collectible magazine seller. All of these shops were closed after hours, of course. Heck, the Three Luck Dragon should be closed, as it was almost ten pm. And there were no other cars on the road, or at least there were no lights visible.

Rafiel put the car in reverse and his foot on the gas and backed up almost a block.

Before he got there, he could tell there was something seriously wrong. That anyone coming down this road wouldn't even notice his car, for the "wrong" in the Three Luck Dragon parking lot. He'd only missed it because he'd been worried.

Otherwise, he'd have noticed it. And also, that the something seriously wrong there was the type of thing that the police always heard about afterwards, usually under the heading of "Corpse found in parking lot" or "Another animal attack on the outskirts of Goldport."

He hoped Kyrie wasn't in the middle of that.

For one, he could hear the sound from above the car, even with the windows rolled up. It was reminiscent of a lot of large, heavy sheets being waved in the air. It might have puzzled him at one point, but as a friend of dragons, he knew that sound well. It was the sound of dragon wings beating to bring the dragon down in record time. Worse, this sound was not of a pair or two pairs of wings, but of.... Many.

For another, the parking lot was already crowded. At night, and with the only light coming from the glowing sign that proclaimed Three Luck Dragon, it was hard to see details on what was going on down there, but ... but there were dragons and humans. Lots.

Rafiel swerved his car to what could be considered parallel parking, beside the parking lot. He didn't dare park in the parking lot, because the next thing you knew some idiot juvie dragon would come for a landing on top of it, and dragon claw marks were very hard to explain to insurance adjustors. He'd tried once. It had gotten written off as "unusual hail dam-age." But the guy had told Rafiel not to ski on top of his car, no matter how high he was.

Rafiel could feel, without being able to explain quite how, that there was trouble in the offing. The back of his neck prickled, and he felt like he might need to shift any second now. Not that he intended to. He had a feeling, not clear but absolute, that if he shifted, he'd be unable to hold the scrabbling in his mind at bay.

He turned off the engine. He could catch the same keyed-up, not-quite-at-ease edgy sense from Cas and Nick.

"Come on," he said, and his voice came out as a growl. "Let's see precisely what's going on."

"Oh, this is going to be fuuuuun," Cas said, in a tone of voice that indicated he spoke by opposites.

Rafiel didn't even bother to acknowledge it. Why state the obvious?

"It's all right," Tom heard his father say, in the most reasonable voice in the world. "It's just a grease splatter. He'll be fine."

He grabbed Tom's arm and pulled him back towards the storage areas while babbling about putting a salve on his arm. It took until he'd shoved Tom into the storage room for him to say, "Don't shift. You'd break things."

"I'm not about to shift," Tom said. He'd taken deep breaths all the way here, and he was almost under control. "Sorry for yelling. It was just– Yes, I heard from Kyrie, but there was nothing– It was like a sheet of glass fell between our minds, silencing her, and making it impossible for me to reach her again."

"But she's alive? And she didn't leave? I mean–"

Tom nodded. "Yeah. Alive. And no, I don't think she left of her own free will. She's–" He could close his eyes and see her surroundings. She was in some sort of cavern, closed with a gate. This brought a memory to mind, but not a memory clear enough to allow him to locate her. "It's some kind of stone cell."

"Cell?"

"Yeah. Someone took her."

His father's eyes were both confused and anxious as they stared at Tom. Tom realized this was often his father's reaction. He loved Tom but was a little afraid of what he'd do. "What are you going to do?"

"Find her," Tom said. And as he spoke realized his voice sounded distant and weird, because he was already going within, to access powers he only dimly understood.

Somehow, in the spring, while facing an ancient foe connected to other, even more ancient and dangerous foes, he'd acquired the powers that were traditionally those of the Great Sky Dragon.

It seemed like the Great Sky Dragon could – at least under some circumstances – control every shifter in the world. This had allowed Tom to call them all to the rescue in the final battle, but–

But it was a complex and confusing power. He could go through the minds of various dragons and other shifters, and get a glimpse of what they were doing, but it was hard to make it controlled and precise, and make it make any sense. He might be able to reach people he knew really well, but mostly the system was wonderful for calling complete strangers and compelling them to come help. Which disrupted the lives of a lot of people, and probably didn't make them very fond of dragons.

As far as Tom could determine, this was the exclusive power of the Great Sky Dragon, and Tom had inherited it because he was the last male descendant, in an unbroken male line, from the Great Sky Dragon.

But he couldn't determine if the Great Sky Dragon also still had the power. It seemed to him if he did, that would be a violation of ancient tradition and possibly the laws of physics. Except what part of being a shifter wasn't a violation of the laws of physics? So many violations it was almost funny.

On the other hand, the GSD had never come to Tom and specifically asked what had happened to his great power, and why had Tom taken it, so he must also still have it.

And of course, the Great Sky Bastard probably knew how to use it, which was more than Tom ever understood how to do. Though there had been hints that even the GSD didn't use it properly, that he never learned enough. Maybe. All of which amounted to not much. Tom knew that he couldn't talk to dragons, not since whatever the saber tooth had done to his mind before he rescued the Great Sky Dragon. But he should be able to see other shifters. And maybe some were near Kyrie.

It felt exactly like tinkering with a machine that was too complex for him. He could sort of kind of see where to tinker, and what would happen. Or at least what he hoped would happen, but it wasn't super-clear why.

He suspected it was, like almost everything about being a shifter, one of those things that you had to experience and practice, until you got it right.

He closed his eyes, and took a deep breath, inhaling the residual stale-cracker smell that seemed to cling to this room. He could sense, without opening his eyes, that his father had straightened up and his gaze sharpened, suddenly paying attention. Tom hoped his dad would not ask if he'd found Kyrie or something equally stupid.

Tom needed to delve into the knowledge inside him that an old shifter had called "the Dragon Egg" and figure out how to locate Kyrie.

It took a while of blind groping. It felt like when he was little and there was a game in pre-school where they'd blindfolded the kids and had them feel around a box with a lot of objects to identify what each was. Yeah, in that case, of course Tom had managed to grimace and wriggle his facial muscles until he could see under the blindfold. Because it was a stupid game, and he didn't know why he shouldn't cheat.

In this case, it was more complex. Particularly because the "objects" he was groping around for were mostly human minds.

In a dizzying kaleidoscope, he found himself in the mind of a delivery man politely waiting for a signature on delivery – almost for sure Paul Orvan, aka Orvan Ox, unless there were a lot more shifters in delivery business in Goldport than seemed likely – then in the mind of someone looking from inside a zoo enclosure at kids – which probably meant another shifter had ended up in the zoo. Hopefully, it would be resolved without much trouble – then in the mind of a very large squirrel writing on a wall with red chalk, "Rodent Libera–"

Suddenly he was in Rafiel's mind, and Rafiel was saying, "Backing up."

And then–

And then Tom was in the mind of a dragon. This shocked him so much that he almost lost the connection.

Maduh, the ancient shifter he'd battled in spring, had severed his connection to all dragons. But he was in the mind of a dragon, with another dragon beside him, and facing a woman on a sort of stone throne.

The woman looked like an ice princess. That wasn't a poetic image. She literally looked like she was sculpted from ice, with straight very pale hair, large pale, vaguely blue eyes, and flawless pale skin.

She had an accent, and she told the dragon in whose body Tom was – he could feel the wings, and the bulk, the accustomed dragoness of it – "Take the girl to the place used by the construction workers. There is no reason to start negotiations with her resenting us. Just get hold of her and fly her to the facilities."

Um ... was Kyrie the girl? There was no reason to think it, except that Tom had been looking for "things that felt like they were in Kyrie's vicinity."

The dragon, large, lumbering, and jade green – at least his paws were jade green – turned sideways and stumbled out of a cave that was probably much larger than it felt to someone in dragon form.

He went along a narrow tunnel and threw open a gate.

And there was Kyrie. She was leaning against one of the stone walls, and Tom wanted to pick her up and bring her home, but his sensing of the limits of his connection with this dragon told him if he tried to take control of the dragon's body, he'd break the connection. And alert the enemy – whoever the enemy was – to his presence.

So instead, he watched Kyrie give the dragon that up-and-down look that meant she was used to a better standard in dragons, and not at all impressed by his amateurish efforts.

"Oh, hello, Fafnir," she said in a bored tone. "Did you come back so I could pee on your shoes? How kind of you. Come closer."

Except that, all of a sudden, the dragon did go closer and grabbed her around her waist. Tom heard her yelp, and it was all he could do not to reach for the dragon's body control. But that kind of touch, for one, could cause the dragon to squeeze. And that would be bad. Very bad.

The dragon had Kyrie and took off from a ledge. Tom could see a porta potty near some construction machinery, and suddenly it all made sense.

That was why the "facilities" and the jokes about peeing on the dragon's – was he really Fafnir? – shoes?

Not really a surprise. Over the last several months, proximity to "facilities" had become vitally important to Kyrie.

But as the dragon flew over red scarps and rock formations, Tom identified the place where Kyrie was kept. Acadia.

It was a natural area that technically belonged to the city of Goldport.

Only the psychiatrists of the original colonists – equally divided between miners and proto-New-Age seekers – could really say why they'd thought that this place of rough boulders and spires was a mythical garden in Ancient Greece. But they'd obviously thought that. Perhaps because the rocks looked like the decayed remains of great buildings.

It had been a tourist spot since then. For a while, there had been an inn on the grounds, which was immensely popular, but lately, some eco-fanaticism had filtered in. Someone had said that the inn and the guests degraded the natural ecology and destroyed the habitat.

The habitat of what, Tom couldn't tell. Not like there were a lot of things that lived in the bowl of red rock. Even deer couldn't find enough to eat there and tended to fan out to nearby backyards. Rattlers and lizards weren't in the least bothered by the inn.

Maybe they were afraid the rocks would die or something? Some of the people moving from California were that nuts. Anyway, they'd decided that the inn must go.

That was why the construction site. They were dismantling the inn with minimal ecological impact, or whatever. Which Tom very much doubted, when you considered demolition and all its attendant noise and debris.

But never mind. Tom should now be able to find his wife.

But just as he thought that, the "sheet of glass" fell between him and the dragon whose mind he was occupying.

Just before it fell, he got the feeling of a feminine exclamation of annoyance.

It didn't matter. Now he knew where Kyrie was. He'd arrange for people to hold the fort and go get her.

4

THERE WAS A WAY to interrupt something suspicious in progress, Rafiel thought, which prevented it from escalating into complete chaos.

It involved what he liked to call "the dumb cop routine" – as in, boldly walking in and being all, "What's going on here, then?" and, "Sir, did you mean to hide your knife in that gentleman's back?" or, "Is that a nasty accident?"

When he was a young cop, and the thing he dreaded most was seeming uninformed or stupid, it had been really difficult to do it. He used to cringe when his older partner did it. But over the years he'd learned to perfect the routine.

After all, "just a dumb cop" was unthreatening, and sometimes even perps who should know better and who had just been caught red-handed thought that they could get away with it, if they just pretended to be innocent enough.

As for the two officers with him, the werewolves did dumb cop so well that half the time they convinced Rafiel.

But one thing is to catch normal perps in the middle of being up to something and call them on it, and another to catch a–

A mass of dragon shifters. And dragon shifters who knew he was also a shifter. And who were neither afraid of nor impressed with him.

And yet. Okay, he'd still have to try it. Because the alternative was having his feet roasted off, if he was lucky.

He'd just have to be.... not a dumb cop, but a dumb lion shifter. He'd be helped in that by the fact that as far as he could tell dragon shifters thought of every other shifter in the world as inferior life forms. Okay, maybe Tom didn't. Maybe. But the Others did.

He got out of the car, his walk deliberately slow and casual seeming. He could feel the wolves getting out behind him and falling into the dumb-and-casual routine.

Of course, if they weren't shifters what they'd be doing is freaking out, because they were walking by shifted and half-shifted people, strolling like it was all a nice Sunday afternoon walk.

Meanwhile, in his head, Rafiel was tagging what was happening around him. Ah, there were the people to approach. He remembered them vaguely from helping Tom with a previous issue with the GSD's people. These were the GSD's handpicked lieutenants, middle-aged and looking harassed like all middle managers.

He approached and said, before he could even think of what to say, "All right, what's going on here?"

He remembered being a little boy and seeing his father, then an officer in the Goldport police, walk casually up to two guys who were doing something to a car door, and saying, "All right, what's going on here?"

That had been enough for the two guys to take off running. With the experience of his years, Rafiel now understood they'd been trying to break into the car parked in front of their house. And that casual, age-old police question had caused them to stop cold.

It worked here, too. Not that the two dragon shifters near the door to the Three Luck Dragon ran. But neither did they look completely unaffected.

One of them turned around, running his hand through his hair, looking at Rafiel with a "What now?" expression. He swallowed, and took a deep breath, "Look, we don't have time to play, officer."

"Play?" Rafiel said. He let a little of the big cat's growl into his voice and raised an eyebrow.

The dragon shifter looked exasperated. Rafiel could feel the werewolves tensing behind him.

"Thing is," the dragon shifter said. "It's not your business. It's ... bigger business than you can know. It's a convocation."

"A con what?" Rafiel said, in a tone that intimated that if it had more than three syllables, he couldn't rightly understand it.

"A call to arms as it were. And this one is dragon's business."

"I beg your pardon," Rafiel's voice acquired the very polite tones that informed anyone who knew him that he was in fact quickly reaching boiling point. "It is also my business as an officer of Goldport. The kind of thing that I see going on here ends up with dead people, and dead people are very much my business."

Another dragon growled and turned around to face Rafiel fully. His face had that elongated "lizardy" look that Tom's got when he was at the end of his rope. "And how are you going to enforce that, officer?" He gestured with an arm, whose hand looked suspiciously elongated and long-nailed. "You know what? Do your worst. With all these dragons here, how long do you think you'll last?"

He was going to fry. And Bea would never forgive him. She'd crispy fry his ashes. And yell at him. Well, at his ashes. And then she would do something unspeakable to them. He didn't know what, but he knew it would be unspeakable. She kept telling him not to get himself killed.

He drew back his shoulders and prepared to make a smarmy answer, when from above came the sound of wings.

There were many, many dragon shifters in Goldport. Hell, there were many, many dragon shifters in that particular parking lot, but the size of the one descending from above and the sheer power of his majesty let Rafiel know, perfectly well, who that was.

Because it wasn't Tom.

And other than Tom only the Great Sky Dragon was that big.

He scrambled out of the way – with a bunch of men and dragons – as the ancient horror came in for a landing.

Kyrie had read the same number and type of fairytales as any other red blooded American woman in her early twenties.

Maybe she had read more, and relied on Disney less. Mostly because the foster homes she'd grown up in hadn't always wanted to spring for her entertainment, but libraries made their books available for free. And she couldn't even remember learning to read, or a time when reading wasn't a major part of her life.

So, she'd read a lot of fairytales, and even some fairytale analysis that had probably been someone's PhD thesis.

This probably accounted for her looking at the woman on the stone throne – and where had that throne come from, since she was sure she was in Acadia? – and thinking "Ice Queen."

The woman was, in fact, pale, with the sort of skin that would be "peaches and cream" if someone had remembered to add peaches. Her eyes were very light blue, so light that they were almost transparent, and the blue in them might not be any more than a reflection of light on ice. Her hair was similarly almost colorless, save for a suspicion of what might be silver.

She wore a silver gown and sat on a black marble throne with eldritch carvings. Like many self-taught kids, Kyrie had never been fully sure of the meaning of some words, one of those being "eldritch" but she was sure these markings were in fact eldritch. Like they had some kind of meaning, but the meaning probably wouldn't be known to any living person, and should you discover it, you'd find it was something weird and unpleasant. Possibly relating to the heart of someone's first born. And then you'd have to sand them off and dip the whole thing in holy water.

And the Ice Queen was staring at Kyrie with a look that wasn't so much malevolent as completely surprised.

As Fafnir – he'd looked so shocked when Kyrie called him that, that Kyrie wondered if it was his real name – once more in human form – and mother naked – stood by Kyrie before the throne, Kyrie kept the expression of extreme annoyance she'd walked in with.

The queen – heaven only knew what she was the queen of, but she was definitely a queen – looked at Kyrie, and when Kyrie was within three steps, lifted her hand, and Fafnir stopped. Kyrie considered continuing walking forward, but decided there was no point and looked up, and spit out, "What?"

The queen opened her mouth, then closed it, then opened it again. "But surely," she said, her voice sounding hesitant and marred by a Scandinavian accent, "you want to bow or kneel or something."

"Not particularly," Kyrie said amiably.

"But–" The woman opened both hands, as though to demonstrate helplessness in the face of such unreason. "Surely you understand I'm your queen."

Kyrie snorted. She couldn't help it. "No. I'm American, we don't have queens."

The queen shook her head. Her voice, when she spoke again, was almost tender, like a mother explaining foolishness to a simple child. "You're a shifter, dear. Shifters have queens. I am Angrboda, Queen of the North."

Something about the name tickled the back of Kyrie's mind. She'd read that name too, and the title, but she couldn't remember when. Something Norse for sure.

"And yet, even as a shifter, I'm an American and we don't have queens."

"That is foolish. Is the young man, my son's son, that stupid also?"

Took Kyrie a moment to figure that one out. Then she remembered that the Great Sky Bastard had once told him that Tom's ancestor had been born from a union with the Queen of the North to establish a truce.

"If you mean my husband, he is also American, yes."

The Queen made a gesture like flicking something aside with her right hand. The effect was of someone casting aside and discarding an invisible veil. "American! That doesn't matter. The nations of mortals don't mean anything to us. What we are and who we are lives longer and endures longer than any nations of foolish little apes. We are eternal compared to them and we preserve the old hierarchies lest the world fall apart. In those hierarchies, the dragons rule, and I am the queen."

Inexplicably, and not because she was trying to be rude, but probably one of those things of pregnancy, Kyrie yawned enormously. She decided not to apologize nor give any hint the insult was unintended. It seemed to her that like the Great Sky Bastard, Queenie needed her ego cut to size. With a rusty saw.

"Look," she said, "I don't know where you came from or where you were born, but kings and queens are a thing of the past. They don't really matter to us now, and Tom and I have absolutely no intention of acting as if they do. So you can get angry, which will give you the option of then calming down or not. Or you can skip the anger. Now, what do you want? I don't want to obey you, but I'll listen to you if you have reasons why I should."

The queen opened her eyes and closed her hands. She closed them really tight and stood up, as though her clenched hands were holding onto a rope that allowed her to stand up. "Sven, Birger, Endreid," she shouted.

Like that, three Vikings came running from what appeared to be a side tunnel in the rock.

"Take this foolish girl to the cell," the Queen said, her voice sounding like the winds howling in a blizzard, "until she realizes she has to obey her betters."

"The bastards ain't been born," Kyrie shouted back, sure that her words wouldn't be heard, much less understood but feeling better for having said them.

It didn't matter much as the four Vikings, who were probably dragon shifters, dragged her to her cell.

And why wasn't Tom coming? She was sure she'd felt him in her mind, and sure that he'd have identified Acadia as the place she was held.

She was hungry and tired and uncomfortable and she wanted her husband.

Just as the cell gate clanged shut between her and the tunnel to the throne room, she remembered where she'd read of Angrboda. Like fairytales, she'd read a lot of mythology. She'd read a lot of everything, partly trying to figure out why she had dreams of turning into a panther.

Now she remembered a book on Norse myth. Angrboda was supposedly the wife of Loki – was Loki a real thing? Was she going to be subjected to Jove and Hera too? – and had the cheerful title of Mother of Monsters.

Oh, Tom, where are you?

****

Tom was frustrated. He'd emerged from the storeroom to a million questions.

Yes, people working in the diner knew Kyrie was missing. He knew his dad had told them, though he wondered what Edward had used as an excuse to those who weren't shifters.

They all looked vaguely worried, and those who were shifters looked at Tom in some alarm. With reason, he supposed, since before, in similar circumstances, he'd drafted them all without their say-so to fight a war against outsiders from space who were inimical to all life on Earth.

But all his employees had questions. Not big, existential questions, but questions about what to do and what was going on. Stuff like, what to serve if they ran out of gyro meat before morning, which looked likely to happen from the way the diner remained full. And what to do for souvlaki, since they were running mighty thin, and–

Some of that was solved by Laura Miller agreeing to stay on and make more souvlaki. And it was agreed that as soon as the restaurant supply place opened, Anthony would go and buy more gyro meat. Tom handed over the diner credit card, and the tax card that would allow Anthony into the supply place.

But then there was an endless number of people who didn't realize Kyrie was missing and wanted to wish him joy. He realized they were being nice, and were friends and people he liked, but it was all he could do not to yell at them.

Finally, he was free, the way open for him to leave. He wrote his hours on the sign in sheet, out of habit, grabbed his coat, and made a run for the slightly-curving hallway that would take him back to the parking lot. He wasn't sure if some policeman or other might not linger back there, so he didn't want to change into a dragon to get past them. No. He'd stay human. He'd take the car, go to Acadia, and find a place to shift.

Just at the entrance to the hallway, someone interposed in his way. "Mr. Ormson?"

Without looking fully at her, he identified a middle-aged woman, a little overweight, in nice clothes, and he almost shoved her out of the way. Almost. Only Tom didn't shove people out of the way unless he were trying to save them from a fate worse than death. So, by an effort of will, he stopped, and looked at the woman.

She was the mother of the family where the .... grandfather? ... had got murdered. The same table they'd been watching, and that Kyrie had been asked to go to.

None of which was what stopped him. What stopped him was something about her dark eyes which, inexplicably, reminded him of Kyrie.

"I'm sorry," the woman spoke very fast, as though she thought she was on borrowed time. "My name is Aurelia Smith, and I have reason to believe your wife is my daughter that I – that I gave up for adoption, shortly after birth."

Tom stopped cold and blinked at her. He remembered the older girl at the table looked like Kyrie. But that would mean that Kyrie's grandfather had found her. And that he'd got murdered. Did that have anything to do with Kyrie? Did it have anything to do with her being taken to Acadia by dragons he couldn't talk to?

He blurted out, "Kyrie was kidnapped," then slapped his hand on his mouth, because it was the weirdest thing in the world to say things before you even thought them. And because he hadn't meant to talk to anyone about this.

But the woman didn't startle. "Yes. I thought that might have happened. I think it's connected to ... is there some place we can talk?" She paused a moment. "You are trying very hard not to become the Great Sky Dragon, aren't you? And not doing very well at it?"

He opened his mouth to ask her how she could know that; to yell at her that Kyrie disappearing certainly wasn't helping. But he didn't know who she was and why she was saying this, so he shut his mouth in a tight line and nodded, a non-committal nod that said they could talk, even while he was trying to figure out how to get to Kyrie, and his mind was already rushing to his wife.

She sighed. "Is there somewhere that we won't be overheard?"

The Great Sky Dragon landed gracefully, but with the impression of an eight-hundred-pound gorilla coming in. Which he was, of course, metaphorically speaking. Realistically speaking, he was way scarier than an eight-hundred-pound gorilla, as he stood there, in the light of the neon sign from the Three Luck Dragon which painted his scales lurid purple and bright green.

He steamed faintly in the cold night. Rafiel, who had been kind of busy, realized that it had gotten hella cold. It had been cold before, but now the snow was heavy, and they were headed for a deep freeze. The temperature must have dropped twenty degrees in the last hour. He had a vague memory of a bad weather prediction, but he had, in fact, been kind of busy.

However, the Great Sky Dragon was steaming, which made sense since they weren't cold blooded. And there was a scent like oil emanating from him. No. Just an oily scent, like you sometimes caught in the reptile house at a zoo.

Rafiel felt paralyzed, which was a feeling rolling from the GSD in waves, a majesty, a feeling of awe. And Rafiel hated it. Just purely hated it. It was more mind control and trickery. At least Tom didn't use that. Not often. And when he did, he could be teased for it afterwards. Most of the time.

Before Rafiel could make his displeasure known – supposing he was allowed to move again – the GSD shifted into a naked, middle aged Chinese man.

Someone came running out of the Three Luck Dragon, and enveloped him in silk robes, embroidered with dragons and phoenixes.

Tying a golden cord about his waist, the GSD turned and stared at Rafiel, "Why are you here, kitten?"

"Sir," Rafiel said and could hear the growl in the back of his throat. "I am not any kind of kitten. I am an adult man and an adult lion. And I am an officer of Goldport, and I would like to know about this assembly, because it seems to me it's not for peaceable purposes. Is it, sir?"

For a moment he faced a look of utter shock, like the GSD couldn't believe he was even being asked. Then the Great Sky Dragon laughed. It was the most chilling laughter Rafiel had ever heard.

"Wait," Tom said. He'd signaled for Anthony to bring them something, which had turned out to be a souvlaki platter and two coffees, and they were sitting in the corner booth, right under the picture of St. George slaying the dragon, with blood and gore splattered all around.

To be fair, the picture was behind Tom, but then he was so familiar with it, that he could see it in his mind's eye, as Aurelia Smith looked up at it with a wandering and somewhat confused look. As if wondering what kind of person – did she know he was a dragon – had put that picture in a diner filled with shifters.

"I thought that Smith was the name of one of the foster families Kyrie lived with?" Tom said, partly to distract his mother-in-law – he guessed? – and partly because he truly was confused.

She gave him a half smile. "I'm sure it was. We didn't leave anything with her, certainly not a name. I thought it would be safer like that. It's just a coincidence. Peter Smith, my husband, and her dad... we got married later."

That was something Tom had been meaning to ask, because he thought maybe it was just Kyrie's mom but not her dad, but– Before he could make her explain, she shook her head and asked, "Did you ever think that that picture might not be the best thing to hang up in an eating area? You... are a dragon shifter? Aren't you? Isn't it a little demented to hang the picture of a dragon-slaying saint?"

He laughed. He couldn't help it. "That's exactly what Kyrie said when I bought it," he said. "But then again, I'd just come back from the dead, so she didn't make too many demands." Which he now understood completely. If – not when – he got Kyrie back, he wasn't going to make any demands, either. He was going to do whatever she wanted, even if it was that bizarre idea she'd had a month ago of painting the bedroom purple with stars all over the ceiling. "And like the painting. I think it's important for shifters to realize what happens if they get above themselves."

Aurelia gave a little shake of the head and sighed. "So, I guess you guys found out about being shifters together, right? No one ever sat you down or told you the rules or anything, right?"

"Oh, the Great Sky Dragon has done quite a bit of telling us the rules," Tom said. His voice came out blasé and annoyed. "For values of telling that once involved eviscerating me with a claw."

She made a sound that might have been laughing. "I see he went to the same school of pedagogy as my *revered* father, who thought a killing blow putting us out of commission for a few days was the way you corrected table manners. Took me years before I figured out what was happening. Though, he did tell us a lot about what being a shifter meant and how to navigate the world of shifters."

"Us?"

She ignored him. "The problem is that it's very hard sometimes to tell Father's charming delusions and deliberate lies from reality. Which is why Peter and I chose to abandon Kyrie. You see, we didn't think she would be a shifter. We didn't know how to tell. And we were afraid Father would eat her."

Tom blinked at her. It occurred to him that "eat her" wasn't metaphorical. But he couldn't even say the words. It seemed outrageous. He had various kinds of beefs with the Great Sky Bastard, but to his knowledge, even the GSD hadn't ever eaten someone. Maybe he had. There were things that Conan had said that might incline that way, but damn it, it had never been that explicit. And he certainly had never threatened to eat any of his descendants for not being able to shift. As far as Tom understood, most of them couldn't. And there was no other male descendant of the Great Sky Dragon that shifted into a dragon.

"I know, I know," Aurelia said, as though answering something that Tom not only hadn't said but had no idea how to say. Then she said something that meant she'd guessed wrong. "I get it, okay? But we were college students. Very young. We really had no clue. And we didn't know Peter could shift – he shifted late for the first time. In his mid-twenties – so we were scared. I mean I was probably attracted to the way he smelled. But I didn't know how shifters smelled. And who would think my geeky blond boyfriend would shift into a big black panther of all things?"

Tom rubbed his hand across his face, realizing he'd now been awake for twenty-four hours. When he'd woken up, it had been with the excitement of getting to marry Kyrie. And now.... "Sometimes," he said, his voice sounding hoarse, "the only person that explained things to us, in a way we could understand, was an old alligator shifter named Joe. And his memory was so glitchy that we never knew what would come up next."

"Old Joe," Aurelia said perking up. "Old Joe is around here?"

"No. He, ah ... there was a shifter named Maduh, and there are apparently some kind of space-alien spirits, and they...."

Her face became very sober. "That's when your merry band came to Father's attention, and then he traced all your backgrounds, and that's when he found out that Kyrie was ... ours. That was a moment. He only didn't kill us for a few days because people would have noticed if we didn't show up for work at the lab. But trust me, it would have been preferable..."

Tom groaned. "I'm so worried about Kyrie, and the power is so close and so tempting. I know if I let myself go...." He took a deep breath. "What I don't understand is what the Great Sky Dragon is playing at. It's like he's pushing me to be ... to become this...."

Aurelia sighed. "It's the games these old shifters play. That's how I could sense that you were fighting not to become the Great Sky Dragon, because I know how their minds work and what they try to make you do. Now mind you, Father never wanted to give up any of his power, but he played mind games with us all the time."

"But you're adults," Tom said. "I mean, I guess so are we, of course, but you're–"

"Old, I know," Aurelia said.

"No, no. I mean, as the Great Sky Dragon says, when you live thousands of years, what's the difference in age between us, but really? I mean, you talk as if you lived under his thumb."

"Everyone who is a lion shifter lived under Father's thumb," she said. Then she looked at Tom. "Except maybe your friend Rafiel, and Father was going to fix that as soon as he got a chance. He seemed to think Rafiel was descended from one of his own by-blows that had escaped being exterminated and he thought the mistake could be retroactively fixed. You really have no idea, do you?"

"Are you ready to cooperate now?" Angrboda asked, coming into Kyrie's cell.

Kyrie wasn't sure. She didn't want to cooperate, but then again, she wanted to go home. For one, she'd slept. Kind of. Crumpled up against the wall was a hell of a way to sleep, but thanks to pregnancy she could sleep anywhere. Including standing up and giving a coffee warm up to a table. She was glad they'd laughed, instead of being mad, when she dropped the coffeepot on the table.

It was like, "I have a superpower. Well, two. One is falling asleep anywhere, the other is peeing myself."

But she didn't say anything, because she wasn't required to admit to weaknesses. And she wasn't sure it was actually a weakness. She could probably fall asleep while the Queen of Evil was talking to her, and wouldn't that be a surprise for the old supernatural biddy? Kind of a psychological coup, wouldn't it be?

The other thing was that she was starving, but she wasn't about to reveal that either. Kind of, because she found that as she dragged herself to standing against the wall, she looked at Angrboda's near-colorless eyes and said, "I've been thinking of fried wings. Fried dragon wings would be really big. And I wonder if they'd be spicy."

To her shock, the evil creature laughed. "That's the spirit," she said. "Eating your enemies is always the best revenge. But I don't want you to think of me as an enemy."

Kyrie's first thought was *of course you don't*. But what came out of her mouth was, "Is it better to think of you as an appetizer?"

And that time the creature was silent, as though confused or perhaps worried. Though what Kyrie, who was wholly human and wouldn't be able to shift until she gave birth, anyway, could have done to worry a dragon was inexplicable.

"I don't know if you realize who I am?" the creature said.

"Sure. You're the queen. I'm not super sure queen of what, but we're getting kind of used to people dropping by and claiming to be the leader of this and the ruler of that, so a queen isn't even a surprise, though I imagined queens always wore funny hats and you don't seem to do that."

There was a sound in the back of the dragon shifter's throat that might have been sheer annoyance. Heck, it probably was.

"I am," the woman said, "the Queen of the North."

"Oh, is that what we're doing now? We're claiming kingship over the directions of the compass? I think I'll be the Princess of the South. Or how does Duchess of the Northeast strike you?"

The smack came out of nowhere, and it was probably a gentle slap, to the side of Kyrie's head. Probably because she knew that old shifters could pack a heck of a stronger punch. But it didn't mean she should like it.

Her "ow" was subsumed into the Queen's, "Foolish child. Do not joke about that which you don't understand."

"I understand perfectly that you showed up, out of the blue, had your minions kidnap me for some reason that made no sense, and then decided to tell me you were the Queen of a Cardinal Direction." And then as a memory flashed, "I also know your name is Angrboda, the Mother of Monsters, who is supposed to be Loki's wife."

"I have no idea who Loki is," the creature said, with a sort of laugh. "I think his legend was invented while I was asleep. Though with my luck he's probably an upstart little shifter who decided to claim to be my husband while I was immured and out of time, in order to get some prestige among foolish mortals. I wonder if he's even a dragon shifter."

"Horse, if legend has it right." And Kyrie was not even going to get into the sex change that went with it, or into the eight-legged offspring. She had the impression that she and the Queen of the Compass weren't just not on the same page, they were probably not on the same book, and might be in different libraries.

"No, really? The nerve." She was silent a long time, then shrugged. "Ah, very good. I'll eat him when I find him."

"Sounds like a plan."

"Now, about us."

"Lady, there isn't—"

"No, there is. You see, I am the Queen of the North, the one that the King of the East made a pact with. He came upon the bridge of ice, and we had a child together."

"Sure. Tom's ancestor."

"Tom? Oh, you mean my son's son, your husband." The creature made a gesture as if that were of the least importance possible. "That doesn't matter much."

It reminded her of the Great Sky Dragon seeming to think the marriage between her and Tom was a thing of no account and transitory that they could deal with at some point in the next hundred years or so. She wasn't going to argue. Again, she had a feeling even all else being the same that this creature was not precisely sane or connected with reality at many levels.

"The child born wasn't a shifter, though, and the King of the East used my state of being unable to shift to get power over me, so as soon as the baby was delivered, he put me and my court in stasis for—"

She got that expression people do when they're doing calculations in their heads. "I think ten thousand years, but it might be twenty. It doesn't matter." She sounded very sad, but at the same time somewhat annoyed. "I am awake now, and we'll see who emerges victorious."

"Wait, what?"

"There is a war between the dragons, little one. And it's time for you to choose sides."

Kyrie's first impulse was to say, "A plague on both your houses," but instead she just stared and blinked. "I have no part in this war," she said at last.

"Oh, but you do. All clan leader shifters do. And besides, won't you have pity on a mother's plight?"

As Rafiel had thought before, the problem of getting so many murders that you got the attention of the local big wigs, in their efforts to "curb crime" was that while it gave you some perks, like a forensic van that could do a bunch of the processing, it also came with .... In this case with a guy who was supposed to be the police chief, and more directly, the head of the Serious Crimes Unit for Goldport and "put the house in order" was what the mayor had said, after he'd dusted whatever old city charter and realized they were supposed to have a police chief.

And he'd decided that, somehow, would stop all the crimes.

Which was mind-boggling, since they had solved every single one of the murder cases that had come up in the last two years, both shifter-related and not. Granted a couple of them hadn't been particularly satisfactorily resolved, not so far as the police knew, since there were things one couldn't put in a police report, such as, "There were two shifter beetles mating, and that's why there were a bunch of corpses buried in the old castle grounds, because that's where they were laying their eggs, and we had to burn everything before they stopped." But the crimes had been solved and stopped.

Not that the mayor seemed to care, and neither did Rafiel's new superior.

Rafiel was reminded of this when – stymied on taking control of the situation – he retreated to the car called in to see if he had a forensic report and was told that the old man wanted to talk to him. That was the other bizarre thing. How had they started calling him the Old Man when he was maybe all of ten years older than Rafiel.

Rafiel groaned in the back of his throat at the idea that he'd have to call his boss, but charged cheerfully ahead, "So, on the forensics?"

"Oh, those are outright weird," the guy said. "Like.... As we suspected on the site neck was sliced clean off. Very sharp blade."

Rafiel groaned. He hadn't wanted the first report to be wrong, and for the head to be bitten off, but... all he needed now was Highlander replaying itself in Goldport. Like shifters weren't enough. "What kind of saber? Can we narrow it down."

"That's the part we're not sure about. The lab is processing it, okay?"

He got all the data, while the two werewolves sat one in the passenger side and one in the back, very quiet, which always disturbed Rafiel. It was like they were communicating silently. Maybe they were. Wolves were pack animals, weren't they? Cas, in the passenger seat, rubbed his hands together now and then.

Rafiel sighed. "That's probably the best we can do."

As he hung up, the phone rang immediately. The display window of the car showed Milagros, M.

Rafiel swore softly. Out in the parking lot of the Three Luck Dragon, more dragons landed.

Kyrie blinked.

Angrboda said, "I realized I have been going about this all the wrong way. You are from a proud people." She paused, and for some reason, Kyrie had the impression the woman – creature? – was chewing on the words, testing their meaning. "And I should not demand your obedience, but rather show you what is coming and the importance of what is upon us, and how much I need your help."

Kyrie didn't say anything, because she couldn't figure out how to say anything. This wasn't helped by the guard who'd come in with her Majesty of the Directions. He was short, which was the first time she'd seen a short guy in this place. And his eyes were dark and strangely familiar. Also, either he was winking frantically at her, or there was something stuck in his left eye.

And Kyrie was almost sure that his armor and tunic were plastic and polyester from a cheap costume rental shop. His lance almost for sure was.

However, the most bizarre thing was his wig. And she was absolutely sure it was a wig, one of those that are sold as "glamour wigs" or whatever at

Halloween. From the look of this one, it was supposed to look like Marilyn Monroe's styling.

Kyrie tried not to look directly at him, because she thought that if she did, Angrboda might also, and there was no way this guy here was a legitimate part of her retinue.

Just as she was thinking this, Angrboda turned to the young man, "Bilbo," she said. "Lead us to the cave of Jörmungandr."

Bilbo? Kyrie thought. Followed by, *Oh dear.* In this context, the cave of terrors worried her less than the complete insanity.

"And in the second place," Mr. Milagros said. "I want to know why you left the diner, the actual crime scene, to go haring off to ... where the hell are you precisely?"

Rafiel seriously regretted having paired his phone with the car. The voice was coming out through the loudspeakers, at the level of a fundamentalist preacher rolling into a demand that everyone approach the communion rail.

Cas, sitting in the passenger seat, looked like he'd been carved from a block of stone, his features looking suddenly sharp and precise, as if he couldn't move without the whole thing cracking.

And Nick had an idiotic smile on his face, his tongue pushing slightly between his teeth. It made him look like a dog does when he smiles, but it might not mean anything more than Rafiel felt embarrassment tinged with a desperate need to bite something.

"We're outside the Three Luck Dragon, sir. There is some sort of disturbance going on."

Disturbance was putting it mildly, as there was a crowd of bodies, bopping and writhing together. And some kind of action – he wasn't sure what, but he swore one of the dragons had just got swatted – that made a bunch of dragons jump back all at once like they were engaged in some sort of odd dance.

There was a long silence, and Rafiel imagined Mr. Milagros holding his breath. He'd have his fancy fountain pen in his hand, and he'd be twirling it between his fingers, while his teeth clamped on his lip. It gave the impression that he didn't want to speak, because anything he'd say would be utterly devastating.

Rafiel believed it too. After all, this wasn't the first time he'd been the object of the Old Man's ire. Or any of them had been such. And the man had a gift of the cutting word.

There wasn't much that Rafiel could say. Yeah, sure, the dragons were about to go boogie, and per their normal procedure, there would be some remains – mostly human remains – that wouldn't simply come back tomorrow. The Great Sky Bastard had a great fondness for reducing to ashes those he meant to really get rid of for good. And there had been a dragon scale in the parking lot of the diner.

But how the hell could you say that to a non-shifter?

****

Tom had a weird feeling. When he was little, he'd been told that there was no end to a circle. It just went around and around and around.

He wasn't sure why, except that his nanny was answering a lot of his inane questions, and Tom suspected that had been one of them. He didn't remember that. All he remembered was hearing that if he walked a circle on the floor, he could walk forever and never reach the end of it.

He remembered it because at five it was the first time his mind had come up against the concept of the infinite. Of something that wouldn't end.

His parent's foyer in their upscale condo was marble, and had, embedded in it, as part of the design, a circle in different-colored marble.

And Tom had started walking it.

In his mind, he had walked it for days, or perhaps months. But he knew very well that at that time an afternoon at the zoo seemed to last as long as the whole summer vacation a few years later. So he suspected he'd walked it for minutes. He doubted he'd made it to an hour. Eventually, he'd fallen asleep, and his nanny had carried him to his bed. He remembered waking up with his nanny telling about it to someone on the phone and laughing at him.

He'd been offended, in the way very young children are, at the adults' total lack of understanding.

But these many years later, what remained clear in his mind was walking that circle, over and over and over again, and thinking it had no end, it was infinite. It would be the same in the beginning and the end. It went on forever.

Right then he felt the same. Without falling asleep in the middle of it, or the milk and cookies afterward.

He looked at Aurelia Smith's eyes, so much like Kyrie's, and he took a deep breath. "What you're describing is something very ancient isn't it?"

Aurelia giggled. Her giggle was also very like Kyrie's, and totally inappropriate for a woman her age but not unpleasant. "I don't know how old my father was. But I wouldn't be surprised if he had served as the model for Chronos devouring his children. Though I suspect he was much older than that."

"And with your father dead, what happens?" Tom said.

She sighed. "I have no idea, precisely. Understand that I really am in my forties. I was in college in the nineties when Kyrie was born. All I know is what I heard around the kr ... around my father's compound, as he was talking to his friends. You see, sometimes ... there are times when the leadership of a clan changes, when all the leaders die or are otherwise taken off power. They called them the changing times. Ragnarok, the people of the North call it. The fall of the gods. I guess primitive peoples thought of shifters as gods."

"And that's where we are?" Tom asked. His mind stretched to impossibly ancient times. The changing times presupposed more than one had happened. Wasn't Ragnarok supposed to be only once? And if it weren't, how would anyone know, if it was far in pre-history?

And then suddenly it all added up: What Aurelia had said, and the call from the Great Sky Dragon about something Tom needed to take part in, and–

He was left with something not a headache. Something that was what the headache would leave behind, if it were one of those headaches that lasted for days: a vague nausea, and a sense that his mind had been bruised and his eyes could suddenly see with unblinking clarity, and he wouldn't be allowed to look away.

"Your father was the chief of the lion clan."

"Yes."

"And Kyrie was taken by dragons. And there's a dragon fight going on somewhere – at Acadia, I assume, but then again, the Great Sky Bastard called me to the Three Luck Dragon, I'm sure of it."

"She was? But then that's not about the lion leadership."

"No," Tom said. "It's the business of dragons."

He was already up, already moving. Apparently, it wasn't just his mouth. His body could also decide that he needed to do things before he thought of it.

"Fascinating talking to you," he said. "But I must go and get my wife back."

"No, wait," he heard Aurelia say, but he was already running for the back door. He decided he wouldn't change. Too easy to manipulate him if he were in dragon form. But he would drive.

He tore out of the parking lot in the supply van without even thinking. It seemed sturdier, and more likely a war vehicle than their little sub-compact.

When Bilbo – that could not be his name! – opened a door in the rock wall – a real door, not one of the gates that seemed to partition the rest of the cave into sections, the first thing Kyrie noticed was the smell.

It smelled like... the snake house at the zoo, if the snake house at the zoo were particularly dirty.

The second thing that was obvious was reddish light coming out.

She could swear Bilbo was grimacing under his fright wig, but it wasn't until the Queen of the Cardinal Points pulled the door open, and looked inside with a doting and fond smile, like an elderly lady surveying a basket of newborn kittens, that Kyrie caught a glimpse of what was inside.

It wasn't kittens.

At first, she couldn't make much sense of what she was seeing, except that there was movement, and ... sliding. There was the impression of dark green and yellow, too, and her first thought is that it was a cave full of lizards.

But the eye has a way of seeing things clearly once the mind has time to adapt.

And the first coherent thing she saw were two eyes. They were huge, oddly human, and looking up at her with an impression of conjoined malevolence and longing.

Beneath it was an open mouth with fangs.

And then her brain suddenly clicked, and showed Kyrie that what she'd thought were multiple lizards were in fact a giant snake, so huge that the coils slid on coils, and it filled the entire cave however large and deep it was

It couldn't be a cave in Colorado. It didn't make any sense for it to be a cave in Colorado. Though she remembered reading somewhere that there were caves in Colorado with shafts so long they went all the way to the Pacific Ocean. She wasn't sure she ever believed it, though.

Now, she wouldn't take a bet one way or another.

She particularly wasn't sure, because, between the stench, the light, and the sense of unalloyed malevolence coming from the dark cavern, she wanted to retch. She had the feeling that a month of dinners was waiting to come out. And the kid must have sensed it, too, because he was kicking up a storm.

Kyrie took a step back but found that the Queen had grabbed around the upper arm.

"It is my son," the Queen said, in the sort of voice someone might have talked about a rosy and smiling baby. "Jörmungandr. He ... something went wrong when he was made. It was early after the last Ragnarök, and something went wrong." She turned to Kyrie, and Kyrie got a feeling she was trying to persuade her by means beyond talking and looking pitiful. "Will you not have pity on a mother's grief? If you do, I will look after you. And your husband."

The baby was kicking up a storm, and Kyrie didn't know if it was because her heart was hammering in her throat, or because the kid could feel the weight of the attempted mind control of the crazy queen, or her malevolent "child". But Kyrie didn't need to know why. What she needed to do was get away from there.

She managed to pull her arm from the iron grip of the pale, manicured hand, and step back, once, twice, till she didn't feel she would just pass out and drop into the cave.

Bilbo's eyes were on hers, wide and concerned.

"Lady," Kyrie said, her voice thick and slurred because she was working so hard not to throw up. "I have no idea what the hell you're talking about or what my having pity on you will do."

In her mind was some story she had seen in a tabloid, years ago, about women giving birth to snakes. And how. Only if the queen had given birth to this snake, it must have taken a heck of a long time.

The Queen of the North turned around to look at Kyrie, her back to the cave full of slithering, smelly snake. Her eyes were wide, as though she were profoundly startled by Kyrie's response. And her mouth had a sort of desperate smile pasted on, the kind of smile you imagined would break into a thousand pieces and fall off her face, like a cartoon character's expression.

"But–" the Queen said. "It is obvious. I want your child's body for my son. It won't mean anything to you. The child won't even be a shifter. He's just human."

She reached out and touched Kyrie's belly. Her hand felt like ice, and the baby went suddenly still.

There were many things she could have done and got a bad reaction from a heavily pregnant panther shifter. This one might have been the worst one.

Since she'd been pregnant, Kyrie had tried to shift several times, and had absolutely no success.

Now, suddenly, she was trying really hard not to shift. It seemed to her like her teeth and claws had both lengthened, and there was an animal growl in her voice when she said, "Hell no."

And as the queen blinked at her in incomprehension, it seemed to Kyrie that her body reacted of her own accord. Her leg lifted and administered a kick to the queen's knee, and Kyrie jumped back and out of reach, only mildly relieved the kid resumed a fanfare of kicking and moving around, like he was trying to escape her belly.

The queen screamed, but before she could react, an alligator tail, seemingly coming out of nowhere, hit her midsection.

The Queen of the North stepped back, lost her footing, and went tumbling into the snake cave.

And the alligator tail closed the door.

Kyrie blinked. There was an alligator, wearing the remnants of plastic armor, a plastic Viking helmet, and a fright wig.

"Old Joe?" she said weakly. "But you're dead."

Rafiel expected Mr. Milagros to come back with the worst possible type of sarcasm, but instead, when the chief spoke his voice sounded genuinely puzzled. "Why the hell are you pursuing crowd control in the middle of a murder investigation?" he asked.

"What? Oh. Because it might be related. We've had problems with triad activity before."

A long silence followed, then, "Officer Trall, do you really think that the death of a middle-aged African-American man from out of town is related to triad activity?"

"Well … could be." Rafiel was desperately trying to come up with a rationale. It would be so much easier to say that whenever something went hinky in town the Great Sky Bastard was in it claw deep, and that right now … right now, given the dead man was a shifter….

Rafiel blinked, as it was getting hard to see outside, for the crust of ice forming on the windshield. But even in reduced visibility, it was easy to see that there were more dragons than before. It was starting to be like the joke about the clown car, only this was dragons and a fairly large parking lot.

It was also really weird to tell whether there were any humans out there, or what the mix was.

"Officer Trall," Mr. Milagros sounded like he was on his last nerve, or perhaps past. "I don't think you realize the politically sensitive nature of this investigation. This is an African-American man in a mostly white town. And he seems to be wealthy and connected and sponsors a lot of charities. When news of his death spreads, we might have a situation on our hands.

"Being from LA, I can tell you that I see this situation very clearly indeed. I suggest you come back to the crime scene, or at least to the lab van, and then question the man's family, and follow through on the statements of those in the diner at the time. In LA , it was always the details that solved this type of crime. Someone might have seen what was going on in the back parking lot, by accident. Or they might have seen someone suspicious walking back there. Look, I know they're saying the man's head was cut off with a saber or sword, but there's no way that's right. I don't trust this kind of lab result. It's probably contamination.

"The size of sword needed to cut off the head of a full-grown male in an area where he could have set up an alarm is more than could have been back there unnoticed. No, he was probably shot, and the head was sawed off, I'm sure. Which means someone carried it, and that someone was likely to be covered in blood. Someone must have seen him or her. Go and sift through those statements. You'll find a lead."

Rafiel closed his eyes, and even though he wasn't particularly religious, sent up a prayer for patience. He desperately wanted to say, "Sir, has it ever occurred to you that there can be only one?"

He wasn't going to. For one, Milagros would probably not understand it. For two, he might and that would be worse.

There wasn't much point, really, arguing with his boss on this point, but seriously? He thought someone had been running around with a human head under his arm and covered in blood and that this was a *detail* that would only show up on careful examination of evidence? Pah. He knew that the mayor had said the man had been Chief of Police in LA before coming here, but seriously? Unless people did more mescaline in LA than could be harvested in a year all over the world, how was it possible that running around with a head under one's arm, and looking like an extra from Texas Chainsaw Massacre was not an immediate and obvious tell, and also something that would be talked about all over town and discovered within seconds?

And then Rafiel thought he really didn't want to know about LA.

He realized he was about to be incredibly disrespectful. He realized that it might lose him his job, or at least cost him a reprimand, or some other kind of retaliation. But there came a point when enough was enough.

And if enough wasn't enough when you were next to a parking lot in which dragons were starting to look like tinned sardines in a peculiarly small can, and when one of your best friends was missing, and when the dragons intimated there was some kind of war going on, when could you actually say it was enough?

"Sir," Rafiel said. His voice came out very clear, and weirdly cold and detached, like he was listening to himself from a long distance off. "Fine.

You do that. *You* put out a BOLO for a maniac carrying a human head under his arm and covered in blood. *You* do it right now."

It seemed to him he heard a squeaked, "What?" from the other side, but he'd already hung up.

He rested his head on the steering wheel and took deep breaths.

After a few minutes, the phone started ringing.

The alligator snapped its teeth, and Kyrie had the impression it was grinning at her.

From behind the closed door came screams of ... not terror. But also, not pleased. Somewhere down a hallway came screams of very angry Vikings. Very angry men. Angry men who were shouting in the kind of language that has a lot of paffs and clangs. And there were sounds of swords, too. Or at least heavy metallic sounds.

"Oh, shit," Kyrie said.

And then she realized Bilbo the gator was doing a dance in front of her and gesturing wildly with his head. If he were a dog, this would be the "Timmy is in the well" dance but in this case, it was stranger and accompanied by the clack-clack of castanet teeth hitting together. The little gator eyes had a sense of urgency.

"Yeah, I think we should run," she said. "Do you know the direction?"

Somewhere – she really had to stop doing random internet dives down strange rabbit holes – Kyrie had read that alligators could run sixty miles per hour for like six-foot distances, but were relatively slow on land, otherwise, only running about eleven miles per hour.

The thing was, while she was sure he wasn't running sixty miles per hour, eleven miles per hour was still faster than Kyrie could run, let alone with the kid kicking in rhythm as she ran. She was torn between the certainty she was going to pee herself, and the fear labor would start. Hadn't they said that violent exercise could cause labor?

It didn't matter, or not precisely, because the sound of angry guys with swords running kept coming closer and closer.

Suddenly, inexplicably, there was a gator tail wrapped around her middle. It was a very large gator tail, and she was very out of breath. Before she could react, she found herself sitting astride a humongous gator who was running hell for leather down one dark passage after another.

And all she could do was hold tight to scales – which were kind of slippery – and try not to scream.

5

"RAFIEL," NICK SAID, HIS voice soft and just above a whisper, as though he were afraid of making Rafiel explode again. "The number is from your girlfriend."

Rafiel opened his eyes to see Bea Ruiz's number on his dashboard screen. He pushed the button to answer.

"Rafiel!" she sounded like she'd been waiting a long time.

"Sorry, babe. I thought you were Mr. Milagros."

"How– Never mind. Where are you?"

"Outside the parking lot at the Three Luck Dragon."

"Uh.... Why?"

"We were coming to interrogate the Great Sky Bastard about Kyrie's disappearance."

"You might want to leave there. Fast."

"Why?"

"Because I'm getting a call to battle, and in my mental map, the Three Luck Dragon is throbbing like a migraine."

"Call to–" He hesitated. "Call to battle?"

"Yeah. Apparently, the Chinese dragons are going to war against the Norse dragons. And I keep hearing the word *changes* in my head. Only I think that's wrong, and I'm only being told that because I don't under-stand Chinese."

"I don't know. Isn't the Book of Changes the I-Ching?" Rafiel asked.

"The what? Oh, I don't like this. And I'm not coming. It's hard to resist, but I'm not coming."

"Good." Rafiel looked out. It was now snowing, and above him there were dragons flying what seemed to be circular patrol pattern. "Please don't come. I think there's going to be a lot of death here tonight."

They were out of the cave now, and the alligator was running, fast as heck, down the almost vertical surface of the cliff the caves had been in.

Kyrie was almost lying down, arms around the alligator's neck. She thought this was undoubtedly something that should appear on the internet as a Florida Woman meme. But in the growing snowstorm, she hoped there was no one out with cameras. And worried that the alligator's metabolism would soon ground them, even if the gator was a shifter cold-blooded blooded, right? How long could he keep running in snow?

Unfortunately, the people in pursuit were obviously used to ice and snow. Fortunately, they were not as fast as the gator was, not as long as the Vikings were in human form. But sooner or later, one or more of them would shift.

"Go right at the end," she said. "Then hurry. There's a construction site. Maybe someone left a truck or something we can hotwire."

She wasn't even sure he heard her, but at the bottom of the hill, he turned left, then ran a crazy route that took them through a hole between two rocks, where the opening was small enough that Kyrie almost became stuck. She realized he was trying to run in the shadows so he wouldn't be as obvious from the air. So, despite the wig and the plastic Viking hat, the gator wasn't dumb. Which figured.

She thought that of course, it wasn't Old Joe. For one because Old Joe would already have shifted back to ask some very strange question. Like if she had souvlaki. But how many gator shifters could there be in Colorado?

As she was thinking this, she felt more than saw the first dragon shadow go overhead and heard the rush of wings.

"There," she said. "Can you get us to that ball wrecker? If I can't start it, we're going to have to go into the ruins of the inn and hide."

The gator came to a sliding halt in a spray of snow near the ball wrecker, and Kyrie leapt in. That is, leapt as much as someone who resembles a bowling ball with feet can leap.

Fear was good for that, because she didn't spend any time at all recovering, but looked at the controls. The key was in the ignition. She'd heard this was normal – at least in low-crime areas – because people often changed equipment and didn't want to spend time trying to start up.

She turned to where a small man, with a blond wig askew on his dark hair, and a plastic helmet sideways on his head, and just enough plastic armor to somewhat preserve his modesty was climbing onto the ball wrecker.

"The key is in, Bilbo," she said, as a sound of rushing wings flew overhead. "Hang on tight. We're going home."

Tom saw it from afar. Felt it too. Ahead was strife. War.

About time you joined us, the old Sky Bastard said in Tom's head.

No, Tom thought very intently. I'm not joining. I'm looking for my wife.

He expected something back, perhaps a scream of rage. But there was nothing.

Probably there was nothing because, from the general direction of Acadia, there was a flock of dragons flying in. Their shapes were distinctly different from the Asian dragons that Tom was used to seeing. Bigger. Thicker. Like they could have graced the prow of a dragon ship. More like his own dragon, though he was a bit more svelte.

The dragons in the parking lot rose up.

And Tom swore that it had suddenly got twenty degrees colder. The van's exterior pinged with cold. Or maybe not, but that's what it seemed like to him.

He wondered where Kyrie was.

This was bad, this was very bad.

And then through the increasingly thick flying snow, he saw a police car weaving. It couldn't be Rafiel, because it was a marked police car, siren screaming.

"If he tries to give me a ticket, I'm going to shift and eat him," Tom said to no one in particular.

"I'm going to shift and eat him," Rafiel said, as a marked police car skidded to a stop, facing his car, and Mr. Milagros came out.

He wore a leather jacket tailored like a sports jacket, and a pair of slacks. On his head was a pair of headphones.

One of his least lovely habits around the station was to wear noise-canceling headphones at all times. He'd once told Rafiel that he used them to listen to time management books and seminars. Which was all very well, except for the fact that he also made himself unavailable and consumed vast amounts of everyone else's time, while they semaphored to get his attention.

Apparently, he'd done that to come out and tell off his wayward senior detectives, too.

Above him, the darkening sky was thick with dragons. A band of what could only be described as Norse dragons was flying in from the East, and a detachment of Chinese dragons was flowing to meet them. And a van pulled in behind Rafiel.

The seeming boxing in of his car would have worried him a lot more, if he didn't recognize *The George* supply van and see the silhouette of Tom behind the wheel.

Mr. Milagros knocked on the driver's window and pulled his headphones down.

"What I can't understand," he said, as if they'd been in the middle of an acrimonious conversation, which Rafiel guessed they were, even if on the phone, "is why all of my senior detectives are here, and all of them are sitting in a car. What in hell is going on? Are you clowns waiting for a delivery of doughnuts? No wonder Mayor Billings hired me to bring some order into this department. What is so fascinating about this place?"

Above, there was a flash of fire, which illuminated the whole area in bright orange. Mr. Milagros didn't seem to notice. "I mean, if you guys are going to get Chinese takeout–" He looked towards the restaurant. And stopped.

In the space between them and a restaurant were about ten dragons, and one of them was taking to the sky, a brilliant green and blue dragon, with lashed markings on his wings. He lifted into the confusion of snow and started winging towards the Norse contingent. And then another dragon, this one red and yellow, took off.

"What?" Mr. Milagros said. "What? Is this some movie being filmed?"

Yeah, because a movie being filmed would have special effects visible to the bare eye, Rafiel thought, as he realized with horror that this was exactly the conclusion that one could expect of a mind which thought that someone with a head under his arm would walk casually past the diner windows.

Behind him, Tom had got out of the van, and was standing looking up, next to it.

Most of the dragons were now airborne, and the flaming in the sky was followed by the thud of bodies in flames falling to the ground.

And Rafiel figured out what the worst-case scenario was. He was not ready to lose his best friend. He said, "Excuse me, sir." Pushing the door open, and the bewildered, perhaps catatonic police chief with it, he jumped out, and ran to Tom waving his arms, "Don't shift. Don't shift."

Tom didn't even move.

Kyrie kept driving, expecting at any minute to be grabbed by a pair of claws from above. At least she wouldn't go quietly. And she suspected Bilbo wouldn't either.

After a while it dawned on her. "They're not after us. They're flying towards town."

"Yes. I think there's been a battle cry gone out by the King of the East." His accent was plummy British, distilled accent of upper class and restraint.

"The King of the East? The Great Sky Bastard?"

The man gave a gurgle of laughter. "Oh, is that what you call him? We usually say dragon, but in my experience, dragon and bastard are equivalent words."

"Not my husband."

"No. Not from what I heard. You guys are all right. Which is why I got involved."

She looked over her shoulder. He'd done something with the scraps of the costume that had remained attached to him, so that he wasn't actually breaking any indecency laws. And he was short, wiry, dark-haired, and dark-eyed. He looked....

"I thought ... did you know Old Joe?" she asked.

His laugh had the sort of upper-class feel of his accent. "You could say that. Though I haven't seen him for centuries. I think the last time we met was in India in the eighteenth century. I was working with the East India Company. He was ... he'd gone a bit native." There was a long pause. "I'm going to miss the old man."

Kyrie navigated from Acadia's path to the road with a noticeable bump. "He told you about us?"

"Oh, it's a little more complicated than that. That stunt your husband pulled, calling every shifter in the world, was when I first became aware of him. He shouldn't have been able to do that. Call it a sign of the times. And for a little while I thought he was my replacement, so I investigated."

"Your replacement?"

"I'm ... uh, the leader of the reptiles. Except for the dragons, and there's reasons for that. I inherited from my grandmother, and I don't object to passing it on, but– Ragnarök is a time of instability."

In Kyrie's mind, as she drove a ball wrecker down the street – mercifully deserted – as the snow flew, and she became aware that she was far too cold, the memory of Old Joe talking about how his mother was the leader of the reptiles clicked. "You're Old Joe's son."

The man laughed, delightedly. "You're very quick. Yes, I am. Have been for ... oh, dear. I can't remember exactly how many thousand years. I always forget to carry a zero or two. But I was very young when leadership of reptiles was dumped on me."

"Surely your name isn't Bilbo?" She was now within view of the Three Luck Dragon on the approach to Goldport and, at first, she thought there was a thunderstorm. But closer up, she realized the flashes of light splitting the sky were dragon fire, as Norse and Chinese dragons fought in the skies above.

"Uh. No. I just love Tolkien, and I figured I was small compared to those Norse brutes, so you know ... dear Lord, is that a dragon battle?"

"Looks like it," Kyrie said, and mentally she shouted, Tom, please tell me you're not in the sky and fighting!

Tom shook himself, with a start, as though someone had dumped a bucket of water over his head. He'd been watching the battle, smelling the fire, and trying as hard as he could to both stay out of the mind of the combatants, and not listen to the Great Sky Dragon ordering him to combat, in increasingly strident tones.

Suddenly he heard Kyrie in his mind and woke up. He shouted "Kyrie, where are you?" while sending it mentally as well.

Rafiel was there, inexplicably. Tom hadn't seen him approach, but Rafiel now grabbed him by the shoulders and shook him. "Tom! Where is she?"

I'm about half a mile down the road, she said. I wondered why the dragons weren't following us. What the hell is going on?

Some kind of battle, Tom said. *I don't fully understand it, but it's taking all of my will power not to join in.*

Damn, Kyrie said. And then, urgently, *Have you made sure that Conan is all right?*

Tom beat himself up for not having thought of his friend. He looked up at the melee. Considering Conan had once been mind-linked to the Great Sky Dragon and to what extent, even if he had been given to Tom as a sort of party favor, he was obviously at risk.

He reached a tendril out looking for his friend, while trying to block out all the other intrusive minds around. It was sort of the equivalent of diving into a room full of people all babbling at the same time, while trying to hear only one particular person. Oh, and trying to block out someone shouting with a megaphone.

And yet, he found Conan. He found him by homing in on plaintive cords played on the guitar. He felt the shape of the mind, and mind-shouted at his friend, *Conan, you're not in the middle of the battle, are you?*

The response came back, plaintive and sullen, *No. Rya locked me in the storage room. At least it's not the refrigerated room, though she threatened me with it if I so much as think of shifting. I don't want to shift. But it's kind of boring in here.*

Never mind, Tom said. And he threw a baffle over Conan's mind, to keep him safe and deaf to the call. *Stay put. I think we have Kyrie.*

As he spoke, a ball wrecker, of all things, pulled up alongside the van, and Kyrie ran out, far more limber than he would expect, given the belly.

Behind her, a dark, short guy of Mediterranean looks slithered out and stood, hesitating, beside it.

He was mostly naked, which didn't mean much of anything since he stank of shifter to high heavens. But why in heavens name was he wearing a blond wig and a plastic Viking hat?

"Sir, sir, it's just a movie. It's special effects," Rafiel heard Cas shout from near the police car.

Kyrie was safe, and frankly she and Tom had got locked in an embrace, and Rafiel felt vaguely embarrassed, as he always did with public displays of affection. The weird young man who shifted into a lion, and who had never imagined marital felicity, found other people's romances bewildering, of course. Even if he had one of his own.

But even he couldn't believe that Cas' efforts at convincing Milagros to believe him, and not his lying eyes, were going to work. Or that Milagros really was going to buy this was special effects.

Rafiel cast an entirely too casual look upward. Weird the things you got used to, right? Above him was a bizarre, massive battle between two types of creatures who were supposed to be imaginary. Fire blazed. Burning dragons fell to the parking lot with enough regularity that Rafiel found himself singing "It's raining dragons" to the tune of *It's Raining Men.*

But most of those weren't completely consumed, he noticed, and certainly not through the head. Which meant most of them were down for the count and incapacitated as game markers, but game markers were the precise analogy. They weren't dead. They'd come back from the dead in a few days. But they were *hors de combat.*

He knew regrowing body parts was difficult, took a long time and was painful. And coming back from the dead incapacitated you from shifting forms.

Which meant one, or from the looks of it, both dragon armies would be greatly reduced. But after looking for a while, he was sure that's all it was. They'd be made incapable of fighting for a few days. But he wouldn't have to deal with a bunch of unexplained corpses.

And this somehow made it all part of life in Goldport, with its infestation of shifters, but not an emergency.

Now the important thing was to make sure Mr. Milagros wasn't completely batty. Or wouldn't be. And that he wouldn't be doing anything stupid that involved the rest of the department.

He approached, looking his best dumb-and-not-excited policeman and said, "Officer Wolf is right, sir. It's just special effects. They .... they have these computers that project images, you know, so that the actors can find their marks and make sure that they are in the right place and deliver their lines with feeling."

Mr. Milagros's dark eyes were huge in his face, as he looked up. "Really? I didn't know they had the technology. I mean, I said it first, but then I thought never–"

"Well, sir, I had gotten notice they were filming this, so I thought I would come out and talk to some people, just in case the crime involved them, since the corpse was from out of town, and well dressed."

"Oh, yes. That makes sense. But you need to sift through the depositions and look at the detail. That's how cases are solved."

"Of course, sir. I'm sorry I didn't explain myself properly on the phone. They had just started this projection, and I also didn't know the technology was this realistic. I was so surprised I wasn't thinking straight." As he spoke, he, Cas and Nick walked Mr. Milagros to the police car.

"I'll go with you back to the station and start on those reports now," Nick said. "How about that, sir?" He smiled. Of all of them, he was the one capable of the most diplomacy and finesse, and he was deploying them for all he was worth. "You know, I probably should drop you off at home. I know how dedicated you are, but rank does, after all, have its privileges."

He got Mr. Milagros in the passenger seat, then got in the driver's seat, gave Rafiel and Cas a mock salute and drove away through the snow.

"We probably should get out of here," Cas said. "Dyce is going to be worried. And I'm freezing. What the heck is with the weather?"

"I don't know," Rafiel said. "Nothing exciting was predicted. Perhaps it has to do with the battle."

"Um ... possible. I wonder if the Old Man is going to be, okay?"

"Oh, he'll be fine," Rafiel gave a grin. "I mean, we did think all conceal- ment was blown after Tom issued that general call, but most people have convinced themselves they dreamed it or something. Milagros will proba- bly be really excited about the technology for projecting while filming, and by the time he finds out it doesn't exist – if he ever does – he'll come up with a better explanation. Hold on."

Rafiel approached the van. Kyrie and the weird guy with the plastic helmet were climbing in and Tom was behind the wheel.

He smiled at Cas and Rafiel. "See you back at *The George*?"

Rafiel shook his head. "No. Let's go to your place. I .... don't know if the diner is safe just yet." He made a head gesture towards the battle. "This might spill over there."

The unknown guy nodded. "Quite likely. It's a known hangout of the *New Dragon*."

Rafiel wasn't even going to ask about that. And Tom wasn't new. He was at best lightly used. "See you there, then. I assume you're not going to get involved in this?"

Tom stared out at the burning, clawing, fighting dragons.

"Not for all the tea in China."

"India, actually," the guy said and smiled.

Rafiel had a weird feeling he was familiar, but had no idea who he was, and could summon no recollection.

"What about the ball wrecker?" Kyrie asked. "I didn't even think of re- turning it."

They were at home, in their tiny kitchen, which meant the four of them barely fit. She and Tom sat at the table, while not-Bilbo stood by the back porch door, and Rafiel leaned against the kitchen counter.

After calling his fiancé and finding out she was all right, and her son was in bed, Cas had left again, to go off to the diner and grab very large orders of takeout gyros and souvlaki. Not-Bilbo was hungry, having just shifted. He'd drunk all of Kyrie's remaining half gallon of milk, and eaten a dozen eggs, raw. He'd also borrowed one of Tom's jogging outfits. It didn't look as good on him as on Tom, Kyrie thought, but then again no one said alligators were as sexy as dragons.

The hard part is that they had promised Cas they wouldn't talk about anything that had happened until he was back.

Part of it had been easy, because Kyrie had gone into the bathroom for ten minutes, then had showered, because she felt gross from the cave and from seeing the thing in the closed-off room.

But now they were sitting around the kitchen, while the storm howled outside, and she was trying to stay awake and not to say anything important till Cas got in. She'd asked Not-Bilbo why the Vikings wore helmets with horns. "I thought that had been invented by the Victorians."

He'd shrugged. "Perhaps ancestral memory. These guys aren't Vikings. The people who served the Queen of the North were gone centuries before the first Viking, but things survive. Names, and ... and such. And trust me, their helmets had horns. The hornier the better."

Kyrie had not said anything about the joke, if it was a joke. Instead, she'd tried to find other things to ask. Which was where the ball wrecker worry had come from.

"Oh, I wouldn't worry too much," Tom said. "People will think it's meth. I mean, that's the easiest explanation for everything that is out of place and broken or really, really weird. I wonder what shifters used before they could use meth as an excuse."

"Opium," Not-Bilbo said. And grinned. His grin was, weirdly, like Old Joe's. Like he had too many pointy teeth for a human mouth but was more goofy than threatening.

She remembered what he'd said, about thinking Tom was his replacement, and having to do something about it. She frowned. Just because not-Bilbo was funny, and had a British accent, it didn't make him safe.

Sometimes she thought no shifters, ever, were safe, not even their little group.

She suspected if Tom had really been his replacement, he wouldn't have been safe at all.

****

"Well," Tom said. "The gang is all here, so can we talk about it now?"

They'd moved to the living room because Cas had come back with Nick, who'd said that "The Old Man went home, and seriously, I can skim the reports of the witnesses and tell him some highlights tomorrow, and he'll think I spent the night poring over the details." And Conan, who said he was really tired of the storage area, and who felt even less like shifting and going to the fight with Tom nearby. Tom made a point of not investigating why he could dampen the call for Conan. Rya had come with Conan. And somehow Bea had materialized at the door, driving Rafiel's father's car.

Which meant Tom's little nothing of a driveway was crowded with four cars, one of them a marked police car. He would worry about what the neighbors would think, except that they were known to have policemen friends, to the point Mrs. Markham across the street had come to them with reports of a prowler last week because "I thought you could tell your nice policeman friend, and that way I don't have to call the police."

Mostly because Mrs. Markham called the police about prowlers so much that they didn't take her very seriously. And they probably shouldn't, since it was all based on motion detectors on her back porch. Though, honestly, it would help if Jason Cordova didn't go through her trash can in bear form. Even if she kept finding and throwing away her husband's half-filled booze bottles.

So, the small crowd had spilled over to the living room, where he and Kyrie were seated cozily together on the futon, while Rafiel and Bea huddled on the floor by the window, and the other guys were distributed around the room.

Conan had brought paper plates from the diner and had taken it upon himself to serve everyone. Kyrie was eating, because frankly these days Kyrie spent a lot of time eating and sleeping, but Tom felt he couldn't take a bite, even if he hadn't eaten much in the last twelve hours or so. He wanted to know what had happened.

There were several alarms going on in his back brain, and he wanted to know what was in play and who all the players were.

Kyrie ate a couple of pieces of souvlaki and sighed, "Okay, this is what happened to me."

It was a bizarre story, Rafiel thought. But then, he couldn't imagine anyone making it up. "So, you didn't see who killed the man?"

"No. I– had a weird feeling from him, but I didn't know him. I smelled blood, probably as I was being grabbed. But it's all confusing because I think I was being mind-controlled."

Tom looked like he wanted to say something but was holding it back by sheer force of will, and Rafiel decided he wasn't going to ask. Though it took effort.

"And you?" Rafiel said, looking at the man in the plastic Viking helmet. "Kyrie said that you're Old Joe's son. But we don't know your name, nor what you were doing in the middle of all this."

The man grinned with too many teeth. He wiped his hands on a paper napkin and stood up. He bowed slightly. "My name is Nimrod, but you may call me Rod. My surname of convenience has been Dalquist for a while."

"Surname of convenience?"

The dark eyes were vaguely tolerant and full of amusement. "I was born in Ur of the Chaldees... I don't remember the year. Under... don't remember ruler's name. For my own peace of mind, I make it a point to shed all but the last couple thousand years from memory, except for very early childhood, of course. I should remember the ruler's name, but I don't. I probably wrote it on a clay tablet somewhere, but no one has found it so far. Probably broken."

Rafiel couldn't tell if the man was making fun of him or now, and felt his hackles rise, even though he tried not to show it.

"Easy," Rod Dalquist said. "I know you're a policeman, and they tend to want everyone's identity. But honestly, it's just that I picked the name up somewhere in the fifteenth century when I was doing business in those parts. Was the name of a good friend, who died of something awful, so I took his name. Most shifters are Smith or Jones, or the equivalent for their areas, and it gets tiring. Werewolves are refreshing because they tend to be Wolf, Lupo, Volk, etc. But no one goes around calling himself Gator."

Rafiel frowned, then nodded. There was no point disputing it. He wasn't Smith or Jones, but his parents weren't shifters, and he imagined if people lived long enough in many civilizations, particularly if they were born before surnames were a thing, it probably didn't matter what you were called. As was, if he and the others lived that long – Ur of the Chaldees, really? – they'd have to find identities to avoid detection, in the modern, hyper-connected world.

Rod sat back down. "It's strange," he said, conversationally. "I don't think I've been around these many young shifters in.... tens of thousands of years. And then it was–" He frowned. "Part of it, of course, is that most shifters used to die really young. The first time they shifted and were caught by someone, that was it. Only a few survived and were canny enough to pass and reproduce." He speared an olive from his plate and chewed it philosophically. "But I wonder if the approach of Ragnarök is causing more of us to be born. It's what woke the queen you know. Probably all started with the New Dragon here."

"You said that to me, in the ball-wrecker." Kyrie sat up straight, obviously making an effort to stay awake. "That it was Ragnarök. Do you mean it? The end of the world?"

Rod laughed. "Oh, heck, no. Not the end of the world, though I suppose the Norse decided that's what it meant, but the ice-heads are nuts anyway. Too much cold froze their brains long ago. No. Ragnarök means the twilight of the gods. And it's giving our kind way too much credit, though I suppose a lot of us impersonated divinities and supermen back in the days, which explains everything you ever wanted to know about the Roman gods, I guess."

"You said most clan heads die, or at any rate, the clans get new heads."

"Yes..." Rod said, suddenly uninterested in explaining more.

"Yes? And you called me the New Dragon. I'm going to tell you to get that out of your head." Tom said. He was sitting up very straight. "Because let me tell you, Rod of the Chaldees, I really have no intention of presiding over a bunch of semi-criminal dragon shifters."

Rod laughed. "Oh, not all of them are semi-criminal. A good number are outright criminal-criminal. And the Norse ones are just nuts. I don't think they're technically criminal, because they haven't been in civilization long enough to realize there are laws, except the word of their queen. They're just barbarians. We were more civilized back in Ur."

"I still don't want any part of them," Tom said. He was now fully alert. Rafiel noted that so was Bea, sitting up.

Rod's smile twisted into something hard to define. "You might not get a choice, pardon my saying so. Though if you try to be head of all clans, you might end up with a fight in your hands."

"What in hell do you mean, precisely?" Rafiel asked.

"Oh, boy. You're a lion, right? Are you in the running?"

"In the running for what?"

"Head of the feline clans."

Rafiel felt something cold in his stomach, and he couldn't explain it. "What in hell is that?"

"The man who died tonight. That's who he was. The lion who was head of them all. And had been for three Ragnaröks. He ate the competition."

Kyrie wasn't even vaguely sleepy, suddenly, "Is that why he tried to get in my mind? And why he wanted to talk to me?"

"Probably. He probably thought you were in the running. And he didn't want you to be. Or he was trying to make a play to stay in the running. I don't know exactly? We lost the jade some time ago, so I don't have all the memories, but..." He huffed. "Look, I was born after the last Ragnarök, so I can't be sure. But my grandmother, who raised me, because dad was... wrong born, and mom died when I was little, said that the lion head hadn't changed for two Ragnaröks, so it was probably the same one. She called him The Old Horror like you call the dragon head The Old Sky Bastard. Though honestly, grandmother might have been that old too because dad always said he was born before horses, and she never disputed it. She might be among the ones who came into flesh first. I just don't know if she was head of clan, or if she just became head of reptiles after the Ragnarök before the last Ragnarök. I know once she talked to me about the gathering place when she became head, and–" He shook his head.

"And?" Rafiel asked. He felt as if his flesh were crawling, and his scalp was moving over his head. It wasn't like shifting, but more like dread. Like his flesh was trying to leave his bones behind and go ... elsewhere. Somewhere that made more sense perhaps.

Rod smiled apologetically. He ate a long strip of gyro in a way that made it incontrovertibly obvious that he was in fact a gator shifter and sighed. "Look, I don't know anything, okay, but I follow pictures of digs and archeology, particularly in the Middle East, because sooner or later they're going to find some stupid thing I wrote in some clay tablet, or someone else wrote on cave wall or papyrus. And then I'm going to have to step in and discredit them. I've considered becoming an archeologist, just to throw dust in the eyes of the busybodies. But, having read the works, I suspect a good number of them already are shifters. Old shifters. They are as busy sweeping oddness under the rug, as we are when we talk about someone on meth moving ball wreckers or something stranger.

"However, when pictures started coming out of the place called Göbekli Tepe. I started recognizing some of the things grandmother talked about. All the pillars, carved with animals, the gathering places for the clan fights." He shook his head. "Not that it matters, does it, after all this time? It's not like we're going out there to fight."

"Clan fights?" Rafiel asked, as his hair tried to stand on end. He still felt something scrabbling at his mind. A sense of nightmare, and of not being in control of his destiny.

Kyrie watched Rod. He stared at Rafiel for a long time, then said "Clan is probably not the right word. Clade might be better, but it's not that either. I never figured out why certain animals go together, such as my having visibility and command of gators, crocs, snakes, and lizards. I think it was a pact made long ago. Perhaps at the beginning. It's like all the birds go together, except the chickens. You don't want to know about the chickens."

Kyrie really didn't want to know about chickens. As far as she was concerned, the best use of a chicken was fried. But she remembered what Rod had said before, his not-so-veiled hostility against dragons, or at least the Great Sky Dragon.

"So, is the dragon clan being in charge of all animals also something that was decided at the beginning?" she asked. "And why did you say Tom might have no choice?"

Rod shrugged. Suddenly he sounded tired. "Because no one really has a choice. One day you're going along fine, living your life, and the next day the... power? Responsibility? Whatever you want to call it, of your particular shifter thing drops on you, and you have to learn to use it on the run." He held his hands out. "I didn't kill grandma. I wouldn't dare because she was cunning and canny. And anyway, I thought the power would go to father. But apparently, someone else killed her, in the last Ragnarök. And power fell on me. The only warning, I had was these ridiculous headaches that seemed to never stop, and a feeling something was trying to get into my mind. And dreams. The horrible dreams.

"Then one day I woke up and I was the leader and being attacked. There were idiots, you see, part of grandmother's advisors, and they– They thought while Ragnarök was on, if they took me down, they'd be leaders. I don't know why they wanted it. I almost died fighting them off."

He sighed. "We never really know who is chosen or why, though it might be more obvious if the clan has its object. In the dragons, it is obvious that the Pearl of Heaven chooses, and if it chose you," he tipped his head towards Tom. "There is really nothing you can do."

"It didn't choose me," Tom said. "I stole it. And then gave it back, before the Great Sky Bastard killed me."

"Oh, is that it?" Rod said and grinned his disturbing too-many-teeth grin. "And you think you could steal the pearl without it having a special affinity to you? Nuts."

He ate a couple of strips of souvlaki while staring at the plate like it might contain all the mysteries of the universe. "Look," he said. "I'm not–" He looked back at Kyrie. "I don't know why the dragon chief has control over everyone else, too. It's not used very often. Which is why when you used it." He looked at Tom. "And I heard the call, and saw the other reptiles get it too, I thought you were my successor as leader of the reptiles getting warmed up. Turns out, no. Not really. Grandmother said that the Dragons had seized the power over everyone illegally, and she suspected them of having grabbed the other ... clans sacred objects, but I honestly don't know."

"I'm not going to fight," Tom said. "And say that the Great Sky Dragon is too honest and upright to do any such thing. I'm not insane."

Kyrie sighed. "Your ancestress on the other side isn't any better."

"Oh... the Queen of the North. No. I didn't know she was part of the Norse myth. Or such an unsavory one. She's supposed to be married to Loki."

"She denied it."

"Okay, maybe. Or maybe she knows him under another name." Tom looked like he had some problem that he wasn't exactly ready to air. She wondered what it was. "So, Rod, if one doesn't want someone else to inherit the power or whatever you call it of leader of the clan, what can one do to avoid it?"

There was a sudden slanty-eyed look from Rod, giving the impression there was really a reptilian brain behind his eyes. "What makes you think one can avoid it? If one is supposed to be a leader I presume you mean?"

"You intimated that when you thought I was your successor getting warmed up, you checked me out. What did you mean to do about it?"

Rod shrugged. "There's only one thing one can do about it, really. Kill the prospective candidate. Half the time, the power doesn't find anyone else appropriate and stays with you. Grandma said that's how clan leaders survive the changes."

Kyrie glared. She felt a weird sensation like she was in danger, but that was silly. She was many things, but never a reptile, and since the thing was ruled by genetics, if admittedly weird ones, the chances of her kid and Tom's being yet a third kind of shifter were almost none. And yet, "How many have you killed to retain your power?" she asked.

"Me?" He set the plastic plate down and opened his hands as though to show he had no weapons: a gesture that meant nothing when you were a shifter, and your best weapons were a shift away. "None. I haven't gone through any changes."

Tom cleared his throat. "You have to have. I don't believe there haven't been any in the enormous span of time since you were leader."

Rod shrugged. "None I'm aware of. And I would have known."

"You want to keep power that badly?" Kyrie asked, thinking that as nice and easy-going as Old Joe had been, his son was a different thing. Though perhaps it was simply a difference in age. And that Old Joe had never tasted power.

Rod laughed. It was sudden, spontaneous laughter. When he wiped tears of laughter from his eyes and looked at them again, he looked more like Old Joe than ever. Tom half expected him to call him "Dragon boy."

"No," he said, somberly. "I actually have very little use for power and would prefer to live my life as just me. I have vague memories of a time when I didn't get sent here or there because some clan thing needed supervising or a member was in trouble, or whatever. It was nice. I could even spend my time dreaming on the mudbanks, being a gator, and not bothering with human stuff if I so wished. No. The problem is, at least according to Grandma, that no one is ever sure which clan leaders will be killed, and which will only gradually lose power to the new one."

"Gradually? What if it's an accident? What if the Great Sky Dragon was temporarily dead and I got the power?"

Rod shook his head. "No. He would still have collected his power back when he woke. Or it would never have come to you. That's why I said it wasn't a choice. And the worst part is, I'm not sure he means to let it go. Not while he lives."

Kyrie's mind had been running fast, kind of like her trying to run after the alligator down dark passages. It seemed to her Rod was talking around things, deliberately avoiding talking about scary or important things.

So, she jumped in, "Is there any chance the mantle of the lions would fall on me?"

There was that laugh again. "Considering you're the granddaughter of the leader, and these things are often hereditary, I would say so."

Kyrie thought she had let out a shout of surprise. Perhaps she hadn't. Perhaps she'd simply imagined it. But everyone was staring at her. And Tom grabbed her arm, "I'm sorry Kyrie. I meant to tell you when we were alone. Yes, he was your grandfather, and those were your parents and your younger sisters."

Kyrie felt– she had absolutely no clue how she felt. Vaguely nauseated, but that might simply be having a bunch of greasy meat on an almost empty stomach, honestly. She blinked several times.

So long, when she was little, she had tried to imagine why her parents had abandoned her, what hideous trait as a newborn, had caused her to be left, less than a day old, bundled in blankets, in front of a church.

Didn't her parents care? Were they perhaps drug addicts, or other people who simply couldn't keep her.

She thought of the family. Not a happy family, obviously, but a family. "My parents?" she said, her voice cracking. "Both of them?"

"Yes," Tom said, and looked like he would say something else, but then didn't.

Kyrie swore softly. Her swearing audibly was unusual enough that Tom nodded as if she'd addressed him. Then he said, "Ladies, gentlemen. There are blankets in the hall closet for those of you who choose to or decide you need to stay. I've been up for nearly thirty hours now, and I'm going to take my wife to bed before I start to hallucinate. If everyone leaves, the last one should make sure that the door is locked."

And then Tom had wrapped his arm around her and dragged her down the hallway into their bedroom.

As soon as the door was locked, she turned in Tom's arms, her head on his shoulder, a maneuver complicated by the hard ball of baby in her middle.

"I guess they just didn't want me?" she said and felt embarrassed that her voice was a thread of a voice, small and flute-like as if she were three or four years old.

She felt him shake his head, though she couldn't see it. "It wasn't like that," he said. Speaking softly, he told her that her father hadn't yet shifted when she'd been born, so her parents had assumed he was not a shifter, and so there was a high chance she wouldn't shift either. And that he had a feeling bad things happened to non-shifter babies in that family.

"They did abandon you out of love, Kyrie."

"But they didn't come to get me later," she said. Then shut up. It was stupid, and she wasn't a stupid person. In a family where children might be eaten for not shifting, what might happen to her, had her parents gotten in touch with her before? She remembered the malevolent intrusion from the old man. "Never mind," she said softly. "I'm exhausted. Let's go to bed. Maybe your kid will stop running a marathon in my belly long enough for me to sleep."

Rafiel and Bea had left, though the others had stayed behind. Rod said he was staying to guard – though no one had any idea if he was guarding Tom from something, or something from Tom. Conan had said – aggressively – that he was staying with Rya to watch over Tom and Kyrie. And Nick had whispered urgently to Rafiel at the door that he would stay to watch Conan, because he might fall thrall to the Great Sky Dragon, somehow.

"It's like a bad spy movie," Rafiel said as he and Bea got to the car. "They're all guarding Tom from the others or something. Want me to drive?"

Bea laughed. "No way. You sound half asleep."

"Nah, I'm fine. I'm a policeman. I have spent many nights awake and live on black coffee." He thought he said coffee, actually, before he fell asleep. He knew he'd fallen asleep, because he woke up with Bea poking at him, and laughing. "Rafiel, you idiot," she said, fondly. "You have to get out and get to bed. I can't carry you."

He stumbled half-awake through his parents' family room, managing a vague smile in their direction, sure that Bea would explain everything to them after he went to bed. She was solid, that woman. He was glad he'd met her. Even more glad he'd convinced her to accept his proposal of marriage.

He walked down the hallway to his room at the end of the hallway, with the single bed, surrounded by bookcases.

As far as he knew he never undressed, just dropped into it, and fell asleep by the time his head touched the pillow.

He was on an arid plane. As far as he could see, humans and animals approached from all directions. Flying up above were dragons. He didn't have to see them to know they were there, or that they were fighting. The sudden flashes of orange illuminating the landscape were evidence they were flaming each other overhead, and sometimes he heard the fall of a body, but he never saw them. Even though he knew he was dreaming and that such things were often strange in dreams, it felt ominous.

He realized he was climbing a sort of slope and that up on a very shallow hill, there was some kind of vast construction complex, and fires burning.

"The dragons, eh?" a voice said from beside him, a voice he knew. The person's – person's? – shadow on the ground was of a minotaur, a human with a bovine head, a large one. Between his horns was something round, like the disks portrayed mostly on the heads of bovine goddesses in Mesopotamia and Egypt. "I understand North, and East are fighting for supremacy again."

Rafiel turned. Walking behind him was Paul Orvan. Of course, he knew the mild-mannered delivery man was a minotaur. Though he couldn't remember if he'd ever seen him minotaur-ing around – mostly he came into the station on perfectly normal package delivery rounds for Fastbrown – it was known, in the way such things were known around the shifter community.

The weird thing is that in this alien setting he wore his Fastbrown uniform: brown shirt and brown shorts and had a clipboard under his arm. His head, too, was his human head, with short brown hair, and mild, curious eyes behind glasses. The shadow on the ground though still showed him with a bovine head and that weird disk.

"It's the sun disk, isn't it?" He said. "Something about the divine cow."

"Beg your pardon?" Orvan said. "Oh, yes, I suppose. The holder of the position was female when those legends were created. It's actually just our thing, you know? We bovines. A polished bronze disk. A mirror, from before glass was common. I normally don't wear it. It has clips for the horns, but it's too heavy to wear all the time. Gives me a pain in the horns."

"I thought all the... ah ... foci for the clans had been lost, except the dragons."

"Not all," Orvan said. "In fact, I doubt most of them have. We just don't rush out to tell the dragons about it, you know? I think your thing is a fetish."

"I beg your pardon?" Rafiel said in turn, feeling vaguely outraged. Sure, he'd had sex while in lion form but that didn't mean that he'd enjoyed it. The creature had commandeered his mind. He had tried to prevent it. He'd found himself powerless over his own body, which was the worst sort of rape. He'd been possessed, mind and body. It wasn't his fetish.

Orvan made a sound. "No. A tribal fetish. I don't remember what it is exactly anymore, but I think it incorporates an antelope horn. It is said to be the horn of the first antelope brought down by the first lion. But you won't be offended if I tell you I think that's nonsense."

"It..." Rafiel felt the bedclothes beneath him for just a moment, as he tried to wake up, but then sank back into the dream. "It still exists? This fetish thing?"

"Oh yes. Or at least I presume so. Enlil... that was his name at one time, the lion boss? He had it. That's how he stayed on top for so long. It told him who'd ascend next. I bet you it brought him to Goldport, and the stupid fool, with all his family pride, meant it would be his granddaughter."

Now closer, Rafiel saw circles of carved pillars. He remembered reading about Göbekli Tepe, and without getting closer, he knew that would be it. He remembered Rod talking about how contests had probably happened there, at the last Ragnarök, or at least that was what Rod's grandmother had told him. That was why each pillar was carved with a creature. He wondered if there was a lion. He didn't remember reading about lions. But then again, maybe there was some other feline.

"You were here, before?" he asked. "At the last Ragnarök? How old are you?"

"Oh, no, no, no. I'm a relative youngster. My story is well known. It's all as it says in the can. The mythology books. King Minos' wife birthed a minotaur. I just want to point out that daddy was a spiteful bastard, and that he was so panicked to hide the strange thing in his family that when I started shifting, he gave out that his wife had betrayed him with a bull – of all things – and locked me up in the damned labyrinth for years."

"But I thought Theseus had killed you!" Rafiel protested.

"Oh, he did. For like three or four days. Evil little maniac, Theseus. I'm not surprised his thing with my sister Medea went badly. And then I escaped before they came in to collect the body. They probably burned something, and my dearest royal father was appeased, assured I was dead. Ah! I was on a ship out of there and working as a deckhand by then. And I had much fun for the next thousand years or so, embroidering on my legend."

"Am I to assume that you didn't take the sacrifice of maidens and youths or whatever?"

Orvan was silent for a long time. Then he said, a bit sullenly. "I didn't eat them, if that is what you mean, no. Not non-consensually. I didn't kill them unless they were the enthusiastic kind who tried to kill me. Mostly we arranged for them to leave, quietly, when cleaners came or something, escaping the crazy parents who'd sent them over as human sacrifices." He was quiet for a while. "I do wonder what legends my father had heard that he thought human sacrifice would help with anything and that I either required it or it would restore me to full human. I never had the opportunity to ask him." Another silence. "I should ask Mike sometime. The centaur, you know?"

Rafiel didn't know. "Perhaps he heard legends of Göbekli Tepe," he said, his voice almost a moan, as he fought against the dream, trying to wake up. He remembered Rod saying something about awful dreams.

There was something like a clarion call, in the background, only it played the Tokens, singing:

In the jungle, the mighty jungle
The lion sleeps tonight
In the jungle, the quiet jungle
The lion sleeps tonight.

The song was strangely apropos, and completely out of place in this plane, illuminated by the light of burning dragons, and the distant light of torches, in Göbekli Tepe.

They were inexplicably closer to the complex. Ahead of them, a creature lumbered that looked to Rafiel's eyes like a frog crossed with an armadillo. And near it, a group of men in tunics that swept the ground walked, speaking a language that seemed to be mostly clicks.

"Perhaps Minos had heard the legends of Göbekli Tepe," Rafiel re-stated a little louder.

Uyimbube, uyimbube, uyimbube, uyimbube, Uyimbube, uyimbube, uy-imbube, uyimbube,
Uyimbube, uyimbube, uyimbube, uyimbube, Uyimbube, uyimbube, uy-imbube, uyimbube.

The sound appeared to come simultaneously from somewhere to his right, and from the firelit city ahead, thrumming with the sound of drums, and the eerie chants of humans. And above, like bugs caught in a giant bug zapper, dragons flamed.

"It's raining dragons," Rafiel heard himself starting to sing.

"Eh. They have one of the most disputed clan leaderships. They've often been divided in two, even though they're actually a single species, and not like the rest of us, shoved in with a bunch of people who don't belong.

Though I think that the lions are single too, aren't they? Tigers and such are in too. I think they count as lions in a weird way because they can reproduce together. Lion and tiger and panther shifters don't seem to be differentiated. Not as shifters. Anyway, they have to count as lions, since Enlil was always a lion supremacist. If they didn't, there would be no tiger or panther shifters."

Near the village, the peaceful village
The lion sleeps tonight
Near the village, the quiet village
The lion sleeps tonight

"What? How? Why are we going to Göbekli Tepe?" Rafiel asked. "What does it have to do with a Ragnarök, a time of change?"

Orvan laughed. "It's where the would-be heads fight, and the losers are eaten," he said. And suddenly, as Rafiel turned, it was no longer Orvan, but the old man from the diner, glaring at him, and trying to reach for his mind. "You unworthy fool," the old man said. "You will be eaten."

Hush my darling, don't fear my darling
The lion sleeps tonight
Hush my darling, don't fear my darling
The lion sleeps tonight

His cell phone. His cell phone was ringing.

Rafiel reached for it before he was fully awake, and brought it to his ear, turning it on, at the same time he pried his eyes open and realized he must have slept all night because it was morning.

"Hello?" he rasped, his voice as thick and hoarse as though he'd spent the night walking a parched plane.

"What in hell are you going to do about it?" Mr. Milagros' voice yelled in his ear.

Rafiel cleared his throat. He pulled the phone away and saw the time. Ten am. He should have been at work an hour ago. "I'm sorry," he said. "I think I have a cold coming on or something. I think I slept through my alarm. Let me grab some coffee and I'll be right in."

"Well. Yeah, okay sure. But what are you going to do about the lioness running down Fairfax early this morning?"

"What?"

6

"**G**ET OUT OF MY way, I got to pee," Kyrie shouted at Conan and Tom, who were blocking the path to the bathroom.

They jumped out of the way, and she had a moment of happiness that she'd heard their voices before coming out of the bedroom and had put on a sweat suit.

After washing her hands, she tied back her hair and examined her face in the mirror. As a married woman, she looked exactly like a single woman, but maybe more rested. How long had she slept?

She opened the door of the bathroom, "Tom? Is the diner staffed? Do they know I–"

"They know you were found or rescued yourself, yes," Conan answered. "And Bea has gone in to help, and I'll be going after I go by home to shower. Anthony is still or maybe again on the job, and James and Jason have come in. They said they're fine till noon. So, you guys don't have to rush in." He mouthed without sound. "Rod is in the kitchen. Wants to talk to you."

Oh, so that part was real, was it? Kyrie had woken up half-convinced that Old Joe's son was a dream or a hallucination. And had Tom really said that her family had found her? Had they been looking? All the years that it would have been her fondest wish, and now it was just one more thing, another complication.

"I need some food," she said.

"Laura dropped the cake and other leftovers by," Tom said. "Let me make you coffee."

Conan headed out the front door, while Tom and Kyrie headed to the kitchen. Rod was sitting at their table.

Kyrie had a moment of panic because she remembered how hard they had to work on Old Joe to get him to leave their cat, Not Dinner alone. But then she spotted the orange fluff ball on the floor, near Rod's feet. Rod was eating Chinese meat dumplings and giving the cat bits of it. Which explained Not Dinner being his best friend.

Rod grinned at Kyrie and showed he'd read the play of emotions on her face by saying, "I don't eat cats. I like them, but not as snacks."

"I'm sorry. Your father was– He– There's a reason we named the cat Not Dinner."

Rod nodded. "Oh, yeah. When shifters get very old, they.... It's like normal humans, you know, but the .... It goes on for a long time. Also, dad was animal-born, so that was always closer. Grandma used to complain she couldn't keep him dressed. Or in human form."

Kyrie wanted to ask other things, like "Do you eat people if not cats?" And "So, my grandfather was very old, wasn't he?" but there was no polite way to talk about such things in the language of humans.

"Look," Rod said, as he popped the last dumpling from the plate into his mouth and chewed. "I don't want to intrude. I just stayed because I thought you guys were too tired to be able to defend yourselves, and then I stayed till you woke up so I could explain."

"Defend?" Tom said from the kitchen and started the coffee grinder.

Rod waited till the sound stopped, and said, "Yeah. Enlil... that was his name when my grandmother knew him, I don't know what name he went by now, but Enlil, your ..." He looked at Kyrie. "Your Grandfather thought you were set to be the next leader. He was old enough; he could feel the Ragnarök coming well before we could. And he came here for a reason. He thought it was you who would be leader next. He probably used his object, if he still had it, and it pointed this way.

"I don't know if I told you that sometimes you can avoid a change of leadership simply by killing the successor? You can. And I think he'd done it twice before. So, last night, that's what he wanted to do."

"I didn't kill him," Kyrie said, defensively.

"No, I didn't think you did," Rod said. "Stands to reason. You're pregnant. Can't shift. How could you face a full-grown lion? Even the Maasai only do that when they're males and in prime form. No. I don't suspect you. He was old, and strong, Enlil. But it's possible someone else killed him, who wanted to ascend."

Kyrie felt her throat close. "But that was his goal, in coming out?"

Rod shrugged. "I.... have a little more experience than you in the politics of shifters and shifting, and I do believe so, yes.

Kyrie was quiet a long while, and then Tom spoke up, "Did her parents know that? Kyrie's parents? Did they know that was her grandfather's purpose?"

For just a moment Rod was caught. Not in a mistake, not in a lie, just in sheer surprise. He stared at them eyes wide. "I've never thought about that, and I don't know. I don't know what the relationship in the family was. I ... don't know."

Tom looked almost scared for a moment, and then his phone rang. He pulled it from his pocket, and held it to his ear with one hand, while he poured Kyrie a cup of coffee with the other. "Yeah? Oh."

"Kyrie," he said. "Your parents are in the diner. Your next elder sister is missing."

In the supply van, because the car was still parked at the diner, Kyrie sipped her coffee while Tom drove. Rod had intruded, sitting in the back seat. "Didn't you tell them to go to the police?"

Tom shrugged. Kyrie knew better than that. For one, no shifter ever would refer a missing shifter kid to the police. Even Goldport police, because it could, and most often would go wrong in the most spectacular ways. But it was okay if you told a friendly officer.

"Your mom said that she'd told the nice officer in the diner, which I assume was Nick, though it might have been Cas if he's given up sleep or something."

"He has been looking tired," Kyrie said, distantly. That she didn't dispute "Mom" worried Tom a little because in a way he wanted her to dispute it so they could discuss the return of her family. It had to be working on her, particularly with all the pregnancy emotions up on top. He'd found her crying because the flea collar on the cat would kill fleas, and what had the poor fleas done to die, just days ago. And now she took the sudden appearance of her family with strange, detached calm.

Rod cleared his throat from the back seat. "To be clear, I don't think your parents wanted him to kill you. I have heard ... I heard you were a foundling, and I believe they did that to keep you alive. I think they must have intended to save you, somehow." He perked up. "Maybe one of them killed him."

"I don't think they left the diner between his leaving and his being found dead," Tom said.

Rod sighed. "That's a wash then. Look, neither of you asked what the dangers are in your situation. Or how this relates to Ragnarök. You see, I stayed last night because I don't trust the dragons not to make another try, or the lions for that matter." He would have sounded pushy – if he didn't so obviously sound reluctant to say anything.

Tom wanted to ask exactly what the idiot Dragon Queen wanting to steal his baby's body for her mysterious offspring had to do with the whole thing, but he'd just resigned himself to never letting Kyrie out of his sight till this was all done.

But what struck him as weird was the mention of the lions. "The lion big bad is dead, isn't he? Why should Kyrie be in any danger now?"

In the rearview mirror, he saw Rod push his lips in and out, as if in deep thought. "Well..." he said. "Here's the thing: the clan will have a leader this week. Has to. The power will find a home. It's designed that way because if the power doesn't rehome, it's a spot of weakness in the fight against invasion by the discarnate ones. You know of whom I speak?"

"Your father talked about them. He made it sound like a bad science fiction movie from the seventies," Tom said. "All these aliens who chose not to incarnate, and who were in some kind of dungeon dimension, trying to come back, or something."

Rod's lips pushed in and out. Two vertical lines formed, one on each side of his nose as he thought. "You know–" he said. "That's essentially correct, kind of though it's far more complex, at least as grandma told me. But that will do because I don't have the vocabulary to describe it any better in your language. The only big difference is that they're not trying to come back. They're trying to come back and destroy everything living, to force every one of their kind on Earth to go back to space with them."

"Wait!" Kyrie said. She almost dropped her coffee cup in surprise. "Are you saying that these creatures are trying to win a fight they lost at the beginning of life on Earth?"

"Sure," Rod said. "I don't think time is the same for them. I mean, they're ancient to me, and I know I'm ancient to you guys. And even just in that difference, I can tell you that a hundred years feels like yesterday to me, and I want to tell people about this great tea I had last century in Calcutta. The clan heads, at the beginning, got together, and put a kind of a lock on Earth, to prevent the others from coming and spoiling their toys. I don't know how all, or really any of it works. I wasn't there. But it seems to lose power at intervals. I never figured out if it's when too many of the leaders die, or if the leaders die because it happens. And then all the leaders need to get together somewhere and renew the protection."

"Yeah," Tom said, pulling into the parking lot of the diner. He was thinking if they expected him to be one of those leaders, they were sorely out of luck. Even the Great Sky Bastard probably didn't know what to do for a case of weakening protections. So why would Tom? "But what the heck does any of this have to do with lions trying a hit on Kyrie?"

"I suspect there are hierarchies of power, and people who expected to inherit the command, and who will feel like Kyrie is in the way?"

"Does it work that way among the reptiles?" Kyrie asked, sharply as Tom stopped the car. They both turned back to look at Rod.

Rod looked wistful. "Sort of, I think. Not really, because we don't– look a lot depends on the personality of the clan leader. Grandma was not a person who had any use for a structure, and for people to come and bend the knee to her, nor did she keep people in thrall and obeying her. I honestly am not very different from her in that respect. Very live and let live, okay? Besides, most shifter reptiles are eccentrics and want to be left alone. Not the frogs. The frogs are pervies and plain weird, but even they don't seem to have a criminal or otherwise cohesive association. They just get together for orgies a lot."

"Frogs," Tom said, feeling as though the last shred of his patience had been stepped on. "Are not reptiles."

"Oh, you spotted that too. Do you know bats are classed under dogs?"

"What?"

"I think this had a lot to do with friendships among the initial clans and whom they liked and whom they didn't like." Rod shrugged. "I told you it didn't make a wit of sense. And I mean, I'm okay with us having the snakes and all, though snakes... it's like the personality carries over and they're all slithery and stuff. I'm okay with us having some of the shifter dinos, though honestly, they should be with birds. But why the frogs?" He shrugged. "At any rate, you know, I don't think reptiles is as disputed as some other clans. Because the leader doesn't have a ton of power. Most of the time I find myself having to rescue some guy in Florida, who was thrown from the roof of a bar after changing shapes, okay? Not the most relevant work in the world. I just stick around to close the wall of the world when needed. And if I get replaced in this go-round I won't even care. Unless a frog takes over." He frowned. "Other clans are weird. And Enlil was plain crazy, so he probably has some odd structure under him. I just want to keep an eye out, okay? Because you guys were friendly with dad, and I heard about the nice memorial service for him. And because you are obviously pregnant. I don't want someone to do something stupid."

He opened the door of the van. "Let's go see what's going on with the young lioness, shall we?"

Rafiel took a shower in record time, and ran into the kitchen, while putting his shoes on, which involved a lot of hopping on one foot, and then the other. He was thinking of telling whoever was in the kitchen to tell Bea – if it wasn't Bea – that he had to go to the station because there was an emergency.

But as he emerged into the kitchen, his parents and Bea were sitting at the kitchen table – in a nook, by the bay window, looking out at the backyard. The backyard was bare, of course, in January, but his mom had put lights on the little metal gazebo and two of the trees, and it looked cheery in the grey winter morning light. They were having – he squinted – pancakes and coffee.

Bea got up, got another plate and a cup, and set them at Rafiel's place at the table.

Rafiel waved his hand in a dismissive gesture, "Can't stop," he said. "Got to go to the station. The chief called to say there was a lioness running on Fairfax, and it's probably one of ours, so I need to go and figure it out before—"

"Chill," from his father. "Nick called. It's Kyrie's sister. Her next sister. He's on it."

"Oh," Rafiel came to a stop and eyed the pancakes. "I still will need to figure out how to explain it to Mr. Milagros. And is the girl a danger? Has she shifted before?"

"Her mom– Well, Kyrie's mom, I guess. I have no idea... Bea says it was her grandfather who was killed? Nick said? Or–"

"Yeah, it was her grandfather." Rafiel's stomach made an executive decision, and he grabbed pancakes and doused them liberally with maple syrup. "What do you think about it all, dad? Did Bea tell you the whole thing?" With his father's experience, it was always worth getting his ideas on any crime. Frankly, Rafiel would have resented it less if his dad, or his dad's partner, had been recruited as police chief, instead of a complete outsider. At least his dad knew shifters existed.

"As much as I understood of what went on," Bea said.

"Anyway," Rafiel's dad said, going back to the thread of the conversation, as he was known to do. "The girl's mom apparently says she has shifted before, with no untoward incidents. Her mom is only worried because they're in an unknown city. They live in Chapel Hills, North Carolina, you know, and there she apparently has access to woods. Anyway, there wasn't even that much panic from a lioness on Fairfax. People here are used to strange things. She should be okay and come home. Her mom says she shifts under stress."

"I see," Rafiel said, though he didn't see at all. Bits and pieces of his dream came back to mind, and he stopped, a piece of pancake to his mouth, and sighed. "The lab said something about animal proteins on the neck of the corpse, and thinking the head was bitten off, but Milagros doesn't seem convinced, and I suspect it's just lion, really. He was probably starting to shift. I'll have to go look at their reports and talk to them."

His dad nodded. "You know," he said. "From what I hear, if I didn't know better, I'd think Kyrie did it. Or at least, it's suspicious that the man dies right after he finds her."

Rafiel shook his head. "I don't think she could have. I have seen Tom interact with the Great Sky Bas– Dragon, and I think that the .... Clan leaders for lack of a better term, have some control over members of the clan, and that Kyrie wouldn't be able to attack him." Of a sudden, it came to him in a flash that if this was true, it was unlikely that he was killed by someone in Kyrie's family. "It's something to verify at least. Which means a lot of interviews. I wonder if the gator knows when the dragons grabbed her, and if he can verify, she couldn't do it." He finished demolishing the pancakes, and almost as a joke, told his dad the story of how Milagros expected them to identify the murderer from talking to diner patrons. "I mean, like someone walking past covered in blood and with a head under his arm wouldn't be immediately obvious."

His dad made a face. Rafiel got the impression that like himself, his dad didn't particularly like or approve of Milagros. Sometimes he muttered something about big city policing ways, so completely different from the police work in their small town. But then he shrugged and tilted his head to the side. "Don't let your dislike for the man convince you that he's a complete idiot," he said. "I mean, sure, the scenario you sketch is ridiculous, and I don't hold it against you that's what you thought of since he doesn't know about the existence of shifters, or what it means, and so his clues might not be the same as yours.

"But perhaps the clues aren't what you're thinking of. Perhaps the murderer isn't a shifter. Seems to me, guy like that, kicking around since the dawn of time, would have a lot of enemies, and some of them might not be shifters. It's possible. And if it wasn't a shifter, it could very well all hinge on someone having seen a stranger with an unusual piece of luggage. Enough to carry a knife and a change of clothes. And bring back a head and the bloodied clothes."

"Oh," Rafiel said. And suddenly felt stupid. Tunnel vision and everything that was going on in the shifter world could blind you. He should have thought of that one.

And he was going to talk to Orvan Ox and figure out if the dream had any congruence with reality. If Orvan really was the leader of the bovine clan– He might know something about inter-clan wars.

The diner was full and several of the part-timers were circulating like dazed bees among the tables. At a glance, Tom saw that a lot of the regulars were there. He wondered why, but then stopped wondering. The shifter world in Goldport worked like any small village. There was a way of transmitting information that was faster than the fastest internet: shifter to shifter, bat to rat, to wolf, to lion, to dragon, to Pegasus. Probably everyone had heard about the young lioness running around town. And he'd bet money most of them had also heard about Kyrie's family surfacing.

For one – Tom cast an eye at the corner booth where Aurelia and Nick were in earnest conversation, and then to the table next to it, where Kyrie's dad was riding herd on the two pre-teens, who were chatting to each other like any two preteens – anyone looking at those kids would know they were related to Kyrie.

Kyrie, Tom noted, went into the diner, and straight behind the counter, where she signed in and put her apron on. Apparently, she wasn't ready to deal with her family. She consulted the shift diagram, probably to see who needed relief. Anthony, at the grill, had circles under his eyes and looked about to drop. Tom wanted more than anything to go to the corner and demand the truth from Kyrie's mom, find out if anyone was really a threat to Kyrie on the lion side, but–

But the diner was his. He was responsible for the grill and the fryer – which was probably already plotting how to blow up – and he couldn't allow Anthony to work himself to death. For one Cecily would kill them all, and probably nail the heads in front of the diner as a warning to other people who might want to work Anthony to death. Or something.

He went behind the counter, signed in, put his apron on, confined his hair, and went to relieve Anthony. That Anthony greeted him with "Oh, thank God. I was about to leave Nick in charge of the grill and fryer."

"Good thing you didn't. I think it would be a conflict of interests to actually employ policemen."

"I didn't think you would pay him."

"Oh, yeah, that makes it all better," Tom said. "Go home, you lunatic."

Anthony went to the place they left their stuff, took off his apron, put his jacket on, then turned around, "I'm glad you found Kyrie."

"She found herself. But yeah, I'm keeping a close eye on her. I don't want her to go to even the storage room by herself."

Anthony nodded. And Tom realized even while he took over the grill and fryer and read orders, he was keeping an eye on Kyrie, who was doing a circuit of warmups, with occasional delays for people grabbing her hand. From the expressions and looks, they were congratulating her on her marriage. Kyrie usually replied with a smile, and displaying her ring, and sometimes with soft looks in Tom's direction.

Tom realized it was going to be really hard to keep an eye on her while cooking, because he didn't want the fryer to explode, but he also didn't want her to disappear.

And then it occurred to him there were solutions for this.

He didn't like his power as, as he referred to it, Beast Master. Rod had implied that the power the dragons had over the other animals wasn't exactly licit or consensual. He hadn't verified Rod's veracity on anything either. For all he knew the leader of the reptiles would be naturally slithery, just like Cas and Nick were somewhat doggy. But if all of what he was getting from everyone amounted to "leadership is changing and will probably fall on you," Tom certainly didn't want to encourage any more of the crazy people to think he would be the next leader of all the animals. Or even – just – of the feuding dragon clans.

On the other hand, a dragon – who should not have had the ability to command a feline, or not like that – had taken over Kyrie's mind and used the control to kidnap her. And Tom remembered what the Great Sky Bastard had told him. Right. His first duty was to Kyrie and his unborn son. He couldn't bear the idea he'd almost lost them both on his wedding day. So, he would use his power as beast master. And that was that.

The diner was full of shifters. It normally was, anyway, but it was even more full of shifters than normal this morning. The smell of shifter was thick in the air. And Tom actually didn't have much issue borrowing the eyes of anyone in his view. He decided he'd take two or three of the people there, so he could always keep Kyrie in sight.

Dr. Roberts, aka Professor Squeak, a professor at the nearby med school, and a regular, was sitting in his corner, sipping his coffee, and reading one of his eternal science fiction paperbacks. He was in human form, not always a given, but always necessary to drink coffee since rats aren't particularly good at things that required lips. Because he was that sort of person, always keeping situational awareness, he looked up from his book every few seconds and swept the room with his gaze. And he was in a corner of the annex, so he would see Kyrie if she went in there.

Ian McMurtrie, a fox shifter a retired officer, and occasional part-timer for the police force, was sitting at the other end of the counter, where he would be able to keep an eye on Kyrie if she went to the hallway that led to the storage areas, and Tom wanted that watched anyway. Actually, he'd drop a word in Ian's ear anyway. That might be more effective than borrowing his eyes. Tom edged that way, refreshed the man's coffee, and said, "If you'd keep an eye on Kyrie. She was kidnapped by mind control yesterday. If you see her walking robotically, would you scream?"

Ian nodded. He seemed to be wholly absorbed in his coffee and doughnuts, but Tom knew he'd notice anything funny in the hallway.

So, now, Tom needed another set of eyes in here. He could, he supposed, borrow the eyes of one of Kyrie's family, but he didn't want to. So, he cast around for someone likely to remain seated a long time, and his gaze landed on Kevin, what the heck was his last name? In Tom's head he was tagged as Kevin Panda, but– Oh, yes. Kevin Denton. He was a dignified white-haired, bearded gentleman and he usually had a leisurely breakfast in the morning, before heading out to his lab nearby. He had told Tom it was part of how he reminded himself other people existed. He didn't need to interact with them. Just sit there, and see a bunch of people having breakfast, and he got his quota of people for the day.

Tom put some eggs on the frying surface of the grill, and a bunch of bacon, then turned around just enough to see the Panda, and reached.... In.

It was weird, kind of like putting a finger in a glove, if your finger were entirely made of thought, and the glove were someone else's brain. So, in fact, not like it at all.

He left the man's thoughts undisturbed and didn't even try to perceive his moods. The time might come, as had come before, when he needed to violate the privacy of someone's thoughts, but that time was not right now, and right now all he needed was what Kevin Denton was seeing.

It took about a second, and then he saw the diner, and Kyrie refreshing the coffee of an old couple, who were telling her how happy they were she and Tom had married, and when was the baby due. They were regulars, and so far as Tom knew, not shifters.

He got two breakfasts plated, then turned and got Professor Squeak in his sights. And reached in.

Dr. Roberts looked up almost immediately and looked at him. There were no mental words, exchanged between them, but he got the impression the man was asking him exactly what was happening there. And wordlessly, Tom conveyed that he wanted to keep Kyrie under watch.

Dr. Roberts nodded. Once. And went back to glancing between his book and the diner.

With his sentinels in place, Tom tracked Kyrie with the back of his mind, while he cooked breakfasts.

And it was through his borrowed eyes that he saw Orvan Ox come in for breakfast. He wore his Fastbrown uniform, but not carrying anything, which meant he probably hadn't gone on shift yet.

He looked around, his face looking as usual, mildly amiable, but Tom had the impression he was registering how many shifters were congregated here with some surprise. Or maybe not. After all, given his occupation, he was a vital part of the network of shifters and usually knew what was going on before anyone else did.

Orvan had just sat down, when Rafiel came into the diner moving fast and with a look of purpose to his expression. He found Orvan and homed in on him.

Tom thought, *Oh, no. Some ox is about to get gored.* And then felt really guilty for the joke.

"Orvan!" Rafiel said, sitting down.

The ox shifter looked up, looking calm. "Yes?"

And then they both stopped, because Jason Cordova was there, with the order pad out. Orvan ordered fried chicken which seemed a very weird order for breakfast, and made Rafiel think of some videos on the net, of cows munching on chickens who strayed in their path.

Anyway, didn't the legends say the minotaur was carnivorous? And yet, though he knew that Orvan was a minotaur – maybe he'd seen him shifted during the great call out Tom had done? – perhaps the whole thing about his being the minotaur in Knossos was wrong? It was just a dream.

He tried to imagine the Fastbrown delivery man stomping and huffing around the dank labyrinth and couldn't.

And Orvan was still looking at him with mild, mildly enquiring eyes.

So, what could Rafiel say? *I dreamed of you last night* seemed counter-indicated. It would have been counter-indicated even had Orvan been female, but as a male it just sounded weird. Rafiel could ask him what he thought about Göbekli Tepe, he supposed. But that–

As usual, when Rafiel was stuck, his mouth made the decision for him. As Jason walked away to get fried chicken and two coffees, Rafiel heard himself ask, "Does the bronze disk really make your horns hurt?"

There was a moment of silence. Orvan opened his mouth, then closed it, then opened it again. His eyebrows shot up. "How do you know?" he asked. "Is this police work or something?"

Rafiel shook his head. "No. I'm not sure what it is, but I dreamed you and I were walking somewhere, and you told me you were the leader of the bovine clan, and also–" He shrugged. "And also, that you were that minotaur. You know, the one in the labyrinth."

"Oh," Orvan said, his alarm subsiding. "Strange dream, but it's a time of strange things happening, I've noticed. I think the changes might be upon us. Are you in the run for clan leader, Officer?" He spoke mildly, as though asking Rafiel what he'd have for breakfast.

Jason came back with their food. As he walked away, Rafiel said, "So you are? That minotaur?"

Orvan smiled. "There is a reason I like Greek diners, even beyond this one, I guess. Are you trying to keep things from being overheard? Because Jason Cordova is one of us. A bear, I think."

"Not trying to keep things from being overheard so much, as trying to keep them from going too far," Rafiel said. "I don't know who the leader of the bears is, and–"

"I don't know either. Like bats, they might be under canines. These things don't make a ton of sense."

"Yeah, Rod told us. Nimrod. Old Joe's son."

"Ah. Him. I thought I'd seen him around."

"You know him?"

Orvan huffed, a sound he made by blowing air out of his nostrils, in what would probably be way more intimidating in minotaur form. "Well, 'know' in a manner of speaking," he said. "When you've been around for millennia, you start to be aware of the faces that stay around that long too." He picked up a chicken leg and took a bite, chewed, swallowed, and said, "So, what can I do for you Officer?"

"You can tell me everything you know about the lion clan."
"Oh, dear."

She was an abject coward, and completely out of patience with herself. Or at least that's what Kyrie told herself. She kept looking at them: her birth family.

Her dad looked like every dad from every benign TV sitcom ever. Maybe the older ones. The new ones seemed to delight in making parents seem stupid, particularly fathers.

He didn't look stupid. He was blondish. Dark blond, with a receding hairline and the sort of thin, aristocratic features that seemed to run in certain New England families. The kind, that is, that had stepped out of the Mayflower wearing top hats and funny bonnets and had rarely bred out since. But that had to be wrong because she understood from Tom that both her parents were lion-ish shifters. Her dad was a panther, like herself. So somewhere along the line some other blood – African? – had dropped in the pot. But he certainly didn't look it. He wore a button-down shirt and slacks, and a zippered sweater in dark grey. He wore glasses, which was unusual among shifters – but not unheard of – and he was listening to his daughters across the table, answering now and then, or reaching out semi-absently to prevent a glass of milk from toppling over, or an over-enthusiastic gesture from sending a pancake flying. He looked worried, but not frantic.

Now and then he looked towards the corner booth where his wife sat, talking to Nick, who kept asking her questions.

She, his wife, Kyrie guessed her mom – Tom had said her name was Aurelia – did look like Kyrie even if darker, and with obvious African hair. It was obvious from the looks Kyrie's dad sent her way that he loved her very much and was worried for her.

Kyrie's mother looked exhausted. Like she'd spent the night awake and hadn't even thought of sleeping. There were dark circles under her eyes, and she seemed to have developed a crop of fresh gray hair overnight.

Kyrie took a deep breath. It was now or never, and if she didn't do it now, she was only going to get more scared. The thing she was most scared of, is that she couldn't tell what she, herself, would do. She might be perfectly polite, or she might lose her mind and start screaming at this woman who had abandoned her as a newborn.

All those years, all those families, the time Kyrie had thought she was insane. All the nights she'd lain awake wondering why she'd been abandoned.

No. She had to go over and say hi. She had to at least talk to them, or she'd never forgive herself. And she'd make a very bad mom if she couldn't face her own fears.

She walked up to the table, holding the coffee pot, and gave both her mom and Nick warmups, before she sat the coffee pot down, extended her hand and said, "Hi, I'm Kyrie. I believe we've met once before?"

Behind her, she was aware of her dad standing up.

Professor Squeak sent a warning to Tom's mind, as though he needed extra words when he saw Kyrie walk towards the table where her mother said. The warning, delivered in a humorous mind-tone was "Standoff at the okay corral."

Tom didn't turn around. He had fries in the fryer, and didn't want to overcook them, and didn't want the fryer to explode either. So instead, he stayed turned but followed it through the eyes he was using.

He could tell Kyrie was tense, as she approached the table. Afraid, he thought.

And as weird as his relationship with his own father was, he couldn't make heads or tails of what Kyrie's feelings towards her family must be. In fact, as far as he could tell, Kyrie was being totally opaque on this, which wasn't quite normal. Normally you knew exactly what Kyrie thought about something. Her face showed it plainly. And if it didn't, she'd tell you.

But she looked like she was holding something in, and Tom wasn't sure what. He saw Kyrie extend a hand to her mother. He saw Aurelia look up, her eyes suddenly soft and vulnerable. He saw Kyrie's dad get up.

And then Kyrie's mom pulled Kyrie into her arms.

Kyrie wasn't a touchy-feely person. Even with Tom, they weren't the kind of couple who were always touching, hugging, kissing.

The thing was she'd grown up in foster homes and learned early that too much touching invited transgressions of various kinds. She hugged Tom, of course, and in moments of great emotion, she hugged her friends. But she didn't run around hugging strangers.

So, when the woman – her mother, really? – hugged her, it first felt like a huge intrusion. In the next minute, it felt like they were family and had known each other forever.

Her mom was slightly shorter than Kyrie and heavier. She hugged Kyrie, awkwardly due to the baby, and held her tight. "Oh, honey," she said. "So many years I wanted to know you."

Like that, all the defenses that Kyrie had built up over the years melted instantly and explosively, like an ice cube in the microwave. She started shaking and felt tears falling down her face, and she was the little girl who'd lain awake in strangers' homes, hoping her family would somehow come to her rescue, somehow claim her.

One word escaped her lips, "Mom."

Then Nick was moving aside, getting her to sit down, and her mom was sitting down across from Kyrie, digging into her purse for tissues, passing some to Kyrie, while wiping her own overflowing eyes.

Kyrie looked up and said again, "Mom," this time with a tremulous smile. She had so many things she wanted to say and ask, but she didn't seem able to say more than that one word.

"I–" her mom said. Her voice dropped to a whisper. "I couldn't find you. If I'd known where you were, I'd have come to find you before. I wanted to tell you we didn't want to ... we didn't want to leave you. It was the hardest thing I've ever done, and your dad probably hurt more than I did. But we were afraid my father would hurt you." And then her tears started falling harder, and Kyrie reached across and grabbed her hand.

"Kyrie." Nick tapped her on the shoulder. "Kyrie, let me get up."

Kyrie slid aside, without letting go of her mom's hand, and then slid deeper into the booth as her dad slid in next to her. From the corner of her eye, Kyrie saw Nick sitting with her sisters.

Her dad put his arm over her shoulder, and said, "I'm so glad we found you!"

Someone, Kyrie couldn't see who through her tears, slid leftover wedding cake, in a big plate onto the table, and a bunch of little plates and forks. Kyrie couldn't see who the server was, but she knew where the cake had come from.

Her very beloved, emotionally awkward husband was convinced everything went better with sugar.

"I'm Peter Smith," her dad said, sounding hoarse. "And I'm very glad to meet you at last."

"No, Dad. You're Dad," Kyrie said, all snuffly. If Tom could forgive his dad and let him be part of their lives, surely, she could forgive hers.

"I can't stand it," Tom said, as Jason came behind the counter. "Kyrie needs my support."

"She's fine. I took the wedding cake over," Jason said, proudly. "And James is taking them coffee. But I agree with you. You should be with them. With Kyrie. Go. I see Conan and Bea coming in. Conan won't let the fryer explode. It would mangle his guitar hands. Go."

Tom went, lifting the passthrough and out to the corner booth, in a rush. He felt weird because they'd just recovered their daughter. The last thing they needed was a freshly acquired son-in-law muscling in on the reunion.

At the same time, damn it, Tom was going to protect Kyrie if it was the last thing he did. Not that he thought she needed protection from her parents, but...

Shifters were strange to begin with, and these were very strange times. So, he was going to see that she was okay through it, whatever "it" was.

As he got close enough, Kyrie's dad got up, and extended a hand to him, "Peter Smith. A pleasure to meet you."

"Tom Ormson," Tom said.

"Ormson?"

"Yeah, stupid, isn't it?"

Kyrie's dad grinned and moved out of the way, and Tom got in next to Kyrie, while Kyrie's dad moved around, to sit next to his wife. James brought fresh cups for coffee, a pot of coffee, and a bowl of creamers, and lingered for only a second, to see if anyone needed anything. Kyrie helped herself to a massive slice of cake.

Her mom was in the middle of a story. "I had no idea he was also a lion shifter, you know? I thought we knew all of those. I mean, they were in and out of my Father's house, all the time, and I would have noticed him." Aurelia's eyes crinkled at the corner. "He was the cutest goth on campus, and he was studying physics. I mean— We had math classes together, and I... then he invited me to come and listen to his band, the Jungle Boys, and—" She shrugged. "I guess we were both nerds. I mean, I knew I was a shifter, and Father... my father was likely to kill him and probably me if he knew we were dating. I told your dad, and he thought my father was some kind of gang overlord, and a massive racist. I guess that wasn't wrong, on either count. But anyway, he understood my need for secrecy after Father sent two guys to punch him up for hanging out with me.

"So, we were secretive and young and stupid, and then I found I was pregnant with you. I arranged to go away and do an internship in Charlotte, so Father couldn't find me. He lived in Savannah. Anyway, I was afraid he'd look at me and figure out I was pregnant, and I was afraid of what he'd do. Turns out he knew, but he didn't care, so long as I didn't try to bring you home. I think he thought I had killed you, judging from his state when he—

"Anyway, when you were born, we were alone, and I only had your dad to help me, and then we wrapped you up, and we thought the obvious place to leave you would be at the door of the church before the midnight mass let out."

"We read in the paper the next day that you'd been found. It hurt, but we always assumed you'd been adopted. I've ... prayed for all these years that you had a good family and been happy. I didn't want to look, because... because our lives weren't wonderful with your grandfather hanging over us."

"You got married, though," Kyrie said, not wanting to tell them about the endless succession of families, and the one good family she'd gotten removed from when they tried to adopt her because the social worker in charge of her case didn't like them.

"Six months after you were born, I shifted for the first time," her dad said. "I had no clue what it was, nor what was happening to me, but it was in the college dorms, and your mom was right there, and she– She talked to me the next morning while feeding me an entire side of almost raw beef." He shrugged. "We still wouldn't have told your grandfather. Your mom told me he was actually only racist against non-lion-shifters. No, not quite. You see lion, tiger, and panther shifters can all interbreed. I'm actually a black panther. But as long as you were one of those, your grandfather was fine with you, for values of fine. He didn't care what color people were, in human or animal form, he just thought he was superior to every non-lion-or-lion-adjacent shifter out there. Once he found out I was, in his terms, cavorting with a lion shifter, he called me in with mind control, and he ordered us to get married."

"He was very upset we didn't produce a boy," Aurelia said. "But the girls are all shifters, or at least he said so, though the younger has never shifted, so they were safe. We always worried about you, but we had no way of telling if you were a shifter. Even shifters can produce non-shifters, and we were afraid your grandfather would eat you."

"Eat me?" Kyrie said.

Her mom nodded. Kyrie reached over and clutched at Tom's hand. "He'd done it before?"

Her mom nodded. "I used to have sisters. I'm the only survivor. He had his own ideas of genetic purity."

Tom could feel Kyrie shuddering through her hand. But she managed a shaky question, which showed, that no matter what, Kyrie always worried about other people. "My sister... she is missing?"

"Oh, dear?" Rafiel asked, turning back when it became obvious that Kyrie's family wasn't going to have a fight in the middle of the diner. "What is so bad about the lion clan?"

Orvan sighed. "Again, I say, Officer, are you in the running for leader?"

"Not that I know," Rafiel said, with perfect equanimity. "Rod tells us these things are usually hereditary, and the last leader was Kyrie's grandfather, so I would think that she was more likely to inherit than I."

"Not necessarily," another voice joined in, and Professor Squeak was pulling back the extra chair at the table and sitting down. "I'm sorry, but I was following the conversation, lip reading mostly, so I'm sure I missed something." His eyes were very intent. He was always very intent, and a world-renowned researcher, who often got so absorbed in his experiments he shifted without noticing and would come into the diner in rat form. He was a human-sized rat, and often wore glasses and a lab coat, which made it hard for people to process that he was actually in rodent form. There was a sort of silent bet among diner waitstaff on whether or not he'd spill coffee all over himself by drinking in a form that had no lips. Not that they didn't try to tell him, but he was normally thinking of something important and failed to catch their signaling. Hence his nickname.

Rafiel wondered for the first time how many times Professor Squeak changed during a lecture and delivered the rest of it in earnest squeaks while scribbling formulas for various medications on the blackboard. He suspected often, but of course, shifters were to some extent protected by the bias of normalcy. No student would ever mention it. Each of them, alone, would assume they were hallucinating.

"You say Kyrie isn't as likely or more to inherit than I? Far more since she is, for lack of a better term, from the royal line of lions?"

Professor Squeak shrugged. He signaled towards Jason who came and refilled his coffee cup. "I'm sorry, I'm not sure I got it right, but you said something about dreaming. Was it a true dream? One during which you acquired information?"

Rafiel looked at Orvan then nodded.

"Ah. Then you're indeed in the running, though I don't know how widespread it is, but I think there are .... Changes. Before you get the full memory of the leader or the full powers. I don't know if everyone gets the full memory."

"Changes?" Rafiel asked, skeptically. "Like, what kind of changes."

"Well..." Dr. Roberts made a face. "I have never been able to dissect the brain of a leader, but I have had a couple of cadavers that I think were prospective leaders." He smiled enthusiastically. "This was a while back when Dr. Branson the leader of the birds died, and there were a couple of students, one of whom I knew was a corvid shifter. Anyway, they fought, and I got the idea they fought to be the next leader, but then– The next leader..." He shrugged. "Chickens are nasty, nasty shifters. Almost as nasty as T-Rexes and dragons. Anyway, the students had donated their bodies to science, so I got to autopsy their brains, and there was a curious structure in the hippocampus, one that I've never found in the brains of any other humans or shifters. There was no explanation for it, and one had a far more advanced structure than the other. I got the impression that this was the structure that prepared you to inherit. And both of them, and many other shifter leaders over the years, had talked about having strange dreams, often about very old structures, and ceremonies." He smiled, beatifically, as though contemplating some beautiful idea. "I always wanted to autopsy a leader. But none of them ever came my way."

Orvan was looking suspiciously at Doctor Squeaks.

And Rafiel wanted to ask him if he had by any chance recently picked up the brain of the lion leader, but his head was pounding like someone was hitting it with a hammer, as his phone started to ring.

Aurelia made a face. "Your sister," she said. "Angela is.... She has shifted before. We told her all about it before it happened since my father said they were all shifters. He could tell when they were born. Or perhaps he was delusional. But anyway, she shifts when she's upset." Aurelia shrugged.

"It's normal for teenagers. Or it was for me. But in the middle of the night, in the hotel – we're staying at the Vacay Suites, you know, at the edge of town – anyway, I woke up with the room door closing, I think, but she wasn't in the suite. And as far as we can tell she didn't take any clothes or even shoes. So, we assume she shifted. I put on a robe, and went looking for her, but couldn't find her. I don't know where she could have gone so fast and besides..."

"Besides?" Tom prompted. He had a feeling his ... mother-in-law? He guessed, he'd better think of her that way. Anyway, he had a feeling she was disturbed in some way by her daughter's disappearance. Not frantic, as a normal parent would be, maybe? Or maybe she was frantic, but when you were a shifter, your options for finding your kid were limited. Putting someone on her track might actually get the kid shot by wildlife patrols or something. It had happened.

Kyrie's mom sighed. "The thing is, in our house, she can get out because there are arrangements with the doors and all. Look, we know how to open doors, go out, and all that, but most adults are more in control of their animal than teens. I don't know– I don't know if that's normal, but when I was that young, I would have been stopped by having to open the room door, let alone elevators."

Tom frowned. Yes. From his memories of a few years ago, that was true. Kyrie nodded. "I could usually find a way out of a private home, but many times I just hid under the bed or something. I presume–"

"Yeah, we checked–"

And suddenly Tom realized that Aurelia was in fact frantic. She was just keeping a tight rein on it because she was trying to solve the problem, somehow. And maybe she thought what was going on, or–"

"You have a theory," Tom said.

"Of course, I have a theory."

"And you know who took her," Kyrie said.

"No, no. But I have a strong suspicion. First, it has to be someone who is in.... who is more powerful than my daughter, which I grant you isn't particularly hard, but maybe someone who is changing to become the clan leader. Second–" She pursed her lips. "Like this. I don't know how it works in the dragon clan. Or most of the others. I've known Rod for years, but he isn't the most forthcoming, you know? And I understand each clan works differently, particularly the ones that had a leader for thousands of years."

She took a deep breath. "The lions have... a group in power. My father had ... helpers and adjuncts. I suspect one of them is in the running for leader and would find it easier to rule if he were uh.... Mated to my daughter."

"I take it," Tom said. "That none of these are teenagers or..."

Aurelia shook her head. She made a gurgling sound in her throat that might be laughter, but if so, was disgusted laughter. "They are all hundreds of years old. Maybe thousands."

Kyrie reached for her mom's hand. "How can we help?"

Aurelia shook her head again. "I don't know." She looked at Tom. "How close are you to the leadership of the dragons?"

Tom had to think. The words weren't immediate or obvious. At long last, he said, "It's complicated. Particularly now. I refused a call to battle of the Great Sky Dragon. He might not take kindly to me."

"Refused?" Aurelia said, confused. "How could you refuse?"

Tom shook his head and shrugged. He didn't want to explain. He didn't even want to think about it. In his mind was Rod's suggestion that the clan itself was unstable, while the two centers of power were divided and Tom had some power he should only have had if he were the leader, and yet the Great Sky Dragon was still in charge.

"Kyrie," he said, putting his arm around his wife. "It is very important that you don't give people the slip. I'm going to leave people in charge of making sure you don't disappear, okay? Conan and Rya and anyone else I can get. And then I'm going to find out if the Great Sky Bastard can help."

Kyrie grabbed at his arm, as he tried to slide out of the booth, "Tom? Is this a good idea? At this time?"

Tom grinned at her, though he didn't feel it at all. "What is the worst he can do to me? Kill me? Like it would be the first time." He kissed her cheek and got up.

Rafiel held the phone to his ear.

"Yeah?"

"Cas. You coming in? To the station, I mean?"

"Eventually. I'm in the diner. Mr. Milagros having a problem with my absence?"

"Uh. Maybe. But that's not why I'm calling. It's... the GSD called."

"The? Oh?"

"There is a meet-up at the okay corral, apparently, and you know, the usual suspects, likely to be some violence."

"Cas? What the hell is wrong? Why would the GSD want me? He got rid of me pretty quickly..."

"Uh.... It's hard to explain."

"Is Milagros listening in? Or have you lost your mind?"

"Yes?"

"Listening in, or is just nearby, and can't hear me, but can hear you?"

"In the proximity, you could say."

"Right, so, let me re-state this: there is a fight among the dragons, and you're expecting the usual crap. Is there some way you can tell me why they're having a fight in plain view in daylight, and what he expects me to do about it?"

"Don't know and don't know. You know these weird ethnic gangs. You never really know what's going through their heads. But you know it could mean anything. They might need uh... a neutral arbiter. Or perhaps."

Or perhaps, Rafiel thought, they wanted to put him in a sack, and use him as a hostage, so they could control Tom.

"What the heck," he said. "If they kidnap me and take me hostage, it's not like it's something they've never done before." In fact, you could say his friendship with Tom dated from such an episode.

"Rafiel?"

"Yeah. That's fine. I'll give it a gander. Meanwhile, can you do me a favor? My dad actually had an interesting idea. Did you go through the records of yesterday's interviews?"

"Yeah, cursory."

"Right. Can you go through again and see if people reported any passer-by carrying large pieces of luggage?"

Doc Roberts and Orvan were engaged in conversation. Weird conversation. From what Rafiel could hear, the professor was trying to convince Orvan to donate his brain to science. Which, as eager as the man was for brains might shorten Orvan's lifespan considerably. Orvan was demurring and looking suitably hesitant.

"Pieces of luggage?"

"Just look for it, okay? If you don't find anything, we might need to interview the people near the windows."

"Okay then."

Before Rafiel got to the parking lot of the Three Luck Dragon, he knew what he would find. What he didn't expect precisely was what he would find.

There was a dais arranged, and the Great Sky Dragon was on a sort of throne, surrounded by his entourage, just in front of the doors of the restaurant. He wore his full regalia, with robes that were last seen in Chinese paintings and embroidery back when Confucius wore short pants. Not that Confucius would have worn short pants, Rafiel corrected himself. He had a hazy memory that children in China, in the past, wore no pants at all.

On the other side – *both alike in dignity*, Rafiel told himself as he pulled to the side of the road in front of the restaurant – was another dais, with another throne-like chair, this one in tones of blue and white. And standing around a beautiful blond woman were a group of comic-opera Vikings, except their helmets were... strangely horned – he'd swear some of them had antlers – and their tunics looked homespun and dingy. Their swords also, he judged, looked dented and ... old. And like they'd been buried underground or in a cave underground a whole time. He remembered the story Ron had told and it was something like a sleeping beauty story.

If the sleeping beauty and her entire court were dragon shifters and had in fact died of starvation, and then been brought back to life through processes that made absolutely no sense. But that was okay, because the fun part – the real fun part – is that right there, within view of the road, with everyone driving by, the two sets of dragons were doing the equivalent of having medieval jousts.

If the knights were dragons and fought by flaming each other in midair.

He had a moment to admire the silken, sparkling wings, the way the more gracile Chinese dragon fought the heavier, more armored Norse one.

One was green, the other gold, and they attacked each other claws first, sparkling drops of blood falling onto the parking lot. And then ....

There was a complex ballet, midair, and suddenly the Norse dragon flamed, the Chinese evaded. It should have been easy to follow but it was not. There were complex figures drawn, in mid-air, and–

A Norse dragon fell flaming onto the parking lot. From the Chinese dais, a cry of victory went up. From the other side, two stoic Vikings emerged to take away the charred but still living remains on a stretcher, which they stowed behind the dais.

And Rafiel paused, behind the wheel of the department SUV, frowning, as one of the Vikings undressed, carefully folded his clothes in a neat pile, then twisted and writhed and coughed, and spasmed, emerging as a gold and red dragon, who took to the sky, to challenge the Chinese champion.

Rafiel frowned. What the GSD expected him to do with this was beyond his guess. He turned his car off while trying to figure out what he could even pretend to do.

As the Chinese dragon fell this time – taken off the parking lot arena, in an orderly fashion, his two halves collected on a stretcher – Rafiel heard himself singing to the tune of It's Raining Men.

Oh, Hi!
It's your favorite detective, Rafiel.
And have I got news for you!
You better listen!
Smoke is rising,
Wings are getting low.
According to my sources,
This is the place to go...
I'm hoping it's for the last time,
Tonight, at half past ten,
But you know right now,
It's gonna start raining draaa-gons
It's raining dragons,
Oh, no,
It's raining dragons,
Can I go now,

It's raining dragons,
Don't wanna be out,
It's raining dragons...

Behind him, he saw Kyrie's little subcompact pull up, and Tom erupt from the driver's seat.

With a forceful curse, Rafiel got out of his car. Now things got serious. He didn't really care how many dragons became flambe. But Tom was different. Tom was his friend. And he'd be three times cursed if he was going to let Tom get killed when everything was insane.

7

K YRIE WAS IN THE storage room and was eating pie. She had no idea how this had come to happen. Or rather, she had a pretty good idea, it just made no sense whatsoever.

No. The truth was that the steps made sense.

After Tom had left, she was visibly worried, and her parents – how strange to think there were people who were her parents, and she knew them – had sympathized, and even understood when she'd said that Tom was going to ask the Great Sky Dragon about her sister, Angela.

But she could tell that her parents were also worried, and then Nick had come over and said something about their going to the hotel, in case Angela returned there.

And Kyrie's mom had sighed. "I suppose we should also keep an eye on the girls, and make sure–"

Nick had gotten the idea from this – not being exactly stupid – and set a guard of part-timers on the hotel room. Kyrie heard one of the names and knew it was a shifter. Ian McMurtrie, a retired police officer, who sometimes filled in the roster of the force when they needed extra help. A deceptively small but dangerous man. She assumed the other ones would be too since there was a tendency for non-shifters to go catatonic when faced with people who became lions or dragons or whatever.

Aurelia – Kyrie's mom – started apologizing profusely for leaving, but Kyrie heard herself say, "No, no. You must keep the girls safe." And if she had a brief twinge of envy and resentment because after all her parents had never really cared for keeping her safe, it was brief, and she realized it was unworthy of her.

They had abandoned her to save her. It was literally like one of the fantasies she used to have when she was very little. Without her being the heir to a lost kingdom and her parents having abandoned her to save her from being married by force to an evil minister.

Maybe. They'd probably just saved her from being eaten. At least that's what they, themselves, said. But if she understood precisely what her mother was afraid of now, the getting married forcibly to someone evil might be on the list of potentials.

Not that she really understood what was going on, anyway. But that much seemed likely.

So, when her family left, the younger sisters looking at her curiously, and waving goodbye, as though knowing she was someone who belonged with them, Kyrie had felt a ravenous need for sugar.

When she mentioned it to Conan, Conan pointed out there were left-over fortune cookies in the storage room, but would Rya go with her to make sure that nothing happened?

This was when Bea Ryu came into the diner because Rafiel had asked her to keep an eye on Kyrie.

Kyrie vetoed the idea of fortune cookies, with a shake of the head, "I'd just stop and read each fortune, and probably get all weirded out."

Kyrie never understood how from this the consensus got to "pie" much less how "pie" became "pies" and "A la mode."

But they ended up sitting in the storage area, around a card table – "So we can talk without monitoring our words" Rya said – on folding chairs, eating warmed-up apple pie topped with vanilla ice cream and drinking milk. Conan, either warned by a supernatural sense or perhaps just aware of their run rate, kept bringing them more pie when they finished one set.

Kyrie told them all her mother had said, and in the middle told them how she'd imagined, when she was a very little girl that she was the lost offspring of royalty, or perhaps a magical being like Harry Potter.

"I think every girl has that kind of dream," Bea said. "And I didn't even have the excuse of being adopted."

"Well," Rya said. "I used to pretend that my dad was the magical one." She perked up, as she shoved a piece of pie, topped with ice cream into her mouth. "And I was right. I mean, okay, so he's just a fox shifter, but you know, he is pretty magical, in that he is always willing to support people, and help those in need, and even adopted Mowgli."

Mowgli was a shifter who was probably older than all of them but born in animal form, and therefore was only now becoming really human.

"He's doing well," Rya said. "He's learned to read, and he's... he's not an animal or a savage, but I think in time he'll just be a normal guy. Which is pretty great considering how he started out."

After a long while, the talk slowed, though not the pie-eating. Kyrie had no idea where the rest of them were putting all that pie, but in her case, she was absolutely sure it was going to the kid, who apparently was fond of it, as the rate of kicks was slower and perhaps not as vicious.

"I wonder," Bea said. "What the GSD wants with Rafiel. Normally I'd say let's go out there and find out, but really, with whatever is going with the lions, we can't risk it."

"No," Kyrie said, mournfully.

Just then, Conan came in bearing a tray of pie slices. He hesitated a moment, after setting them on the table. Then he sighed. "Okay, for what it's worth?"

"Yeah?" Kyrie said.

"Nimrod and Orvan are guarding this corridor, one on either end. I don't know why, but I'm not going to ask. However, given those two, I'd guess that they're worried about you and about what might happen."

Kyrie swallowed "At least tell me they're in human form."

Conan waggled his head. "For now. But you can tell it's straining them."

"Do you have any idea what's going on with the Great Sky Bastard?" Rya asked.

"No. I think Tom is stopping any transmissions to me. You, Bea?"

"Yeah. I think he's blocking us, or perhaps it's more accurate to say protecting us, personally."

"So, we have no clue? What could be so urgent about the GSD and Rafiel?

"You?" Tom said. "He wanted to see you? Why on Earth?"

"I have no idea," Rafiel said. He'd grabbed Tom's sleeve as he walked past. As Tom looked at him – straight on – Rafiel realized Tom hadn't even seen him before. Which spoke to Tom being so focused he'd not notice just about anything else. "You know Kyrie didn't disappear again, right? She was in the diner when I left."

Tom rubbed his hand on his chin, and it made a sound. Rafiel realized Tom was on his way to more than a five o'clock shadow, not that Rafiel blamed him, given the crazy events of the last few days.

"Look," Rafiel said. "I came because the old Sky Bastard called me."

Which had brought them to the question, and Rafiel looked at the dragon.... Jousting, and frowned. "I have no idea. The last time I tried to get in front of dragons massing for war, it didn't go well."

Tom smiled. Oh, not a full smile, just a twitch of the lip at the corner, which if anything indicated more amusement than a full-on chuckle. "What? You were told not to meddle in the affairs of dragons, for though art crunchy and good with catsup?"

Rafiel shrugged. "Probably worse, honest, if Kyrie and you hadn't shown up."

"Um..." Tom undid his ponytail and redid it again, something he did when he was thinking.

Rafiel frowned because it was impossible the other dragons hadn't seen him. They were right there, right past where they'd parked the cars. The Great Sky Bastard was facing them. So, why were they being ignored?

Tom sighed. "I've come to ask about my sister-in-law, I guess. Kyrie's little sister. There's reason to think she was taken by a member of the lion clan. Some sort of dispute for the leadership. And I thought the GSD might know where she is and who took her."

"Can't you know?" Rafiel asked. "I mean don't you have–"

"Yeah. Kind of. I'm still not good at directing it. And I have– I don't want the Great Sky... I don't want the old man's attention right now, not with this going on." He waved at the battles in the sky and sighed again. "Yeah. Not a good thing."

"So, we go and beard the dragon in his lair together?" Rafiel asked, cheekily.

The corner of Tom's lip twitched again. "You know what? The lair might be safer. I have no clue what this is even. Come on."

They approached the Great Sky Dragon, Rafiel thought, like two guys walking across a parking lot. Which is exactly what they were. The fact that the parking lot had been taken over by two medieval courts of dragons made him twitchy, but Tom – still wearing The George apron – seemed completely casual. Maybe it made a difference when you had what Old Joe was fond of calling "The Dragon Egg" – whatever the power of dragons was – inside your head.

Rafiel thought of everything that Rod and Tedd Roberts had said and sighed. If he was about to get a lion's egg – strange as such a thing would be – he'd refuse it. His head was enough of a mess without it, thank you so much.

When they reached the line of what Rafiel knew from previous encounters was the Great Sky Dragon's outer ring of bodyguards, he expected something. And they almost got it. He could see the bodyguards considering blocking the way, then sort of hunching their shoulders and stepping aside, inclining their heads at Tom.

Had they received word from the boss, mentally? Or was it a precaution because Tom might be the big boss within days? Was the whole thing that unstable?

The Great Sky Dragon saw them when they were within steps of his throne, and turned around, smiling at them. He had Kohl around his eyes or something like that. It didn't look in the slightest like girly makeup. More like something barbaric and war-related And a sort of weird gold and ruby diadem that looked like he was protecting his nose from breakage, but might be symbolic, as it had a little horn at the tip of the nose. In either case, the two things made him look ghastly.

"Ah," he said. "The dragon child and the lion-head."

"I'm not the lion head," Rafiel said, sullenly.

The Great Sky Dragon lifted an eyebrow. "Are you not?"

"Not that I know of."

"Ah," the Great Sky Dragon said. "Children often don't know what's right in front of their faces, but I thought–"

He looked at Rafiel for a long, long time. Then shrugged. "So, you are not the one who ordered the interference with my tribe?"

Rafiel choked. Definitely, this *crispy and good with catsup thing* was on the program, and he didn't even like catsup. "Interference with your tribe, Gr- Sir? I don't understand you."

The Great Sky Dragon turned towards Tom. "Do you vouch for this? That the lion remains your friend and is not attempting to wrestle power from us?"

Tom looked sideways at Rafiel, and for a moment, for just a moment, Rafiel imagined that Tom was going to say something like "I have no idea who this man is or what he wants." But instead, Tom shook his head, not in denial, but in an obvious attempt at clearing it, and said, "Rafiel is as he has always been. I don't know what you think he's seeing, but he's himself, and he's not betraying me in any way."

The Great Sky Dragon drummed his fingers on the golden arm of his throne. Not precisely his fingers. His hands were encased in a.... glittering sort of finger cover, with six-inch nails on the end. *I wonder what would happen if he shifted? Wouldn't that break his fingers?* Rafiel thought. *Or would it be hanging from his dragon claws?*

"I know he's the lion leader," the Great Sky Dragon said, glaring at Tom before turning baleful eyes on Rafiel. "And that he's hiding it is cause enough for extreme suspicion."

"How on Earth do you know something that's not true?" Rafiel asked. His tone came out more baffled than outraged.

"Because I can't reach into your mind, lion, nor that of my descendant Beatrice Ryu, who is mated to you."

Rafiel was not sure, exactly what the creature meant by mated, and felt himself grow very red. Bea and he had not in fact slept together, partly because she was much younger than he, and he hoped to wait for marriage, and second because he had remaining trauma from his body-control episode with the creature who had compelled him into sex, and he was afraid that the PTSD would force shift or worse from him in an intimate situation. He wanted to marry Bea, of course, and he was almost sure that he could handle intimacy at this point. But giving it a few more months wouldn't hurt.

However, the Great Sky Dragon referring to Bea as mated to him made him squirm, and probably made him look guilty as hell, except Tom said, "I am shielding Bea and Conan."

The Great Sky Dragon looked at Tom and his eyes widened, and for just a moment Rafiel braced, and could see Tom brace, too, for an unpleasant reaction.

But the thing was... something weird must be going on because the Great Sky Dragon made a sound like 'tcha' and looked away from Tom. "I see," he said. "I did give him to you, and I wish you luck with her, as could get no obedience there, but what about this one–” he pointed one of the weird gold claws at Rafiel. “Why is his head opaque to me?”

Tom looked over at Rafiel, for a moment, and squinted, then looked back at the Great Sky Dragon. “I don’t know,” he said. “It is not opaque to me.”

Rafiel didn’t think he had actually either cowered or made a sound of fear. When he said they were going to beard the Great Sky bastard, he hadn’t meant it literally.

He must have managed to appear outwardly impassive because neither of the dragons turned to him. But the Great Sky Dragon looked momentarily so annoyed that Rafiel swore he could see smoke curling off his nostrils.

Then he looked impassive again. “Very well,” the Great Sky Dragon said. “I suppose you came to protect your friend, and that’s admirable. However–” a look at Rafiel. “Should he become head of the lion clan, he should remember what we did the last time someone took the Pearl of Heaven.”

“The Pearl of Heaven is missing?” Rafiel asked.

“I did not say that,” the Great Sky Dragon said. “Can you not keep your pet still, Child?”

“I am not a child,” Tom said, very calmly. “And he’s not my pet. And also, I did not come to protect him. I came to ask you if you know the whereabouts of my sister-in-law.”

“Your sis–”

“Kyrie’s younger sister. I’m sure you heard of a young lioness striding along Fairfax Avenue early this morning. She is Kyrie’s sister, and we are looking for her.”

“Um....”

“But since you don’t know who is even striving for lion head, who thinks he might bolster his claim by marrying my sister-in-law, I suppose it is all for nothing,” he said and started turning away.

“Wait!” the Great Sky Dragon screamed, as Tom started to turn away. Rafiel felt vaguely discomfited by it because frankly he had never seen the GSD look like he’d lost control. He started edging away.

Tom turned around, and heard his own voice, almost supernaturally cool "Sir?"

He too had caught the Great Sky Dragon's loss of patience. He could feel fear coming off the man, and it was a thing he'd never thought to feel. This man, this creature, had controlled a vast organization with an iron hand for centuries.

Tom knew for a fact that he hadn't even sounded this out of control when the Pearl of Heaven had been missing. So, even if it was missing again, why should it be working on him this way?

"Wait," the Great Sky Dragon said. "We'll send two of ours to search for the child."

Tom considered. Then inclined his head, in a gesture reminiscent of his elder's. "That would be acceptable," he said. "Provided she's returned to her family whole and unharmed."

The Great Sky Dragon inclined his head in turn. *It's like we're rival diplomats,* Tom thought. "We will not harm the child," he said. "And will preserve her from harm if possible."

Tom inclined his head. "It is acceptable then."

Across the parking lot, he could see Rafiel take his phone out of his pocket and answer, and he wanted to know what was being said, but–

He turned around to the old dragon, "Is the Pearl really missing?"

The GSD's face contorted. "Yes," he said. It was almost a whisper.

"And you don't have any idea who took it?"

The dragon shook his head. "Not even an inkling, but I thought for sure it would be the next lion."

"Rafiel wouldn't. And neither would Kyrie, but as it happens, sir, I'm going to be looking for the former head's second in command. I think it's highly probable he has my sister-in-law. If he has the pearl, I'll know it. As you know, I have an affinity with the object."

The Great Sky Dragon opened his mouth and closed it.

Rafiel was getting into his car when Tom approached.

"Rafiel, hold on."

Rafiel held until Tom caught up with him. "The phone call," Tom said. "Did it relate to the missing girl?"

Rafiel shook his head. "No... the murder." And seeing Tom staring expectantly, he smiled, maliciously in turn, "What, can you just get it out of my head?"

"Don't be a fool."

And Rafiel laughed because it was as he expected. It wasn't that Tom couldn't reach into his head. Rafiel knew he could. It had happened before. It was that Tom wouldn't. And that Rafiel hadn't felt it, which he would have. So, Tom's answer to the Great Sky Dragon had been a masterful bluff.

"Yeah," Rafiel said. "So, I had Cas comb through all the depositions, to see if anyone mentioned seeing anyone suspicious and carrying anything that could conceal a sword, or for that matter a head."

"And he found something?"

Rafiel frowned. He still had a bad feeling about the whole thing. "It's Professor Travis Lee Clark. The name seems familiar, for some reason, but I can't remember why. Cas looked him up. He's a professor of art history, specializing in non-Western art, particularly South America. He–" Rafiel shrugged. "It's probably nothing, but he's the only person who walked past the windows carrying anything – a rolling duffel bag, in his case – large enough to hide a sword. Also, he was wearing a dark overcoat. Of course, it's been cold as heck, so it probably doesn't mean anything. He's probably just carrying an art project or something."

"Or to add to the complete mess in this city, we now have Highlander playing out as well. *There can be only one,*" Tom said, miming holding a sword.

Rafiel laughed. "Thank heavens I'm not the only one who thought that," he said. The truth was that he'd been feeling weird. Between the Old Sky Bastard referring to Rafiel as Tom's pet, and the entire insanity of the last few days, he'd been feeling uncomfortable. Like something fundamental had changed in their friendship.

Truth was, that much as Tom had tried to make people forget that he'd commanded all shifters – all of them – he had in fact done so. And Rafiel had always wondered since then what the limits were to his friend's power. He trusted Tom. Trusted him unequivocally. But all the same, how much power did Tom have?

And seeing the Great Sky Dragon treat Tom with kid gloves – like Tom was unexploded ordnance that could go off at any time – hadn't helped that feeling. But having Tom fall seamlessly into the same pop culture reference he himself had conjured up did. Whatever else Tom was or was becoming, he was still Tom, and they were still friends.

"Well," Rafiel said. "It did occur to me. Seems like a crazy thing, but ..."

Tom rubbed the middle of his forehead, like someone trying to ward off an impending headache. "But on a scale of normal to pants on head, how insane is it compared to say, shifting into a dragon, particularly a dragon with the power to command all other animals? To get in the minds of people halfway across the world?"

"And do you still have that?" Rafiel asked.

Tom gave him a look. It was as obvious as any yes.

"All right then," Rafiel said, frowning.

"Don't," Tom said. He put his hand on Rafiel's shoulder and squeezed. "Don't even. If you go all strange on me now, I'm going to crack. I need you and our friends to keep me human."

"As much as we can," Rafiel said. "As much as any of us is human."

Tom let out a long-suppressed breath. "Human enough," he said. "Hopefully human enough."

Tom stepped back as Rafiel got in his car. "Let me know what you find," he said.

When Rafiel droves away, Tom stood poised in the parking lot. Behind him, Eastern dragons and Western dragons fell from the sky in flames.

"It's raining dragons," Rafiel sang under his breath. After a moment he put in a call, "Nick, can you meet me at Prof Travis' office? Apparently, he should be in the university right now. We're going to see what he had in the bag."

And so, help him, if this was all going to go Highlander, he'd take a few heads himself.

Kyrie sat in front of several demolished slices of pie. The kid moved slowly in her, like a swimmer tired from doing laps. She tapped her belly. "Estivate at will."

Then started thinking. There was a logic to this. There had to be. So, who would have an interest in one of her sisters? A barely pubescent one?

Unless, of course, her sister was destined to be the next lion leader herself. And there was a pretty scary idea. Who the heck wanted a teen girl leading what amounted to a stone age organization? Tom had once said that the fact that the dragon triads were criminals wasn't strange, since they came from a time before law was invented. She'd bet the lions were the same thing.

So–

In either case, they'd need to know who the next in command of her – had the creature been her grandfather, truly? – yeah, okay, grandfather had been. Because one way or another, either they'd kidnapped her sister, or she had to intend to use them.

She pulled over a napkin and started writing. She might not be able to do much in the way of investigation or fighting, but surely, she would be able to think, right? Okay, provided she didn't fall asleep.

The napkin was covered in questions, by the time she heard Tom's incredulous voice from the door. "Babe!"

She looked up. Tom had opened the door and stood framed in it, looking aghast.

Looking down, Kyrie realized the card table had at least five empty pie plates piled one on the other and her current plate, and the napkin she was writing on.

"I didn't eat all of this," she said, defensively.

"I don't think you can claim the baby ate most of it!" Tom said, but there was laughter in his gaze as well as a sort of fascinated horror.

Nick was waiting outside the strange building that housed the department of arts of CUG. Or to be precise, he was standing back, with his head slightly tilted.

"Hi Rafiel," he said. "I can't figure out whether the place is being built up or falling down."

Rafiel grinned. The building had been much praised even before it was built, and it was indeed a weird shape, supposedly meant to mimic a crumpled sheet of art paper. In reality and made of glass and tiles, it looked like had started collapsing in various places and was being held together with hastily put-up metal rods. "Ah, Nick. It is art. You just fail to get art."

Nick made a weird sound in the back of his throat, which might be laugh or choking. "Can we go in? He asked. Or do you think it will collapse on two cops walking into it?"

"I suspect," Rafiel said. "It will hold okay."

They went up the stairs that looked like they led to a blind corner. At the last minute, they saw there was a sliding door, set at a weird angle. It opened at their approach.

"Phew," Nick said. "I thought we'd have to chew a way in."

Inside the hallway was completely normal, with the windows evenly spaced and casting bright light onto the polished white floor that did an okay job of mimicking marble. "At least the inside is in a normal shape, and I don't have to feel like I'm drunk," Rafiel said.

Mentally, he was counting doors and looking at numbers. Cas had said that Travis' office was B 13.

It was a little brown door, made of the sort of composite that didn't quite look like wood. Rafiel lifted his hand to knock and stopped. There were weird noises in there. It sounded like "chuff, chuff, chuff" and "knock, knock, knock" Like the man was making some weird construction project composed of toy trains or something.

Nick's look said he was just as worried, and his hand had gone towards his holster, but Rafiel shook his head, lifted his hand, and knocked.

"Yeah?" came a voice from inside.

"Uh... Professor Clark? We'd like a word."

"Sure," the voice said, and it sounded oddly impaired. Like.... Rafiel thought. Like he was talking around a mouthful of pins.

Rafiel opened the door cautiously. And jumped back.

It wasn't that anything about the office was threatening precisely. Maybe the carefully arranged stack of skulls on the side wall. But all of it was unexpected. And the ceiling was ... gold. Yeah. Gold was the best way to describe it, as his eyes had trouble adjusting to whatever was up there, all contorted shapes.

Doctor Clark himself was a handsome man in his forties. Surprisingly white, given his specialty, Rafiel thought, with the kind of disappointment that came from hoping that the man could solve his problems with the obviously African lion clan by being one of them. Then again, Rafiel was a lion, and he was blond. And Clark reeked of shifter.

He was short for a man, about Tom's height – which had taught Rafiel never to measure a man by his height since Tom – without meaning to – packed enough menace for a whole battalion of six-footers– with light brown hair, and glasses.

His hair was normally, probably, brown.

Now it was streaked in various colors. As was his face. And his glasses. And the provenance was clear enough, since he held a bouquet of brushes in one hand, removed a set of detail brushes from his mouth with his other hand, and attempted to push his glasses back into place, causing yet more paint transfer.

Now that Rafiel was getting used to the room, he realized there was a desk in the middle of the room, and a chair behind it, both covered in clear plastic.

The ceiling was very gold because it was full of pipes. The chuff, chuff, chuff noises came from the pipes. Which someone – judging by paint transfer, the professor himself– had painted gold and used some kind of panel and trim to make it look like a carved baroque ceiling. The illusion would probably be more complete if the pipes didn't chuff, and if all of it were painted. As it was, the parts that were done looked like the ceiling of a Spanish church circa the 16th century, covered in New World gold. The other parts looked like... a cleaning closet, with water pipes crossing the ceiling.

Clark looked up, as Rafiel did "I'll probably paint mosaic on the flat panels later when I have time," he said.

Nick coughed, probably from the overwhelming smell of turpentine, and Rafiel looked around the walls. Almost completed was a mural, going around the walls which represented... it looked like Mexican temples, not that Rafiel was an expert in them. But the murals were perfectly done, with Trompe l'oeil so exact and detailed that when they were complete people would feel like they were in an arid area surrounded by monumental, slightly unsavory buildings.

But one of the walls, the one that had a carefully constructed rack of some sort, supporting a lot of skulls in front of it, had only drawings of what was to be painted on it. A folding ladder was at the beginning of it, and a lot of paint pots on the ground.

"Do you like?" Professor Clark asked with a broad grin, as though he were showing off his place to casual guests. He rubbed his hands together.

"Uh...." Nick said. "I guess if you're an artist you have to create art."

"Oh, I'm not an artist," Clark said. "I'm just.... An art historian, you know. But they gave me a converted mop closet as an office. Me. The head of the Mustelidae." He grinned happily. "I can tell you since I know you're both shifters, and you–" He looked at Rafiel. "Are the New Lion. You'll get how much of a slap in the face it is to be given a ridiculous office. And at this time. It would just give people the wrong impression, so I have to make sure I don't give the wrong impression."

"The head of the–" Rafiel said.

Clark whirled around, extending a hand still holding brushes. "I presume you know what I mean," he said, as he extended his hand, as though to shake hands, realized he was holding the brushes, and set them on his desk. His nose twitched, oddly. "I mean you know."

Had everyone but him known that each set of animals had a head? He'd thought it was just the dragons, which was explained by their being mostly – or at least ancestrally – Chinese, and therefore full of order and classifications and stuff. Once, when Tom was particularly pissed, he'd said that Confucius had probably been a dragon shifter.

Clark wiped his hand on an already paint-stained white T-shirt, then extended it to Rafiel again, "Travis Lee Clark, head of the Mustelidae and assorted congeners. Otter shifter."

"Rafiel Trall, investigator in the Serious Crimes Unit of the Gold-port Police Force. Lion shifter." Rafiel shook the hand, resigning him-self to having paint on his own hand.

Nick just smiled in that way he did when he wanted to look like he had too many teeth. "Nick," he said. "I'm a wolf."

"I see," Travis said. "I don't know why you've come, but I presume it's related to the changing of the guard, eh? I just want to say I will not hurt the mink. I don't think she has a chance anyway."

"The.... Mink?" Rafiel asked, blinking rapidly, and feeling like he must have stepped through a rabbit hole somewhere because suddenly he was in wonderland without a map.

"She thinks she can take my place as leader of the Mustelidae. Ah. She's an idiot. I never even understood why we got the minks, you know. And—" He waggled his eyebrows. "They're only good for one thing, right?"

"Er... rage?" Nick asked.

Clark looked confused. "No, man. Fur coats."

Rafiel blinked, unsure how this was supposed to mean he shouldn't suspect the professor of murder. Sometimes, just once in his life, he'd like something to happen in the shifter world that was completely nor-mal and explicable and that led to his only or even mostly interacting with normal human beings.

But it was never like that. It was like being a shifter made people more than slightly crazy, and then anything that happened just sent them over the edge.

"Uh... We came about the murder," he said.

Clark blinked at them in genuine confusion. "What murder?"

"The..." Rafiel decided to throw caution to the winds. What the actual heck? No one would believe the professor if he started raving about murdered lions. Likely. It sounded like he already lived in a world of his own, and anyway, he was an artist, whatever he said, and most artists were ten seconds away from a straitjacket. "There was a gentleman murdered in the parking lot of The George, last Friday."

"Oh? They have a decent lamb special for lunch on Thursdays, but this murder thing is becoming a habit, isn't it?"

Rafiel shrugged, refusing to get baited. "Probably," he said. "Because The George is a gathering place for shifters, and there is a lot of turmoil in the shifter world right now. The gentleman was... the head of the lion clan."

"The head of the–" The professor looked struck. He backed up and sat on his chair despite its being covered in plastic. "Enlil? Old evil Enlil."

"Did everyone know him but me?" Rafiel asked. "And I a lion shifter?"

Clark looked up. He had gone considerably pale, but a smile formed on his lips, nonetheless. "That is because you're a youngster," he said. "I mean, I'm used to people talking about me as if I were a toddler, and I'm just over three thousand years old. But you? You're just a baby."

"Thank you. But by human reckoning, I'm fully grown and an officer of the law."

Clark took a deep breath. "Yeah, I suppose you are. Which explains why you've never run into Enlil or his evil, crazed minions."

"You have?"

Clark shrugged. "Not enough to have a personal grudge, if that's what you're looking for, no," he said. "But enough to have got an idea of who and what he was. Some of my... subordinates had experiences with him, in Europe, during World War II that don't bear thinking about. There is this badger, one of my people, who is a tailor, and he dated one of Enlil's daughters during World War II in France, and you know, when he's drunk – the tailor, not Enlil – he talks about what a bastard Enlil is." He grinned. "Only when he's really drunk, he becomes a badger and then he continues trying to tell the story in growls and hisses." He sobered up. "But I think he's really traumatized, poor bastard." He stood up. "That's that. Ding dong, the evil lion is gone. And if we're lucky," He looked at Rafiel. "You're not half as evil, and you'll hold on. Not that I'm sure there is anyone half as evil." He stood up. "How may I help you?"

"You see, sir," Nick started.

"Someone saw you walking away with a duffel bag, and wearing a trench coat walking by the diner, the night of the murder."

"And?" The professor looked genuinely confused.

"And you see, the man was decapitated with a saber, and his head was taken away. And we figured you ... that is?"

"Oh. No, you see." He smiled. "I just had skulls in the duffel."

"Skulls?"

Travis sighed, as though it was a great imposition to explain. Then he grinned. He went over and threw back the plastic. "I probably am violating some sort of 'disposing of human remains' thing, who knows, but I think these were long forgotten, all of them more than a hundred years old, and I'm making something glorious of them. Behold, the tzompantli."

Rafiel blinked at the skulls neatly arranged into a wall, on a rack of pipes painted to look like stone. "I'm sorry, I don't–"

"It was a Meso-American thing," he said. "If you wish, I'll send you my YouTube video explaining it. I have quite the following for my recorded lectures."

"Er.... I imagine." Rafiel looked at the skulls. He guessed they were all really old, just from the color and general look. "Are you robbing graves?"

"No. Though there's Butterpark, you know, it was converted from a cemetery to a park, and they never removed the bodies, so I suppose I could. I hear sometimes people will fall through the lawn into open caskets still with remains in them. But no. I find them in rivers and lakes. A lot of prospectors and natives died without anyone noticing. So– now I make something glorious from them. I mean, if you're going to take issue at–"

Rafiel shook his head. He probably could, and maybe should take issue. But he had enough trouble punishing the serious crimes of shifters without outing who committed them or why. He wasn't going to risk exposing the whole shifter thing by making a point of punishing an otter who liked using forgotten skulls to make some kind of symbolic art thing. "No. I don't think it's worth bothering. I'm not going to– You know unless you add new ones. So, you don't know anything about the lion? The murder?"

Clark tilted his head sideways. "I can put the word out if you wish. My people hear a lot of things." He made an odd undulating gesture with his hand. "They're nimble and they slither, you know? They go places." He rubbed his hands together, in a way that Rafiel remembered seeing otters do at the zoo.

"Thank you, I'd appreciate it," Rafiel said.

Outside, in the sun, Nick said, "Okay, that was creepy as heck."

Rafiel took a deep breath. "Yeah. I mean, in a way. Though I suspect his subject is in general creepy as hell. Meso-America and all that, you know."

"Yeah, I guess, but skulls?"

"I don't know," Rafiel said. "He impresses me as a weird mix of completely innocent and totally fascinated by his subject. It's normal for geniuses and artists, and despite his saying he is no artist, I'm going to guess he's both. His subject is creepy, but I don't think he's a danger to anyone. Unless you are a mink."

Nick cackled, but Rafiel only barely managed a smile. He felt like a supernaturally strong headache had come out of nowhere to crush his head in a vise.

Should he really worry about the safety and health of mink shifters, now? Was that something he needed to do?

Where to look for the murderer next, before Mr. Milagros lost patience? And before the dragons did... whatever the dragons were about to do? And where was Kyrie's sister?

"Look, it's no lead at all, and I have no idea how you'd find this, except through the shifter's network, but can you figure out who the shifter badger is who was in France in World War II? It's a remote as heck chance, but if he's held a grudge against Enlil this long..." He shrugged.

"Yeah, remote as heck chance," Nick said. "And I'm not sure I can figure out anything, but I'll go shake a few of the rodents painting graffiti. One or more of them might know something."

Tom looked over the napkin. "No, hon. I don't think we can go to Savannah and knock on doors to find your grandfather's associates."

She smiled. She'd explained to him that Bea and Rya had eaten pie with her. Now they were back in the diner. "That's not what I meant. I think my mother and father must know them, almost by definition. But more importantly..." She paused and made a face. "I'd like to know what my sisters know."

"What do you mean?" Tom said. "You can't think they know something that their parents don't know, can you? They're just kids."

"Of course. And think about what shifter kids in shifter families must know." She felt her hand coming to rest on her belly, as though trying to figure out what she would do if their kid were a shifter. He wasn't supposed to be, at least if what Old Joe had said was right. Because they were shifters of such different types, the genes just weren't there for a "joint" shifter cohesion.

"You mean, they'll have to know to keep quiet about it and all?" Tom said.

"Yeah. We'll have to teach the kitty dragon that, I suppose," she said, smiling at his worried expression. "Not to talk about shifting, I mean."

Tom sat across from her at the folding table, as though the thought overwhelmed him. It was as if he'd never thought about it before. Really? Kyrie supposed that men really were different. She had been worried about it almost from the beginning.

"I suppose when they're very little people will just assume they have a great imagination," he said, pensively. "And then..."

"And then we can tell them not to tell. Yes. But in our case... how do I put this? It's not like the life my parents described having, where everything revolved around being a lion shifter, and the lion shifter clan, and where my grandfather didn't have any kind of compunction about killing them for a few days."

Tom rubbed his chin, with a sound like sandpaper, caught it, and grinned "Yeah, I'm going to need to shower and shave one of these years. You married a hobo, honey."

She laughed. "Not hardly. But the thing is that the kids must have a different view of all of this than the adults do. I think my parents were so worried about being destroyed, or worse having the kids destroyed at any minute, that they didn't really see much of what was going on, but the kids probably did. I don't think my parents realized that Enlil meant to kill me, for instance, but I bet the kids did."

"So," Tom said. "For all I know you might be right. But what do you propose to do about it."

"For one, you can't leave me locked in here forever, under layers of guards."

"Oh yes I can when the alternative is letting an ancient serpent birthed by an evil blond take over our kid before he's even born."

"Yeah, but that's not the alternative. Look, I don't mind if you send someone with me to keep an eye, or whatever, but I can't stay here, while all that stuff is going on out there. I'll just eat pie till I blow up or the kid grows to be three hundred pounds." She saw him look at the table with amusement, and rushed to protest, "Not that I ate all of that. All the girls helped."

"Right, right," Tom said, making a gesture of appeasement and somehow managing to convey he didn't believe her. Not for a minute. "But Kyrie, there's real danger out there, and I get terrified of something happening to you while you can't shift."

She sighed. "Tom, most people can't shift, and they are still perfectly safe. I'm not sure why you think that my shifting into a panther is a plus, let alone absolutely necessary to keep me safe."

"I didn't say that."

"No, but it's how you're acting. I can look after myself."

"Sure, but you're my wife."

"And?"

"And I'm not absolutely sure I can look after myself, without you," Tom said disarmingly. "I have to deal with all these crazy ass shifters. I don't think I can still be sane if something happens to you. Kyrie, you're the best part of me."

She couldn't help but kiss him.

And that's when Tom's phone rang.

Rafiel had just gotten in the car when his phone rang. He answered it, half expecting it to be Milagros, and without bothering to look at the number. He just clicked the button that brought the phone over the car's radio.

And he got heavy breathing.

"Hello?" he said, alarmed.

"Rafiel!" it was Bea's voice, and she sounded stressed.

"Yeah? What's wrong?"

"Well..." She said. There was a sound like she was trying to catch her breath. A roar came through the phone. A loud roar. Like a thoroughly pissed-off lion.

"The hell?" Rafiel said.

"Yeah, you're not going to believe this, but the house– Your parents' house is under siege– There are six lions outside, prowling. One of them broke the picnic table on the patio by jumping on it. I don't– I don't think it was meant to take a full-grown lion."

"It sure as heck wasn't," Rafiel said.

The roar came again.

"Are you guys safe?" he asked. Which was a stupid question. He didn't think his parents' house, of sixties vintage, in suburban Goldport, had been designed to withstand a lion attack. I mean, could they just jump through a window and break it while being relatively unscathed? He was fairly sure he could.

"We're in the basement. Your dad says it used to be a nuclear shelter and that door will resist just about anything. But–"

Yeah, but– But Rafiel was going to have to go fight this on his own. One against six. He didn't like the odds. But he wasn't about to let his parents or Bea die.

He hung up and dialed up Tom but it rolled straight to voice mail. He left a message and sped on toward home, where his parents and Bea were under siege.

Tom picked up his phone and frowned at the screen. "Wasn't Dad in the diner?" he asked Kyrie, before answering.

"Tom?" Edward Ormson sounded like he'd been running.

"Dad?"

"I have escaped. They grabbed me from the diner and were dragging me to a van in the parking lot, but I escaped and I'm–" Long sound of drawing breath. "I'm under a car on Fairfax. A parked car. But they're overflying and looking for me."

Tom blinked. He felt his face lengthen which was always a very bad sign. "Dad," he said, speaking very carefully. "Who tried to take you? From overflying I assume they're dragons?"

"Yeah, but not... they don't look like the usual crowd. For one, I got a feeling that they don't speak much English. They said they were taking me to the queen."

"Son of a bitch," Tom said, then controlled himself again. "Total idiots. What block of Fairfax, Dad?"

"About two blocks East of the diner. It's a blue suburban. What I'm under."

"Right. Hold on. I'm coming." He looked over his shoulder at Kyrie, as he was running out the door. "I'll be right back. Don't leave."

Rafiel drove by the house first. He had Bea on the phone, and she kept updating him, but Tom hadn't called back.

Outside the house, there were two cars parked, one with Georgia plates, and one with Louisiana plates. What a time to be alive. Lions traveled by car, of course!

But this meant, from what he'd gathered in the last few days, that the lion clan – or clade, or Sunday afternoon go meet, for all he cared – had driven here from their center of power. Did they have the young lion-shifter? Or were they just after him? Why would they be after him? Because he was the New Lion? He didn't want to be the New Lion. If possible, he wanted it less than Tom wanted to be the New Dragon.

The thought that he was next in line for the lion throne – for lack of a better term for it – did not fill him with warm fuzzies. Or any kind of fuzzies. Frankly, it made his stomach clench, and feel like he'd swallowed a whole bottle of ice, whole. All he needed on top of being a lion shifter and a policeman was to be responsible for a bunch of crazy and aggressive people all over.

But he also remembered the thing about seeings that were true and strange dreams, meaning he might very well be in the running.

He took a deep breath in through his nose and out through his mouth. "Okay, Bea. I'm going to go around one more time and see if I can get help," he said.

She was silent so long in response, that he wasn't absolutely sure she had heard him. Or that the phone was still on.

"All right," she said. "By the sound of it, they're in the house and ripping things up. Your dad wants to go out and shoot them. I'm trying to convince him this is not a good idea."

"Not a good idea at all," Rafiel said. "Unless he's sure of blowing out their brains, and even then, it's not guaranteed. It might just piss them off. Dad, stay put," he said. "I'm going to try to get help. Give me at least half an hour before you do something stupid."

He hung up, closed his eyes, and sent a sort of half-coherent request for help to the divinity above. Okay, it was more along the lines of: *Not my dad. Please, not my dad.*

His dad was crusty and jaded, and had a cool view of human nature but ...

But he was in some ways Rafiel's moral conscience and his anchor. *Please, not my dad.*

And then he hung up and dialed Kyrie. Tom hadn't answered yet, but Kyrie almost for sure knew where he was.

*****

Kyrie answered the phone, but had no time to speak, before Rafiel's voice came through, with an edge of hysteria, "Kyrie, where's Tom?"

"He went to rescue his dad, from... I suspect Norse Dragons. Why?"

Speaking at the speed of light, Rafiel poured out the story, about his family being under siege, his parents and Bea in the old bomb shelter.

For a moment – for just a moment – Kyrie almost said she'd come over. It would be like the old days. And if they could also have Tom, there was no way that between the three of them they couldn't take out six puny lions.

But the kid kicked, just in time to remind her she couldn't shift. If only she could–

The thought was half-formed before she could fully articulate it. "Rafiel, give me your parents' address. I'll tell you as soon as I have reinforcements."

And holding her breath, praying she would have reinforcements, she dialed her mom's number.

Aurelia had given her the number, putting it in Kyrie's phone while they'd talked that morning. Ostensibly should Kyrie need anything, but maybe so Kyrie could tell her if she found her kid.

Kyrie felt a little guilty. Because she had no news of Angela. But she did need her mom. And after all, when had she ever asked a favor of her parents? Whom she'd met today?

She dialed the number, and was surprised her mom greeted her by name – presumably having added her to her phone – as that was the first thing she said, "Kyrie? Did you hear about Angela?"

"No, Mom," Kyrie surprised herself with the word tripping off her tongue. She'd not called anyone that since the foster family that had wanted to adopt her when she was twelve. "I'm sorry. We haven't heard anything. I know the police are looking, and Tom has put some dragons on it. But the thing is... We need your help."

"Uh. How?"

She told it almost as quickly as Rafiel had.

"All right, give us his address. And he's in an SUV, you say. Uh-uh. Unmarked, police SUV. Your dad and I and Carol will go."

"Carol?"

"She's a mature fourteen, and she'll be with us. Better than leaving her here tearing herself apart with guilt because she didn't wake us when she heard Angela slip out. I'll leave Gia behind. But she knows to keep the door locked."

Uh-oh, Kyrie thought, as she hung up. She tried Tom's phone, but it rolled right over to voice mail, leaving her anxious and uneasy.

She sat there, in front of the card table, with the empty pie pans. Absently, she picked at the crumbs. Then she sighed and stood up.

Screw this.

Tom was in trouble, and Rafiel was in trouble. She had to do something. Even if she had to do it as a human.

Tom saw the wings ahead of him before he saw the blue Expedition with an unmistakable Edward-like shape underneath.

He shook his head. Of course, Dad would get that wrong. The man never could tell the difference. To him all cars in a class were alike. Maybe Tom should talk to him about reading the badges of cars before diving under them.

The problem with Dad hiding under a car, of course, was that sooner or later the car's owners came up. And right now, there were two people coming towards the Expedition. He could kind of see the shadow of his dad under there, and above he could see and feel the wings of dragons, circling, waiting to dart in at a sign of movement.

The people walking towards the expedition were a man and a woman, her carrying a bunch of books, him drinking some kind of fancy take-out coffee. Both of them laughing.

He started running, but before he got there, the woman got in on the driver's side of the expedition. And Tom's father came running out. And a dragon shadow dove from the sky.

Shitshitshitshitshit, became a refrain at the back of Tom's mind, and he was running and stripping as he ran. And coughing as he stripped, his mind willing his body to shift into the dragon.

Cough, cough, and his face elongated, every muscle and bone on it aching with unbelievable pain. And he had The George Apron off and stretched an elongated arm, to hang it from the branch of a tree. There was a good chance, this being close to The George, some strolling good Samaritan would find it and return it. The rest was all disposable, from his tenth-hand T-shirt to the equally much used jeans, and the cheapest cloth sneakers on his feet. They bought this stuff from thrift stores by the dozen. He loved his leather boots, but he never wore them when things were going weird. Which meant almost not at all lately, of course.

His last conscious action, as Tom, before the dragon took fully over, in the pain of stretching bones and rearranging muscles, was to take his wedding ring from his finger and the phone from his pocket and slip them, into the pocket he had attached to his arm with a flex-plastic bracelet, in a spiral form. It was his only way to keep the phone safe. He closed the pocket, gave a quick thought that it was weird that he could walk, sort of, along the sidewalk, while looking like a half-reptilian monstrosity, his clothes bursting off his body as he went, and no one seemed to pay any attention. The few people who looked his way looked quickly away again, in the same kind of look people used to avoid looking at the profoundly deformed.

And then the dragons were down, and one of them grabbed his father by the middle, talons wrapped around him.

Tom made a sound that, had he still been in full control of his mouth and human would have been "Ah, no you don't, Sven." And then he jumped and was airborne, barely making it, flapping his wings a mere inch or so above the trees planted along Fairfax Avenue, and making speed toward the two light blue dragons flying away with his father.

Tom wasn't about to let them do that. Edward Ormson might not be much of a father, but he was the only father Tom had. And frankly, he was the best of the two parents he'd been allotted. And Tom was going to make sure he stayed alive.

"Your mom?" Rafiel asked when Kyrie called him.

"Yeah, and my dad, and my middle sister."

"But... Kyrie, this is war."

"They know. Rafiel, I wasn't spawned from nothing."

He nodded to the phone as though she could see him and took a deep breath. "Okay, I'm waiting out here. I guess I'll be ready when they come."

And by ready, he meant what he was already doing. Removing his phone and wallet, and putting them in pockets, attached to him by flex bracelets. He'd learned this was essential the hard way when an ancient shifter had tempted him to the wilderness and left him for dead.

And taking off his good jeans, and his shoes. The T-shirt he didn't mind about as much, and he figured the underwear was toast. Which is why to him underwear was listed in shopping as "consumables."

He was vaguely amused at the thought that if any of his brother officers – much less Mr. Milagros – who weren't shifters came by and saw him sitting in his drawers in his police car, they'd have questions. And he really couldn't tell them anything but a lame "I was hot" or perhaps "I was trying to bait some prostitute to come solicit." Which was, to say the least, unlikely in his parents' quiet suburban street.

He saw a car with North Carolina plates park ahead of him, and held his breath, till Kyrie's mom, dad, and younger sister got out. They nodded to him, opened the door to their car, and started, with a quick look each way, to go through the same motions he'd gone through, taking off everything they didn't want ruined.

His phone rang.

He picked up. It was his dad. "Son, we're going to have to go out."

"Dad, don't. You have no reason to. They can't get into the bomb shelter, can they?"

"No. But we haven't maintained this as a safe room. Okay, something to do after. But Rafiel, we don't have any water or anything in here, and the temperature control is broken. We're baking. I'm going out. I've got my gun."

And by my gun he meant one of about seven, Rafiel assumed. Rafiel closed his eyes. "Dad? I'm here with reinforcements. And I don't want my friends shot."

"Oh, don't worry about that. This place has monitors and cameras on the rest of the house. I know what the bastards look like!"

Rafiel closed his eyes and prayed, really hard. Because would his father be able to tell one lion from the other? Rafiel wasn't sure he could, except by smell.

This whole thing had the feel of something that would go suddenly very bad.

And then exploded out of the car, changing into a lion at the same time. He was aware of Kyrie's family falling in behind him more by smell and feel than by knowing them.

Older black panther male, an older female lion, and a barely grown female cub.

He had a moment of surprise that Kyrie's dad was a black panther, but he didn't know why that should surprise him.

And he was running as fast as he could up the steps, past his mother's rose garden, now dormant, and into the porch door that the bastards had punched a big hole through. In the cozy, woodsy living room with the fireplace and all the shelves, he stood and roared a deafening roar.

His mind was blood-red. This was his territory, and the intruders would pay.

Kyrie got out of the storage room, noting the various people carefully watching her. She went across the hall to the ladies' room, where she took some extended time to make sure the kid was not going to make her pee herself at an inconvenient time.

Then she washed her hands, splashed some water onto her face, and thought, *some bride I make. I look about eighty* and set tasks straight in her mind.

She was going to have to figure out where her sister was first. Mostly because Rafiel and Tom would probably get themselves out of trouble again. They'd done it before, they'd probably do it this time. But Angela was a kid and in a brand-new city. She remembered her sister liked the natural history museum. The story about the argument before the murder, which she now thought meant something else completely different, was that she'd wanted to go to the Museum of Natural History, but her grandfather hadn't wanted to go. They wouldn't make that excuse unless the kids really had wanted to go there.

And maybe Enlil really opposed it.

He was probably afraid of facing the bones of some of his old murder victims, Kyrie thought uncharitably. Would Angela have gone to the Natural History Museum? Going that way on Fairfax was consistent with that.

It had been months since Kyrie and Tom had spent time at the museum. They never had much free time. But she had some idea of dioramas and places a young lion could hide if she didn't move around much. Most of the

African and other habitats dioramas were usually empty of visitors anyway. Tom and she had sat there and talked for a while.

Yeah. She thought she was going to the museum. Maybe her sister wouldn't be there, and it would do no good, but it had to do more than staying here and eating her heart out. As her mom had said about her middle daughter, it did no good to sit and feel guilty.

She poked her head out of the bathroom and spotted people looking at her. Six of them, all of them thinking they were completely unobtrusive.

Dear Lord, were all her friends simple?

There was Conan looking back over his shoulder while wiping a table, with the cloth about three inches above the tabletop. There was Rya behind him, just standing there, blinking at her.

Dr. Roberts was at the counter, and he'd shifted again without noticing. A giant rat in a white coat. He held a coffee cup and was going to make a mess when he took it to his non-existent lips.

And then there was Orvan, looking nervous, just outside the back door. He was pacing in circles, and she wondered exactly what orders he thought Tom had given to stop her.

She chewed on her lip, but it was only part annoyance. The other part was to fight her terrible need to laugh.

"Insane, aren't they?" said Rod's voice. And Kyrie jumped. He was standing in the shadows of the men's room, with the door just cracked. Enough to see without being seen, with the light open. Okay, so he wasn't stupid.

She could admit he had startled her. Heck, he knew that from her jump. But she wasn't about to admit it. Instead, she shook her head at him. "You're not much better, Bilbo," she said, and then turned her back on him, and walked up to Conan.

"You!"

Conan was as he'd always been. He blinked and shuddered and swallowed hard. "Kyrie. I– Tom said."

"I'm sure he did," she said. "And I'm sure you can see a distinct lack of Tom around here. I don't know where he is and he's not answering his phone."

"Kyrie, I can't–"

"Wanna bet? What if I should go into labor? I think I feel a twinge starting. Go and find my husband for me, Conan. And take Rya to protect you from the Great Sky Dragon."

"I–" Conan said, and he looked so apologetic and guilty that Kyrie felt like she was kicking a defenseless puppy, but she really needed to know what was happening to Tom. And anyway, she needed to thin down the ranks of her protectors.

She could imagine herself driving down Fairfax with all of them flapping behind the car, holding by one hand. Probably in shifted form, too, because they were that insane. Just no.

"Come on, Conan," Rya said, plucking at his sleeve. She looked both worried and somehow a little afraid. "She's right. We need to know where boss Dragon is. Without him, the other guys could pick on us."

Kyrie turned from them, on a path, seemingly, back to the storage area, and passing Dr. Tedd Roberts whispered at him, "You're in rat form. You're going to make a mess when you drink."

He started, looked down at his cup, started shifting, and she legged it.

She legged it all the way down the hallway, running incredibly fast for a woman who had a massive beach ball affixed to the front of her stomach, a heavy one that kept kicking at her in excitement at the idea of an outing.

Rod made a reach for her but missed, and she hit the back door at a clip, missing Orvan's outstretched arm.

But as she opened the driver's door of the car, Rod was opening the passenger door, his mouth curling in a grin that could only be described as alligator-like.

She made a sound that was supposed to be "stop it," but came out as "Umph" because she'd lost all her breath and was upset she'd never even seen him coming.

"Wait for the ox, or he'll be upset," Rod said. "And he's a good egg. And the bovines are influential and powerful. We're going to need as many leaders as we can."

She saw no point in protesting, as Paul Orvan opened the back door, looking vaguely apologetic as he always seemed to in human form. He peered at Kyrie from behind his glasses – did he really need those glasses? And what did he do for them when he shifted? – and blinked. "Look, if you must go somewhere, you must go somewhere, but whatever your husband is or isn't, he has a lot of power. And he might very well be the leader of the dragons, either now or soon enough. Let us protect you." He opened his hands. "Ox is slow, but not that slow. Ox doesn't want to be gored, much less roasted.

She repeated "umph." And turned the key. "Hold on. We're going to the Natural History Museum, to see if my sister is hanging out there."

"Oh," Rod said. "That would make sense."

Being the lion was always odd. It came at Rafiel as slices of sound larded with sharp pictures, all of it overlaid with smells that his human brain couldn't understand at all, but the lion processed without a hiccup.

In the family room of the house, he could smell six – very powerful – male lion shifters. He could also sense them, with some other power he wasn't aware of ever having possessed.

They were ancient, all of them, as opposed to himself and Kyrie's family, who were all relatively young, definitely less than a century.

He also knew that Kyrie's family – his pride – were waiting for a motion from him. And the lions were heading towards them, at a run. All but one, who was waiting at the door to the safe room.

And Rafiel didn't know how he knew that, because he had never been able to distance-see before, but now he could, in almost exquisite detail. He could see the basement clearly as though he were there, staring at the door of the safe room, a big concrete slab that slid into place.

He realized he was seeing through the lion's eyes, as the lion roared in frustration.

Then he realized the other lions were almost upon them. Without speaking, he thought at the other three that they had better be prepared to fight, and then, as a large, sleek lion with a dark mane came around the edge of the fireplace, Rafiel jumped.

He raked his claws across the large lion's eyes, fast. He pushed, to over-turn the lion, with him on top.

But it was never as easy as it seemed. The other lion must have more experience with a lion fight.

They were clawing and scratching, and there was a pain in Rafiel's gut, which he suspected came from an eviscerating claw.

From somewhere came the "Bam" of a shot, and Rafiel lost his vision of the basement.

And from behind him came a high-pitched scream of a wounded lion.

And that's when all hell broke loose, because he heard wings, and there was a smell of burning.

And then the "Bam" of a shot and the lion fighting Rafiel went berserk.

Still shifted, his eyes feeling like they couldn't focus, Rafiel was aware of his dad striding up, holding a rifle he'd never seen before, putting the rifle to the lion's head and shooting.

Maybe that shot, or the lion brains and fur splattering him and everything else around, or maybe he was bleeding too fast, but Rafiel's consciousness went to dark.

8

TOM FLAPPED HIS WINGS as fast as he could and was catching up to the Norse dragons, each of them built like the figure on the prow of a raiding ship. His dad was squirming, one fist balled and beating at the ankle of the dragon holding him. This made him halfway proud and halfway scared. For one, what kind of insane person tried to hit something that was probably ten times or more larger than him? His father, of course. He'd come a long way since he'd been so scared of Tom in shifted form that he'd ordered his own son out of the condo at gunpoint.

The other part of the terror that made Tom's mind go blank, was what would happen if the dragon dropped Edward. He had a memory of reading about raptors dropping tortoises from a height to kill them, so they could eat the soft, gooey insides.

The memory put speed in his wings. He overtopped the dragon carrying his father and made a dive at his neck.

His father screamed.

Tom dove again, grabbed Edward just in time, and twisted, to find the other dragon's mouth maybe a foot from Tom neck.

Being startled he flamed, and the other dragon dove, with his neck ruffles on fire.

The dragon's companion turned on Tom. A burn hit Tom on the wing. He felt it, and screamed, but turned fast, and burned his adversary with a hotter flame than ever before.

The other dragon's wing membrane melted, like wax in the sun, leaving the wing bones, like elongated fingers bones, shining stark white. Suddenly the enemy dragon was flapping, helplessly as he lost altitude. He wouldn't chase Tom that way.

Tom made for the diner, carrying his father.

It was twilight, the mountains gilded by the sun, but a cold wind was picking up, and there were masses of clouds forecasting a storm. Tom's wing was still smoldering, and it hurt like crazy.

He wanted to go home, put Edward down, and have some coffee. Maybe he'd fight Kyrie for some pie, too.

The last thing he expected was the flight of dragons circling over the parking lot.

All of them Norse dragons, curse his luck.

There were at least fifteen of them, armored, shining in the winter light. And people had gathered around the diner, pointing up.

Cameras were snapping. Wonderful.

Just perfect.

The Natural History Museum and the zoo were in a sprawling park complex. In summer, when school was on vacation, the parking lot was full, and kids ran around getting splashed by the fountains in the planted areas.

Now it was half full, and the planted areas looked brown and forlorn.

Not that Kyrie spent time staring at them. It was just before closing, so she hurried remembering something she and Tom had found out a few months ago and had been a wonderful thing, as they were pretty broke.

The last half hour at the museum was free entrance. This meant she could go in and look for her sister without lining up for a ticket.

She plunged through the gate at a clip, getting a very odd look from the number counter at the gate. In a rush, she said, "I have a craving to see dinosaurs."

He, a bearded middle-aged man, nodded sagely as though this made perfect sense. Maybe it did.

And then she was on the escalator up, moving on a memory of where the dioramas were.

But at the top of the stairs, she was hit by the smell of lion shifter. That is, it smelled like Rafiel, in summer, when he'd been in a fight. The smell of shifter and the smell of musk, together, practically screaming "I'm male, and a lion."

And it was coming from the room to the right, which was – as far as Kyrie could tell – a room the museum rented for meetings and such.

The room was shaped like a beetle, with windows all along the side not attached to the museum, and a wide balcony off it. The last time they'd been in, in the middle of a snowstorm, just before Christmas, Kyrie had thought that given some outdoor heaters, it would make a pretty amazing space for a New Year's party. Not that she and Tom would ever have the kind of money it took to rent it.

She started to turn that way and found herself blocked by a large back. A really large back. Orvan had shifted, and was now full minotaur, walking ahead of her, head slightly lowered. She'd seen pictures and drawings of bullfights, and she half expected him to drag his foot on the ground a few times.

To her other side, a slithering sound told her that Rod had also shifted.

Ooh, boy, was she really bringing a gator and a minotaur to a lion fight?

"Hold on," Rafiel heard his dad say. "Damn it, hold on." Then there was something at his lips. He realized he was being supported by a warm body, and something pressed against his lips. "Drink," his dad said.

Rafiel took a drink. Vanilla and ... something slimy. But the moment the liquid hit his tongue, he realized he was both parched and starving, and drank all of it. As he opened his eyes, he saw his dad pulling the mixer container away from Rafiel's lips, and handing it to someone in the background, "More."

Rafiel shook his head "What was–"

"Cream, eggs, and protein powder. Take it easy. That bastard about gutted you."

Rafiel looked down at himself. He felt pain, but he'd been feeling pain all along. It clouded his mind, but–

"We've called Doctor Nik," his mom said. "He's on his way. With his wife."

"I don't need a doctor. It will heal," Rafiel said. "Tom was–"

"You don't have time to be dead," a woman's voice he didn't know said. Or rather he knew the voice, but not well, and she sounded like Kyrie and– He turned his eyes to see Aurelia Smith standing there, wearing a jogging suit that must be Rafiel's mom's and was much too big for her.

In the back, indistinctly, he saw two figures, carrying a third.

"Justin Harcourt wasn't here," she said.

"Who?"

"The.... My father's right hand. The pretender in chief. He wasn't here. That means... he's up to something. We have no other casualties." She looked worried. "Well, except you. But we don't know where Harcourt is, and he is trouble. I hope Angela–" She made a face. "We're calling Kyrie, but she hasn't answered."

Rafiel wanted to tell her that Kyrie was probably asleep. It wasn't that rare these days. She seemed to fall asleep in all sorts of positions, including while carrying trays. But he had a bad feeling.

And besides, before he could answer, his father had the blender container at his lips again.

"That truly is a vile concoction," he said.

And then Doctor Nik, all six foot of Indian male was there, casting a dubious look around, at what must be a hell of a scene of carnage if only one lion escaped.

He looked at Rafiel and his eyes widened. "Alex," he said. "I need your help, we need to get him patched up fast."

And then he injected Rafiel with something, while Rafiel tried to protest.

The world faded to black again. He took a sense of annoyance into the dark with him.

Kyrie found herself looking at a man, which is not what she expected. The smell of lion had been so pervasive, that a lion is what she expected to walk in on. Instead, she walked into the room, to find a man standing there.

He was middle-aged. Probably around fifty. The back of her head informed her that was nonsense, but that's how she perceived him. Even if he was much, much older, he looked middle-aged, with light brown hair. He wore a suit, which was another surprise, though, on second look, she realized the suit didn't fit quite right. It was short on the ankles, and weirdly rumpled like he'd stolen it off someone, Kyrie thought.

As he turned around to look, when they entered, his eyes were oddly light. Really light, a transparent pale blue she'd rarely seen. For a moment she thought he was blind, but then he grinned and somehow managed to give the impression of way too many teeth even more than Rod did.

"Why, hello there. You must be old Enlil's oldest, lost granddaughter, the one he set out to find." He gave Kyrie a look from head to toe. His eyes lingered on her belly. "I suppose my rival got you knocked up. It's just like these young cubs who know nothing to take liberties. It's fine. We can kill it when it's born. You and I, we can start a dynasty!"

Kyrie realized she'd growled at the back of her throat, but the idiot was approaching, gliding towards her, as though this was some grand seduction ploy.

Were all these ancient shifter males insane? Did they not take into account what a woman might or might not want? Wait, of course, they didn't. Throughout most of history, it hadn't mattered at all, had it? And they were old. Really, really old.

She growled at him again, and sliding up, on either side of her, came a minotaur, head lowered, and an alligator, swinging his tail. And yeah, now Orvan was scraping the mosaic of the museum with his right foot, which gave the impression he was about to dance.

The man looked at one of the guys, then at the other. His mouth dropped open, he was that shocked. He looked back at Kyrie. "What the– What are you trying to do queenie? Start a fight between clans?"

Rod was smiling, which was way more disturbing in gator form. His tail slashed forward, almost snagging the man's leg. The man jumped back, "Damn it, Nimrod, you know the rules. You don't want to start a fight between our clans."

Step, step, step, the alligator stepped forward, and his jaws opened. His tail swished merrily. At the same time, the minotaur charged, head lowered.

The man jumped back.

"Where is my sister?" Kyrie asked.

"What? The kid? I smelled her in here, but not that strong. I–"

Orvan charged again.

The lion shifter barely evaded him, and then, in a heartbeat, shifted and jumped over the railing, headed towards the door, leaving behind a suit, on the floor.

"Come on," Kyrie said.

She ran down the down the escalator and tore through the lobby where people – fortunately not many these late – were still clutching each other.

Normally, she supposed, a pregnant woman pursued by a gator and a minotaur would cause some sort of raucous, but she would bet most people there never even saw her because they were still clutching each other in fear of the lion who had run through the lobby.

As she ran out the door, a woman called, "Kyrie."

She turned.

Aimee Morgan stood just outside the door. She looked like she had dressed in a hurry, and her hair – normally in a neat bun – was disheveled, forming a halo around her head. She was also shivering, in a T-shirt and jeans, under light snow.

She wrapped her arms around herself and smiled tentatively at Kyrie. "I didn't expect to see you. I suppose... it's about the young lioness?"

Aimee Morgan. Aimee Morgan was a secretary bird shifter and a suburban mother. In her human persona, she was as happy and easy as her animal persona was high-strung and forever on the attack.

She had a home and a life – with her emu-shifter husband – but she spent a lot of time at the zoo, when the kids were in school, or when her husband took the kids hiking or something.

Technically, in her human form, she was a volunteer. Actually, if shifters had counselors or peacemakers, or something, she would be one. Because a lot of wounded, lost, or otherwise no longer able to cope with reality shifters ended up at the zoo. Also, some families chose to live at the zoo, and there were often clan feuds, or worse.

Aimee listened to everyone and had stopped one or two blow-ups in the past, simply by being able to speak for or to the lost shifter.

She also knew for a certainty how many and which shifters there were at the zoo at any given time; information that evaded the zookeepers for the obvious reason that most didn't know there were even shifters, much less that their zoo might be infested with them.

Despite being only in her thirties – or looking that age – Aimee was one of the most motherly people Kyrie knew.

She looked at Kyrie, smiled at Orvan, and widened her eyes at Rod. "The lioness is fine, Kyrie. I think," she tilted her head. "I think she's related to you?"

Kyrie nodded. "My sister. Why did you come–?"

"To the museum? Angela said the … she called him the bad lion. She said the bad lion was here. I came to… not to confront him. Not if what she said was true. I wasn't about to leave my kids motherless. But I came to smell around and see if it was true, and I was going to call the diner, or Rafiel for help if it was true." She put a hand on Kyrie's arm and squeezed briefly. "You really shouldn't be running around. You could go into labor early."

Kyrie shook her head. "You saw–"

"The lion come tearing out like a bat out of hell. Yeah, I saw." She shook her head. "He looked… he felt like a whole lot of bad." She put an arm around Kyrie. "Calm down, hon. Your sister is okay."

Kyrie took big gulping breaths. Aimee had her arm around Kyrie and was pulling her towards one of the secondary entrances to the zoo, the ones that the volunteers had entrance cards for.

"At the zoo?" Kyrie asked with a squeak. "She's in danger. The lion will try to–"

"That's why she left the museum and came to the zoo. She felt him enter. I left her with the spider monkeys."

"The spider…" Kyrie lifted her eyebrows. It was a weird choice. It was a weird choice if you didn't know spider monkeys. After all, most people would think the cute, small, sweet spider monkeys would be no match for a lion shifter. They'd be wrong.

The zoo was inordinately proud of its spider monkey exhibit, which was healthy, thriving... and completely composed of a vast extended shifter family. Obviously, they didn't know that. But they should long since have got suspicious of the fact that they never seemed to be able to send any of the monkeys away or bring monkeys in. They tried, but monkeys disappeared, monkeys reappeared, and in the end, they ended with the spider monkeys that wished to be there.

In human form, they went under the name Singe, and Kyrie saw them around now and then. There was a young couple who came into the diner for the lamb special on Thursdays, and she was almost sure that one of the nurses at her obstetrician was a member of the tribe.

In the zoo, it was something different. And it was a little weird too. Instead of being with the other primates, the spider monkeys occupied a spacious enclosure in the aquarium. This meant a complex of artificial caves, taking up a good half of the aquarium building, and stretching, outside, to a netted wooded area the size of a suburban family's yard. The setup was so bizarre that Kyrie had often wondered if there was a Singe in the zoo planning commission.

It was of course incredibly convenient. After hours, the family could be in any shape it very well pleased, as there were no humans around in the aquarium, and the one fish shifter was not talkative. As for the crab shifters, they also tended to keep to themselves. So, in that enclosure, the spider monkeys could do as they pleased.

Had they been with the other apes, an area rife with shifters, they wouldn't have been able to be so comfortable or to do as they please.

Also, there would have been a lot more monkey on monkey or monkey on ape, or ape on monkey violence. Because the truth was that – except for Aimee, and their own vast and fertile tribe, and that not always – the spider monkeys didn't like or get along with anyone.

The spider monkey tribe was the Montagues and everyone else in the zoo was forced into the role of Capulet. Their tiny cute little hands were against everyone, and in self-defense, everyone else's was against them or at least said "whoa, stop that, you violent little maniacs," and then ran a good distance away, and if possible, armed themselves.

The elephants – real and shifter – cowered inside their little man-made cave and cried when they saw one of them approach. The Lions piled in a big bunch with the largest female up front roaring like crazy, to try to get the keepers to come to save them.

Once, the tigers had escaped their enclosure because two spider monkeys had got in. And the camels had once kicked the wall of their enclosure down, in an effort to escape a single spider monkey.

In their relentless insanity, the loud, fractious family had only one friend: Aimee. Even they seemed completely unable to resist the motherly secretary-bird shifter. Or perhaps they were afraid because in shifter form, she managed to out-psychotic them – though not usually without a purpose – but the result was the same. She gave rides to their babies and scolded the so-called adults into better behavior.

And apparently, she'd talked them into hiding a young, frightened lioness shifter.

"Is... will my sister be safe?" Kyrie asked. "I mean, from the spider monkeys."

"Oh, yes," Aimee said. "I explained what was happening, and they took her in, and said they'd protect her." She rubbed her nose. "They don't like lions much you know, much less jumped-up lion shifters who kidnap other lions."

"They're not liking lions much is what I was afraid of," Kyrie said. By her side, she felt more than saw Orvan nod.

Aimee laughed. "There is that but... let's say they're willing to like her, and even you, if it means they get to spite a bigger and badder lion."

"Come on. I'll take you to her." Aimee, led them in through a little gate, using her volunteer card, and around a bunch of machinery. One of the spider monkeys was on the lookout and very excited, jumping up and down on the fence.

"What?" Aimee said as if the half caws and clicks of the monkey were understandable. "The.... He got in? And– Oh good."

She turned to Kyrie, "He got in and smelled her all the way to the spider monkeys enclosure, but the boys, you know, the young gang chased him away. Jeff here says that Mike, Peter, and Titus are still pursuing, but he's cut and beaten and knows he's been in a fight. Come on honey."

Kyrie shook her head as they went. Honestly, the lion probably didn't know what hit him.

They walked through the zoo, with Kyrie being escorted by a mino-taur and an alligator and wondering if she had lost her marbles or if everyone else had. Only people did look at Rod, with something like fear, until Aimee said, "He's okay. He's fine with people. He started as a pet," And Rod would goofily clack his jaws in agreement.

And then a couple of kids stopped by Orvan and said, "Cool cos-tume" and as he patted them on the head, she realized of course that's what people thought. What were they going to think? That they were looking at a real live minotaur? People who weren't shifters and didn't know shifters would have that completely off their radar.

They made fast time, with Jeff leading the way, leaping from fence to tree, and tree to enclosure, stopping along the way to chitter insults at some animals.

Kyrie caught a brief glimpse, as he perched on the edge of the ele-phant enclosure and made a very rude gesture at the young elephant. The poor elephant looked startled, which probably meant he was a shifter. Or maybe not. Maybe even regular elephants understood that particular gesture and wondered what they'd done to deserve it.

Before the elephant recovered, or Kyrie had repressed her smile at the elephant's expression, Jeff was off chittering, and jumping, to scream abuse at the wild donkey. They followed.

The spider monkeys enclosure was entered via the aquarium, but they were at the end, facing the snakes. As far as Kyrie knew, the paltry snake collection at the Goldport zoo had no shifters. On the other hand, some of the snake habitats seemed permanently empty, so who knew?

A capybara got to live with the spider monkeys for reasons no one understood. No one but the shifter community of Goldport knew he'd recently married a daughter of the spider monkey tribe, in a crazy elope-ment that had stopped just short of Romeo and Juliet. The fractious tribe had finally accepted the marriage, provided the new son-in-law became an honorary spider monkey, living in their enclosure.

And someone, somewhere, got the zoo to agree to it.

Now, there were ten spider monkeys at the entrance to the aquarium, having left their enclosure. Weirdly, not even the most dedicated zookeep-ers or volunteers bothered them when they wandered around like this. They were, Kyrie thought, all riled up, and all prime fighting age. Which made sense. Two were watching down the zoo walkway and chattering animatedly.

On seeing Kyrie, they shifted instantly into human form.

Kyrie was envious She could never fully understand how other people could shift that quickly and painlessly. She and Tom always seemed to have pain in shifting and the weird cough. But the monkeys seemed to take a deep breath, and suddenly were two middle-aged people. Liz and Arthur standing where two lookout monkeys had been.

Kyrie surprised herself by remembering their names as she greeted them.

They smiled and shook her hand, and said, "Come, come."

There was no one else in the aquarium, partly because it was just on closing, of course. And partly, probably, because the monkeys had gone on a tear and chased everyone out.

They led her into the exhibit by a side door that Aimee opened with her volunteer card.

Within the complex of artificial caves, there were much deeper caves than anyone would expect, and then, one of them did something to some protuberances on the wall.

A part of the wall slid open, and Kyrie realized she had gasped when Liz turned back with a smile. "You know, one must have some creature comforts," she said, as she gestured Kyrie into the spacious, mirror-lined elevator. The elevator had two floors down, basement and sub-basement, Kyrie guessed.

Kyrie looked back at her own bewildered expression, and Arthur laughed out loud, delightedly. "You know, our cousin, Johnson Singe, is a contractor. It took a little maneuvering, but he got the contract for this. Fortunately, none of the zoo board has any idea what things actually cost, so he could hide all this under material costs going up, and labor being crazy."

Well, Kyrie thought, Johnson Singe must be very good at hiding things, because when the elevator stopped, they were in what looked like an upscale family room, with a vaulted ceiling, and sofas occupied by people and monkeys in confusion. Most of them were watching a nature program on the vast TV over the fireplace.

On the floor, a young girl and a young male monkey were playing with a toy train.

Liz and Arthur led Kyrie through. She could see hallways that led to doors, and Liz waved at them with "Dormitories. Mostly for the kids."

Then they took another elevator, this one not disguised behind a fake-rock wall.

And landed in what looked like a modern office, with various desks and computers. All were unoccupied except for one in the corner, at which sat an adult male spider monkey. He sat on the desk, itself, not the chair, typing very fast on the keyboard with his tiny little hands, and pausing periodically to take a sip out of his coffee cup, which said "World's Best Grandpa." In big, bold letters.

Liz waved at the hallway to the right, "This is the married quarters." She waved to the left, "And this is guest quarters. We put her in a room by herself, away from our young ones, because..."

Liz looked embarrassed, but Kyrie understood completely. One thing was a Capybara who could be adopted into the family, the other one a young lioness with ties to the leader of the lions. They were not about to encourage any interest, or even an acquaintance, with young and eligible monkeys.

As they turned towards the guest quarters, two naked women came out of the elevator, and each sat down at a desk. They seemed to be discussing accounting.

Kyrie wondered momentarily if people had become nudists after coming in contact with families of shifters and thinking this was an interesting way of living. As though they did it on purpose, and not just because after a while you got tired of ripping clothes when you shifted and having to get new ones. Even used, they were a significant part of Kyrie and Tom's monthly budget.

The guest hallway was much longer than Kyrie expected. There had to be at least thirty doors leading off from it. It was carpeted in industrial carpet and had anodyne abstract art on the walls. Lights came on with the movement as they walked down. It looked, and even smelled, like a hotel hallway.

At the very last room, Liz paused and knocked on the door.

There was a shuffling noise from inside, and then the door opened. Angela managed to look younger than the last time Kyrie had seen her. Someone had got her clothes. A sweat suit, dark red and loose, and obviously not her size but decent. And the same kind of cloth gym shoes that she and Tom had defaulted to wearing around the house and at work.

Angela was visibly cringing into herself, and her face looked like she'd been crying ugly.

When she saw Kyrie there was something like a flinch, and at the same time as a startle. For a moment, Kyrie thought that Angela was going to scream and run. Or something worse.

Kyrie had experience with younger kids who were scared and traumatized. Her upbringing had been great for that, if not for anything else. She stood very still, and looked at the girl with a reassuring smile, while speaking in an even, soft voice, "Hi, Angela. I'm your eldest sister, Kyrie. I don't know if Mom told you about me?"

"Only... only after Grandfather— After he died. She said you were our oldest sister, and that she and dad had to abandon you so that grandfather, so that he—"

"Wouldn't eat me?" Kyrie said, smiling to indicate that she understood. "Yeah. They did the right thing." She paused for a minute. "I've been looking for you. Mo—Your mom is very worried."

Angela stood, poised, an arm slightly behind, a look of doubt on her face. For a moment there, Kyrie thought she'd get the door slammed in her face. Liz had stepped away and was examining, with all appearance of great attention, one of the paintings on the wall.

Suddenly Angela's face crumpled, and she lunged at Kyrie. She hit with an impact that made the baby kick, and she threw her arms around Kyrie, crying, sobbing, and taking the deep breaths of someone almost drowning.

Kyrie didn't have much experience with physical contact. In the foster homes, it hadn't been safe. Not to let yourself be touched, and not to touch. So, she hesitated for just a moment. And then something cut loose, and she hugged her sister. "Shhh," she told the distraught kid. "Shhh, it's going to be all right. I'm here. I'll protect you. I'll take you to Mom and Dad. You're safe now."

Angela was... not mumbling. There were shrieks in there, but she was crying and saying something at high speed, something about "He made me— He—"

Kyrie patted her back, hugging her, saying "There, there," as she did when Tom thought the fryer would explode, though to be fair, Tom rarely cried over it. "You'll be okay. It's all fine now. You'll be fine."

Liz materialized by their side, offering Kyrie tissues from a box she'd seemingly retrieved from midair. Kyrie wiped at Angela's face.

When the crying slowed down some, she lifted the girl's face up, fingers under Angela's chin. "Let's go now, okay? I'll take you to your parents."

Angela nodded. She had the hiccups that often followed on hard crying.

Walking through the office space, Liz ducked away for a moment and returned with a water bottle, which she gave Angela, "Here, honey," Liz said, managing to sound maternal and not like a member of the little maniac tribe. "Sip this. It will help."

In the family room area, the spider monkeys, both in monkey form and human form stood around, solemnly, staring at them, like they were enacting some kind of play.

Kyrie put her arm around Angela's shoulders and led her to the elevator. They emerged into the upstairs – the official part – of the spider monkeys enclosure, and there were more monkeys standing and staring, this time all of them in monkey form.

And there was Aimee smiling at her and Angela like something very important had been accomplished. "Okay," she said. "I take it you want to go home."

Which of course was when Tom shrieked in Kyrie's mind, a deafening scream of anguish.

Rafiel was on an endless, arid plane, lighted by a red sun. In the distance, there were pillars that seemed to go up to the sky.

Bizarrely, a voice sounded, just like a carnival barker, "Step right up! This way to the Ragnarök. Come one come all. All contestants in one place!"

And then without warning, he was in the depths of a labyrinth. It was stone, and humid, and it looked like it had been standing there forever. Or sinking. Meaning it didn't seem to be above ground. It smelled of salt and humidity.

There was the sound of waves breaking, nearby. There was moss on the rocks.

The only light came from guttering torches in wall consoles.

Rafiel wondered where this was, and why he was here, when he saw, projected on the wall, a silhouette with broad shoulders and horns.

"Orvan?"

Orvan came around the corner. He was not wearing the moon disk between his horns, and he looked... Rafiel was not going to try to imagine how a thing again one and a half times the size of a man, with horns that could kill you with a careless motion, and – for heaven's sake – the face of a bull, could look sheepish. But that's what Orvan looked like. Sheepish. Rafiel half expected to see his right hoof tracing an embarrassed circle in the dirt underfoot, like a school kid, embarrassed, in his Sunday go-meet clothes. Not that he wore Sunday go-meet clothes, he wore a tunic and a kind of cloak. However, squinting, Rafiel could see a circlet of gold on his hair. Which, he guessed, made perfect sense, since Orvan was all things taken in account, a prince. A very ancient prince. Orvan of Knossos, son of King Minos.

"Orvan," Rafiel said again.

The bull-man looked up, his eyes half lidded. "Yes. But this is very strange, I tell you. I don't like this role they've cast me in. I can't be a psychopomp. I'm not even psycho."

"A what?" Rafiel said, but before the words had quite left his lips, a college class in mythology was coming to his mind, like the acid reflux from a bad plate of souvlaki. "What? A guide of the soul? Do you mean I'm dead?"

The bull man shook his head, sending crazy horned shadows playing off the walls. "No. Or then again yes."

"Argh," Rafiel said, feeling the irritation that this kind of answer always brought. Of course, normally this answer came when he was investigating someone's death. It would be something like: *Mr. Higgins, did you put the knife in Mr. Brown's back? And Higgins would answer: Officer, you see, no. But then again yes.* And the explanation would be, of course, that while he'd put the knife in Mr. Brown's back, he'd only done it because he'd seen the devil look out of Brown's eyes, or else that the voices in Higgins head had guided his hand. Or something equally ridiculous.

"What do you mean, precisely?" he asked Orvan, in the exact same tone he'd ask a murder suspect. He felt like he should have a notebook and be taking notes. At least it would make him feel better, and more grounded in his role as policeman. A living policeman, who would go back to being alive. Hopefully.

"Uh... so, when you're clan leader, there's... dimensions of you that aren't part of your physical being."

"I think everyone has that. It's called soul," Rafiel said.

Orvan tilted his head to the side, which looked funny with those massive horns. "Well...." He said. "Yes, I suppose so, but this is different. Clan leaders take particular responsibilities, when they ascend, and duties to allied clans and such. And we ... we have avatars of ourselves, who are in ... you can think about it as other dimensions, okay?" he shrugged. "I don't know how to explain, but when our ancestors incarnated, they kept access to ... planes of the spirit. This is one of them, though the manifestation is just something I supposedly feel comfortable in, and also a reflection of some old human imagery, you know?"

"Kind of," Rafiel said. And it was true, he kind of got it, but only because he'd grown up reading a lot of fantasy. He'd call this a "magical, not quite physical realm," in those terms.

"Well, then. That is what this is," he said. "And I've undertaken to be your mentor, so you don't lose the fight for leadership of the lion clan and die for real."

"The bovines are allied with the lion clan?" Rafiel asked.

"Oh. No. Oh, very no," Orvan said. "We're.... Look, no one was allied with the lion clan. Not under its old form. Enlil was not a reliable ally. But it is in the interest of the bovines and allied clans to have stable leadership in the lions, and you're pretty much it for that. So, while you're... slightly dead, I brought you here to get some training in lion fighting. Because, frankly, you suck at it. If you go in as you are, you're going to end up dead."

"I don't have time to be dead. Even if I come back right away. Three days without shifting? I don't have time for that, not with Highlander playing itself out in Goldport, and crazy lions rampaging around. I don't have time for this."

Orvan tilted his head slightly sideways and advanced his lower lip in a very human expression. "Now," he said. "You see, I wasn't talking about the temporary death. I was talking about something rather more... permanent."

Rafiel felt his eyes widen and could smell the salty moisture in the walls. What was the legend again. Sure, Orvan had said he didn't do that. That he didn't eat the youths and maidens sent to him as sacrifice in the labyrinth. He'd made some joke about not non-consensually. But was it true?

People were sent to the labyrinth to be sacrificed.

Then again, wasn't that in Minos, long, long ago? This was a different plane. A magical plane let's call it.

"I don't understand," he said, and despised the fact that his voice shook. "Am I a sacrifice?'

The Minotaur closed his eyes hard, as if he had an unbearable headache. A very human hand came up and covered his eyes. "No," he said. "Or then again yes." And immediately on the tail of that, as though he could read Rafiel's mind "Don't hit me."

"I don't have any intention of hitting you," Rafiel said which was not precisely true, because he very much wanted to slap some sense into the bull man. But he also knew that his hands would barely be felt, and he didn't want to get speared by those horns. "But I want answers, not riddles."

"That's... difficult in the labyrinth, but let's say, lion-boy, if you want to be the leader of the Krall, it is like dying. In a way. You will get different memories, and definitely a different life."

"The Krall?"

"The lion-house."

"But I don't want to," Rafiel said. "I can't be the leader of the lion clan. I don't want the job. I'm already a policeman."

The minotaur sighed, and it was like a gust of wind making the torch light quaver. "You have to be." His hand, large and very warm came to rest on Rafiel's shoulder. "The alternative is forever death."

Tom, or as much of Tom as remained in the wounded dragon, screamed in frustration at seeing all the Norse dragons in the parking lot of The George.

He retained just enough of his humanity, of his sense of self, that he knew he could neither drop his dad, nor take him into the middle of what was sure to follow.

With what felt like the last shred of his self-control, Tom tilted for the lone tree on the edge of The George parking lot, near the dumpster. It wasn't the healthiest of trees, what with all the transients who used it as a convenient urinal, and occasional leaks of oil from the dumpster, but it was far enough from the center of dragons with their necks extended and flapping wings, making hostile noises.

He extended the claw holding his father down towards the tree and prayed in incoherent panic that Edward was awake, and would hold on, and that Tom wasn't just dropping him towards his death.

But the other dragons were starting to flap their wings in the aggressive manner that reminded Tom of chickens in a mood, and Tom couldn't really wait, because if they came for him, his dad was dead anyway, right?

He flapped away from the tree, quickly, as all the dragons swiveled their heads towards him like falcons following a wounded pigeon with their eyes.

Somewhere in the back of his head, the human Tom who owned the diner was yelling they couldn't have a fight of dragons right here, in the parking lot, in view of everyone. It would ruin the business as much as the fryer exploding would. People would talk about this. They'd talk about the diner as the place where dragons might attack you at any time of day or night, and no one would come in for their excellent "always fresh, never frozen" fries.

Yet, the same human part at the back of the dragon's head felt weirdly resigned. After all, what could he do? The dragons were here, and he would have to meet them and fight them here.

As he circled just out of their reach, and the idiot Norse dragons tried to flame up at him, he heard police sirens. Which was all they needed.

Tom hoped that whoever was in that police car understood he shouldn't meddle in the affairs of dragons.

One of the Norse dragons flew up to Tom's level and flamed. Tom dodged by flying backward, which shouldn't even be possible, and coughed out his own flame, more in reflex than out of meaning to.

The other dragon screamed, and fell backwards on fire, on top of another Norse dragon, who exploded.

A lot of people screamed on getting showered with hot pieces of recently dead dragon.

Human-Tom-the diner owner was going insane in the dragon's mind, screaming that they might as well hang out a sign saying, "Here be dragons, no, for real." And then what? At best we'll get cryptozoologists. At worse, no one.

He could see the diner with a closed sign, and looking all dusty, with broken windows. How would Kyrie and Tom, and the baby survive?

From the crowd came a loud voice, explaining, in a very assured manner "No, really, this is the new type of special effects. It's just a movie."

People removing bits of flesh and bone from their hair looked unconvinced but interested.

And Tom screamed his frustration.

Then, from the tree, his father's voice sounded, "Damn it, Tom, use the force."

Kyrie took a deep breath. She had heard Tom's scream in her mind, a combination of frustration and perhaps fear. But what did Tom have to be afraid of? He commanded all the shifters, didn't he? The only thing she could think was that the fryer had exploded. But that made no sense, because if it had exploded, with Tom manning it, as he usually did, Tom would probably be dead. At least temporarily.

She looked at Aimee, who had paused, a look of concern on her face, and Kyrie didn't dare ask if she too had heard Tom scream in her mind. Maybe she had but seriously, encouraging the zoo shifter to think Tom was weak wouldn't end well. Next thing you knew, the little maniacal spider monkeys would be trying to take over the world, thinking they were the ultimate force of the universe. Which they might very well be, but they still wouldn't be allowed to run rampant as long as there was authority over them.

Kyrie hesitated. She looked at Aimee. If Tom was scared, if there was some great mess, should she take Angela into this? "Aimee, I don't suppose my sister can stay with the spider monkeys while–"

Before she had finished, Angela was holding tighter to her, and shaking her head just a little. And Aimee's eyes widened. "Well.... I could try, but

"No," a voice said, behind them, and Kyrie turned to see Liz, the spider monkey. She'd changed into a jogging suit and flip flops, and she looked very determined, shaking her head. "Look, it's not that we have anything against the young lady, but if she shifts and goes wild, I can't swear she won't get hurt. Some of our young men... and that's the other thing. We already have an unfortunate match in this tribe, and she's young and pretty enough. I'd rather not."

Kyrie almost laughed at the idea that the spider monkeys were telling her they thought Angela a bad match for the spider monkey tribe, like she was some kind of derelict, trying to raise her fortunes, but then she sobered. It seemed there was a special kind of racism that hit only the shifter tribes. And perhaps it made sense, since cross-shifters didn't breed true. Probably.

Most shifter tribes seemed to hate it when their young people married out. The dragons had sternly objected to her. And she suspected the lions would also have objected to Tom, if her grandfather hadn't seemed to have objected to everyone, lion or not. And again, perhaps it made sense, in a preservation of the shifter kind thing. Particularly if a certain amount of shifters were needed to keep the world safe. Not that she intended on giving up on Tom, in either case, but she understood the concerns.

"I see," she said. "Well. We'll have to risk going on then." She looked at Orvan, who looked like he was doing some kind of deep calculation in his head. "We'll have to go to the diner and see what's going on with Tom," she said, and smiled at Tom and Rod, who had shifted back and managed to grin in a way that made him even more of an alligator than when he was in outright alligator shape. "If you'll guard us"

Both of them nodded, Orvan looked worried, but Rod looked supremely confident.

Liz nodded and said, "Let us get you out of here the back way."

The back way involved going into a walkway that was closed off with construction barriers, and a sign q "zoo personnel only", then out a gate that Aimee opened with her volunteer pass.

"I'll escort you out," Aimee said. "And keep an eye out."

Kyrie heard chattering behind her and saw seven young male spider monkeys perched at various improbable places in the nearby tree.

As they took the walkway the gate led into, which turned out to be a sort of alley behind enclosures, the monkeys followed, chittering, and climbing to high points to look out.

At one point they went behind the lion enclosure, and Kyrie could hear the large felines scrambling away from the wall that divided them from the alley, as though afraid the monkeys would come through it.

And going past what she thought – from the brownish pond in the middle, and the general smell – was the rhino enclosure, a whisper came from behind a probably artificial rock formation, "Jesus. It's the spider monkeys."

Their little group continued towards the side entrance closest to Kyrie's car. The spider monkeys didn't stray from the path to torment the other animals, which must be the first time. Doubtless they intended to do that on the way back.

As they walked, they fell into a more or less natural grouping, with Orvan in front and Rod, in alligator form, keeping the rear guard, perpetual grin in place. Ahead and behind them, the spider monkeys went, chittering and babbling, and occasionally – Kyrie thought – making rude gestures.

They were almost at the entry, when Aimee leaned in and whispered, "I thought Old Joe was dead?"

"He is," Kyrie whispered back. "That's his son, Rod. Nimrod."

"Nimrod?" Aimee asked. And Kyrie would swear she blinked sideways, with inner eyelids, like cats and birds did. "Meaning *Great Hunter*?"

"I don't know. He seems to be– I mean, I think he's okay. For a definition of okay for a very old shifter."

"Oh," Aimee said. "Like him?" Subtle gesture of the head towards Orvan. "You keep an eye on those people. I'm not half as old as they are, but I know the times they lived through. Even the best of them can be... odd. And all of them will do what they have to do to stay alive and keep power. No matter how nice they seem."

The Force. Tom spun mid-air, burning at an oncoming dragon before the Norse dragon could get a good grip. The dragon screamed and waved his paw in midair, making it burn worse.

Tom flew out of the way and surveyed the scene. Too many of them. Too many of them and he was wounded.

The Force. The problem was, of course, that Tom's dad lived in a fantasy world. No, that wasn't true. The problem is that he lived in a fantasy world that had no relation whatsoever to the fantasy world that Tom lived in, and which happened to be true. Mostly. Sort of. In some ways.

Tom was not about to entertain a fantasy of Star Wars as well as Highlander.

And in the middle of the thought, while flying sideways and upside down to avoid becoming crispy fried dragon, the idea came to him that he did have a force of sorts.

He'd promised – himself more than anything – that he would never again call all shifters from all over the surroundings. That little excursion had been almost impossible to cover up and apparently had got him all sorts of notice from people he'd rather didn't notice him, from the Queen of the Ice to Kyrie's grandfather.

But–

But he could call the Chinese dragons, couldn't he?

9

T HROUGH HALF LIDDED EYES, to protect against the light of his enemies burning merrily, he realized he'd have to, because over the horizon there came more dragons. From their shapes, Norse dragons. His cousins on the other side, he supposed.

They did say family feuds were the worst. And he remembered some talk from the dragons about how the dragon feud had, in the past, almost destroyed the world. He burned two of the nearer dragons who had ganged up to attack him, but if he didn't call for help, he was going to die.

And he couldn't die. If the diner was going to be ruined, he'd have to find a job to keep Kyrie and the kid from starving. His son was, if he had anything to say about it, going to grow up in a traditional family and with a father who looked after him.

He blasted out a call to all of the Great Sky Dragon's people, and in return, in his mind, heard the half-triumphant, half-impatient Great Sky Bastard, "About time."

Kyrie really could have done without the talking. It was bad enough that Angela was in the passenger seat, the two guys crammed behind, and driving through Goldport rush hour, not having the slightest idea what was going on with Tom, except that the scream had – she was sure of it – come from the diner.

But she didn't need Angela to start talking. Perhaps it would be better for everyone if she hadn't talked. Because Kyrie couldn't shift. And it was going to be really hard to go punish Justin Harcourt, let alone kill her grandfather again, since the coward had had the foresight to die before she could kill him.

It had started .... Almost normal. Angela had sniffled, clutching the bunch of Kleenex Liz had given her, and whispering, "Thank you. I didn't know if you'd be mad at us, because... because Mom and Dad left you. They told us why, but–"

"I'm not mad at anyone," Kyrie said, driving down the tangle of little streets named after presidents. It looked like everyone was heading out from the museum or the zoo. The streets, which like Kyrie's street, were often parked on each side with the cars of the residents but with very little traffic, were bumper to bumper, while dodging the parked cars.

To add to that, there were kids crossing randomly, laughing, and chasing each other. By the look of them elementary school kids, probably on vacation from schools. For the first time in her life, Kyrie highly disapproved of school vacations.

"You shouldn't be," Angela said. "Because Granf would likely have eaten you. He kept threatening to eat us."

"Uh– I–"

"Like he ate Mom's sisters."

What? Kyrie almost bumped the car ahead of her and stopped just in time.

"He said he did, before Mom was born that he'd eaten others of his daughters before, and he said that if we didn't obey him exactly, he'd eat us."

Were those shadows of flying dragons going over the street? Really? What in holy hell was going on? Kyrie tried to reach her mind towards Tom, but all she got was a searing of panic and light. Was Tom on fire? It was, after all a hazard of being a dragon, but she didn't want him burned up. The great sky bastard had managed not to burn up all these centuries. Why shouldn't Tom manage it?

She felt both worried for him and vaguely mad at him. What the heck was he doing, catching fire?

And to make things better, the kid was playing soccer with her bladder, which felt like it was about to burst. She was going to pee herself, and then they'd never get the smell out of the car seat.

"So, he said I had to marry Harcourt. He said that's how we'd have a dynasty. And when I told him I was too young to marry, he said the monkey laws didn't matter and the monkey–"

What poured out made Kyrie's hair try to stand on end. She'd heard of worse abuses, of course, of young girls way below the age of consent being the "brides" of much older men. She was even sure that had been going on in her third foster family with some of the girls, only fortunately she'd been too young there to attract anyone's attention. But Angela was her sister. And this was not a foster situation. She was with family. And Harcourt was hundreds, perhaps thousands of years older than Angela. It was– Kyrie didn't need to feel nauseated, on top of needing to pee.

Angela cried, wiping frantically at her eyes with the balled-up tissue, and Kyrie reached over and patted her leg, because the last thing they needed was for Angela to shift and for them to have a car full of young lioness. In her mind, she imagined Angela's shift causing everyone else to shift, and the minotaur's horns punching through the roof of the car, while Rod chomped onto the back of her seat. The fact that Rod was smiling like a loon back there didn't help. Did he really have extra teeth? Had he heard anything Angela had said? Did he think it was funny? Or was that weird smile his horrified reaction.

She now understood what the spider monkeys had been upset about and why they were afraid of Angela's shifting. The girl was overwrought.

"Mom doesn't know," Angela said. "Because I was afraid if she did, she'd go toe to toe with Granf, and he'd kill her and eat her. Don't tell her."

"I won't, I won't, but honey, you're safe now," Kyrie said, as she dodged a parked car and just avoided crashing into the back of the car ahead. Turning onto Fairfax, she realized there were three police cars ahead of her, and she swallowed hard. What in living hell was going on here? Why were there police cars headed to the diner? Please let no one have been murdered again. Particularly not Tom, or any of their friends.

"I don't know if I am," Angela sniffled. Harcourt .... He commanded my mind. He–" She gave a little scream that sounded like a lion's growl translated to human voice. "He–"

"It's okay," Kyrie said. "We'll protect you from him."

"Mom says you married a dragon."

"Yes."

"And Mom says he's okay, but don't you know you'll have all the clan against you for marrying a stranger?"

Kyrie laughed. She laughed and she couldn't stop laughing, even though Angela looked at her with huge eyes, in complete confusion. Everything she'd gone through, everything she and Tom had survived, like she'd be afraid of a single clan, even if they were all lions.

"Oh, honey," she finally said to the startled teenager. "Let them come the lions with their claws. While I have Tom at my back, I'll be fine."

But she wondered if Tom was even alive still. She thought he was, because if he weren't she'd sense it, right? But holy heck, she couldn't turn her back on that man without him getting in some kind of trouble.

Then again, he probably said the same about her. And he was not going to be happy at all about her having escaped her minders. Even if she'd taken the minotaur and the alligator with her.

Rafiel looked at the Minotaur. "Okay, then," he said. "I'm a dead-alive lion, who is competing for clan leader, which is like dying, but it will be worse if I don't."

Orvan gave him a grin with dazzlingly white human teeth. "Good. You got it. It doesn't really matter what you are in the corporeal world. You are here now. And here and now you need to train. The real matter, the reason you were sent to the labyrinth and a memory-avatar of me–" Deep sigh. "Was sent to instruct you. You see, if you go up against Harcourt right now, on your own, you will die. Nothing else will happen. You will just die. And we can't have you die."

"We?"

"The..." Orvan waved his hand vaguely. "The totality of the clan leaders. It's not actually all of them, because there's always been rogues, through the millennia, but... a ... you could say a quorum. We call ourselves "We Who Live""

"Good name for your rock band," Rafiel said. "I suppose it's better than We Who Are Dead. Or We Who Are Dead Alive, which is the name of my rock band, should I ever have one"

Orvan gave him a weird, embarrassed smile. He felt woozy and not at all happy about this. Was he dreaming?

This didn't feel like a dream. He could smell the salt and moisture, ancient, penetrating the rocks. He – extending a hand – could feel the moss on the walls, a slimy wet feeling. This was like no dream he'd ever had. Worse, he felt bruised from his real-world fight. His body hurt from under his neck to his belly button. Where he'd been ripped.

Orvan shook his head at Rafiel touching the walls, and said, "Yeah, they haven't done maintenance on this for centuries, I think. Oh, not the one in Minos, of course, but the real one. You know, the eternal, primeval one."

And that was something that Rafiel wasn't going to touch with a six-foot horn. Whatever primeval and eternal meant in this place, he didn't even want to know. "Well," he said. "Then whatever am I supposed to do and how do we do it?"

Orvan gave him a dubious look. "You up to it, lion boy?" he asked. "You look green. And honestly, not very well. Like you're about to throw up."

Rafiel didn't ask green in which sense. Frankly, it could be either. And no, he didn't feel great, but what was he supposed to, sit here, in the dream labyrinth and try to will himself better? No. "I'm as good as I'm going to be," he said. "It's not like I'll get better, just sitting here waiting."

"If you say so," Orvan said, but before his words finished sounding, Rafiel was on the big red plain, and the carnival barker was yelling stuff, but not stuff he could understand. The language wasn't English, but something barked with a bunch of consonants, which made him think of some author or other referring to "sadly vowel-deprived languages."

He was in lion form, standing, roaring. Another lion – a huge, magnificent one – charged towards him.

And Rafiel knew he was going to die.

Tom had become a spectator in a giant battle of the dragons, and he didn't like it. He didn't like it, because this was sunset, and rush hour, and Fairfax was chockablock with commuters who kept stopping to watch. There were three police cars, which meant there were some part-timers there. Probably all of them standing around, watching, open mouthed.

Frankly, he was surprised that some policeman or other hadn't wadded into the parking lot, amid pieces of burning dragons, and burning men that the dragons turned into after dying, and said, casually, "What's going on here, then." He half expected it at any minute.

Meanwhile, a growing crowd gathered, commenting, screaming, or just staring in horror.

Tom-the-diner-owner was having kitten fits in the back of Tom's head. And Tom himself was quietly panicking.

For centuries their kind had lived in hiding, after – presumably – living more or less in the open as some kind of gods.

He and the shifters he knew had kept everything hidden for years. It hadn't been easy. They'd lived around the edges of normal society and hidden what they were. They had policed their own, dispensed their own justice, and more or less got along without the normal humans. But something like this could not be hidden. Not even in Goldport.

At least the one time he'd called the massed shifters had been in the middle of the night, and people could ignore it. But this was still in daylight, and people had gathered, despite the blowing snow and horrible cold. He was terrified that if they were exposed, the normal world would rise up against them and destroy them. And he'd somehow be to blame for all the destruction.

The Chinese dragons had formed an honor guard around Tom, defending him, so he couldn't even fight. They were circling and flaming, and the only thing holding shifters from becoming obvious and known by all – the only thing – was the policeman at the edge of the parking lot telling one and all about this new special effects technique that made holograms visible to everyone. This caused people near him to ooh and ah, and, as that version spread through the crowd, the screams stopped, in favor of the appreciative sounds at the amazing technology.

But sooner or later people were going to realize that there were no cameras in view.

Probably the only thing holding them from realizing that was that they were all so dazzled by the dragon fight, but this was going to break. Had to. Humans weren't stupid. If they had been, they wouldn't be the dominant species on the planet.

And Tom had to stop shifters from being discovered. He had to stop the whole thing from blowing wide open. He had to stop it.

It came to him, like a realization from someone else's mind suddenly implanted into his, that he *could* stop it. There was no reason he couldn't command the Norse dragons as well as the Chinese ones. Obviously, whatever the ancient shifter had done to his head to divide him from dragon-kind was now gone. So he should be able to command all of them. In fact, he'd been created solely for the purpose of commanding both sets of dragons. A designed breeding experiment, you could call him. Or Tom to his friends.

He almost sent the command out, telling everyone to stand down, when another thought intruded. Once he stopped the fight, the only thing keeping people from freaking out was going to go away. Instead of a bunch of dragons in spectacular arial battle, he was going to have a parking lot filled with naked people, some of them dead. And that was not going to be pretty in any sense of the word.

There would be screams and– The police would be right there. At best, at the very best, they'd all be arrested for indecent exposure, but it would also become obvious the fight was no special effects.

Tom realized he had shifted. He was naked and standing in the shadow by the back door into the diner. Fortunately, everyone was looking at the dragon fights. And there was a line of Chinese dragons in front of him.

Which gave him an idea.

Kyrie pulled up next to the diner. There was no way to go into the parking lot, because there was a full-fledged battle of the dragons going on. At rush hour. With half the population in the neighborhood looking on, open-mouthed.

What the actual hell had broken loose?

Then she spotted Tom, hiding in the shadows between the wall and the door. As she was staring, in relief and disbelief combined, he went into the back door of the diner.

She stayed very still, chewing her lip for a few moments. All right. So, she could go in. Maybe. Or she could stay out here, until some dragon came over and flamed her. Right.

"Okay, Angela," she said. "We're going to go inside, okay?"

The kid had just stopped crying. Her face was blotched with tear tracks, but she nodded. As best Kyrie could tell, she'd reached that point of crying and confessing, where she felt empty and too tired to be able to argue, and whatever Kyrie said, they were going to do.

She opened the door and walked around to open Angela's. And Angela saw the dragons. She shrieked and pointed, her eyes wide. "Dragons. So many," she told Kyrie.

Kyrie looked over. There were easily a hundred of them, and– both kinds. She blinked. Oh, hell, this was about to be a shit storm.

"Yeah. Dragons are showoffs." She pulled at Angela. "Let's get inside."

They dodged around the Chinese dragons who seemed to be defending the diner. The dragons didn't even look at them, and one stepped with a claw on Kyrie's foot, which made her swear under her breath. It didn't penetrate the shoe, but the beasty was heavy, even with just a claw.

Rod and Orvan were there ahead of her. They opened the back door of the diner for her and Angela. Kyrie hesitated. She had a feeling there was bad stuff about to happen, and she wanted to make sure Angela wasn't caught in it.

When she dove in the door, she pushed Angela into the storage room. "All right," she said. "You should call you– You should call Mom. Here's my phone." Then she rushed out, closing the door behind her. On second thought, she locked it with the key they kept on the wall. And she put the key on the wall hook again.

Anyone who didn't know who they were and what they did would think the entire arrangement silly, but it was there for those rare times they had to keep someone prisoner in the storage room. Which was not exactly it, right now, but it might keep Angela from wandering out under mind compulsion.

She figured that the phone would keep Angela busy a little while. And maybe the evil lion, Harcourt, wouldn't find her here. Oh, he'd probably come here sooner or later, but maybe not for a little while.

She wondered how Rafiel was doing, and if he could protect Angela.

Rafiel screamed, as a paw full of claws disemboweled him. He bled onto the sands of the eternal arena. He could smell his own blood while he writhed in pain. He could feel his body grow dim and distant.

And then he was standing again, his body whole, even if horribly painful, while he waited for a new adversary who was rushing towards him at speed.

He decided this time he wasn't going to let himself be flipped over.

He heard, distantly, as though spoken in a place far away, "I can't get him to wake up."

"I think," it seemed to Rafiel that it was Doctor Nik's voice. "I think that he's doing deep work, of the kind that you can't really– I think he's doing work at a level he can't be awakened. I don't think this is a normal coma. He's.... I think it's clan leader thing. Not that I'd know anything about it."

From the tone of voice, Rafiel could almost see Dr. Nikhil's eyes shifting and wondered how much he really knew about all of it. Was he the bear clan leader? And would he tell if he were?

Rafiel didn't like all the leaders stuff. He didn't like it one bit.

And then suddenly he was in the labyrinth again, and Orvan was yelling, "This is not working."

"This is not working," Tom said. He'd been standing in the shadows, just inside the men's room. And he'd just seen Kyrie lock her sister in the storage room. He came out, and she turned to him. "It really isn't working," he said. He sighed at Kyrie. "I'm on just about my last nerve. I'm going to.... Have to put on the Great Sky Dragon. And take it off again. And I'm not sure how strong I am. I don't know if I can keep it off once I put it on."

And then he realized Kyrie looked like she was somewhat past her last nerve. It was a look he'd only seen since she'd gotten pregnant. Exhaustion that went beyond exhaustion. As though something behind her eyes had just collapsed utterly, and she only remained awake by will power. "I'm sorry," he said. "I know what it must be like for you, but–"

"Forget what it will be like for me," she said. She looked, not exactly angry, but very irritated. "What the hell is going on out there? How could you let it get to a full-on dragon fight, in the open?" She grabbed onto his sleeve. "Tom, this is very bad. It could blow everyone's cover wide open."

"I know." Tom said. "And I realize how bad it is. They ambushed me. There wasn't much I could do. I think they took my father in order to setup this ambush without my catching on. At least I burned them." He shook his head. "Now there's only one way out of this mess. I'll have to assume control. I'll just have to do it. I think it's what the Great Sky Dragon is trying to do."

He said it as casually as he could, but she gave him a darkling look. "If that means what I think it means, I can't say it's my favorite solution. The Old Sky Horror is driving you, and I don't understand why. Maybe so he can kill you. I wish he'd stop his games. It's like he's looking to take offense."

Tom said what the Great Sky Dragon could do with his offense, then apologized, "I'm sorry, but– I don't know what else to do."

"I don't think there's anything else you can do." She sighed and took her hand to her forehead. "I think before this is done, all of us are going to do things we never wanted to do. But ..."

"No, listen, I just came inside to look for Conan. I need a distraction."

Kyrie's eyes widened, and he had a sense she felt guilty about something but didn't have time to ask her what. He charged ahead, "I really need a distraction. Big hairy, important, calls all eyes to itself distraction. If I don't have anything to direct people's eyes to, then when I stop the fight, the people who are now convinced this is special effects – God alone knows why – are going to see a lot of naked people, and a lot of dead people. And that will be even worse than seeing a big scaly dragon fight right there in the open."

"Conan..." Kyrie looked like a kid with her hand caught in the cookie jar. "I might have sent Conan away."

"What? Conan? In heaven's name, why?"

"I sent him to look for you. I sent Rya with him, to make sure he didn't get in trouble," she said, defensively. "Look, I was afraid– I needed to go get Angela."

He thought he was going to be angry, but then, in the end he just felt guilty. He'd asked people to look after Kyrie. No. He'd asked people to keep Kyrie safe, which in the current situation might as well be asking them to keep her prisoner. Yeah, he'd had good intentions, but what had possessed him to tell Conan to look after Kyrie? The poor man was a talented singer, but let's face it, barely competent to look after himself. They'd all felt very relieved when he'd started dating Rya, because at least he had someone to look after him.

Kyrie apparently interpreted his silence as complaint. "I took Rod and Orvan with me."

"It's not that," Tom said. "It's just that I need a distraction. It's not like you can shift. I don't know where Rafiel is, or even if he's alive. I ... sense something bad that way. I've tried to reach for his mind, and I get... dead signals. And anyway, I'm afraid that nothing but a dragon will work."

Kyrie sighed. "How about Orvan and Doc Roberts?"

"What?"

"Look, don't you think a fight between a minotaur and a giant rat in a lab coat will capture people's attention? I mean, we could also ask Aimee! A giant rat, a minotaur, and a secretary bird!"

Tom put his head down and tried not to cry. Dragon leaders and beast masters didn't cry.

"This is not working," Orvan said. He looked exhausted, as if he carried all his millennia of existence upon his shoulders. "Lion boy, do you not want to live?"

Rafiel didn't know if he wanted to live. He'd been gutted and bled on the floor of an existential – or eternal and primeval – arena for what felt like centuries. It was like a version of hell. Something he couldn't escape.

No matter how fast he moved, how much he tried, he would die, again, and again, and again, and the voice speaking in a strange language would crow triumphantly over his broken body.

And now he was back in the labyrinth, human and broken, huddled in a corner, shivering.

Supposedly the dying was metaphorical. Supposedly, he wasn't really getting killed. Not in any way real. He shivered. His teeth hit and clacked together, and it resounded inside his head with a noise like castanets. If it wasn't real, it shouldn't hurt. And it hurt so much, it was all he could do to stop himself from keening. "None of this is real."

The Minotaur looked worried. Something like a wind sighed through the ancient labyrinth, and the torch flames wavered. "It is, and it isn't lion boy. Your body might not be here, but your essence, your... how do you say, *psyche*.... Oh, yes, soul, is bleeding out again and again, and when it's all gone you won't survive. Not even shifters survive without... how say... anima. Spirit."

"I don't want to fight."

"That's not a choice, lion boy. You're a good boy, lion boy. Young. A nice kid, really. But you're not taking this as is. All this modern stuff of choosing your life... you don't understand that you don't have a choice. Your only choice is to fight and take the mantle of clan leader, or to die. The... the alignments... the shield on the Earth, the genetics, the things you can't control have chosen you. And now you only have that choice. Only that one."

"Then I die. I'm going to die anyway. Must I go through a million combats, and slowly bleed to death? Can't I just give up?"

The minotaur looked concerned. Suddenly, he squatted, huge body very close, and smelling weirdly both human and bovine. He brought his face so close, that Rafiel could see little bronze flecks on the dark irises of his eyes. "Listen, lion boy: in the labyrinth, in the arena, in the final fight you'll have in the ... body world, if you get back there, if you win your way there, the fight is not physical. That's what you're doing wrong."

"Those claws eviscerating me felt pretty physical," Rafiel protested.

Orvan sighed. "Yeah, but not. What you fight with in the labyrinth is everything you love: all the reasons you shouldn't die here. All the reasons you need to be in control of the lion clan. Because if Harcourt gets control, all of your family will die. Everyone. Relatives you don't even know you have will die, so that your line doesn't arise to challenge him again. Do you understand?"

He waved a hand in the air, about three inches from Rafiel's nose, not like he was trying to fan him, but more like he was an orator reaching and trying to bring back the right word, "You see, you have reasons to live. I don't know what they are. But inside each man there are... images, ideas that make him want to live, to achieve: mother, wife, love, country, a favorite place, the friends who support you. You are not an empty man. I have met such, and they're poor things, but you're not that. What are you, Rafiel? What are you made of? I know you love dragon-girlfriend, and you love your friends, and you love your parents, those are all important. But if we tore you apart, what would be written in every fiber of your being?"

Rafiel shook himself. He took a deep breath. Put like that, there was only one thing. "The law," he said. "Justice."

"Don't go," Tom said, grabbing at Kyrie's hand. "Hold. Is someone guarding this area?"

"Rod and Orvan are guarding the entrance from the diner. And the Chinese dragons are guarding the back entrance."

"Um... so, don't go and call the minotaur yet. I know Doctor Roberts would cooperate, and Orvan would give it his all, but I don't want–" He shook his head. "There is one thing I can do."

Kyrie blinked. "There is?"

"Yes, I can find Conan."

"Oh, no. You're not going to go out."

"Not on your life. I'm going to the bathroom. You go and deal with the diner."

Kyrie blinked. "The bathroom?"

Tom smiled. "It's private. Go see if you can get the tables around the corner booth cleared. I will need room for a conference with two idiots."

Kyrie lifted an eyebrow "The old bastard and the Ice Queen?"

"See," Tom tried to quiet his qualms about what he'd have to do, and kissed Kyrie on the nose. "This is why I love you, my wife. You know exactly what I'm thinking. And maybe tonight we can actually sleep."

Her eyebrow remained raised. "You only wish we could sleep. Something else will happen. I don't believe in this sleep thing anymore. I don't think it exists. It's a lie perpetrated on the young. We only think we slept in the past. It's all an illusion."

They both laughed, even though Tom knew it wasn't precisely funny.

Rafiel drew a deep breath, "The law. Equal justice under the law."

Orvan smiled. "There you go, lion boy. Equal justice under the law would be amazing in the shifter world. I don't think it has ever existed. It would be great if you could make it exist. And you can. Or at least you can try as lion leader. Go. Fight for that. Let your essence shine through your whole being and light the world."

And like that, Rafiel was in the Arena, but he was–

He was huge, and strong and confident, and he did indeed seem to shine with a light from within.

Orvan was right. There had never been law or justice, or even an attempt at justice in the shifter world. The lions, and for that matter the dragons, and ... all of them, had been led like feudal kingdoms, where everything hinged on the will of the king, and whether or not the king liked you.

That was why he must win leadership of the clan. He was the law. And the shifter world desperately needed the rule of law.

Rafiel allowed the need to win to grip him. When the other lion tried to flip him, Rafiel jumped aside. When the murderous claw came for his throat, Rafiel wasn't there.

His mind ran on a drum beat of "I have to survive. I have to survive so shifters can have justice."

With sudden assurance, he hit his foe sideways, and swiped a joyful front claw across the enemy lion's belly then jumped on the foe, while a back claw ripped the foe's innards.

The enemy bled onto the sands, and faded, like a cloud on a clear day, then scattered as a strong wind came out of nowhere.

And Rafiel stood in the arena and roared his defiance, smelling blood and heat and triumph.

The weird language all consonants declared him the winner.

From the unseen stands, came many animal noises of applause, and – he would swear – a plummy British voice shouting, "Well done. Oh, well done, that bastard."

Until he woke with a sore throat. Like he'd been trying to roar through an all too human throat.

Tom closed his eyes. He'd promised he'd never again send out a general call. Okay, mostly he'd promised it to himself.

But he could feel all the minds he could reach, right there, and surely, they would cause enough of a distraction.

The alternative–

Suddenly the threads in his mind became very clear, and he could feel the one that led to Conan's mind.

Conan, he said, sending his words through the link.

Apparently however this communication didn't go both ways because Conan sent back only confusion with a bit of fear.

Tom opened his eyes. He stared at himself in the mirror, bleary eyed. His blue eyes stared back at him, near-sightless with confusion and pain. Which was odd because he wasn't aware that he felt pain until he saw it in his face. And then he squinted at the mirror reflection. Right. Why was he naked? How could he have forgotten to get dressed? And what the heck was with his left arm? He remembered his wing had got flamed, but it must have caught his front paw and arm. It was a horror. As was his back where the wing came from. He could feel it. A good thing that he hadn't gone into the diner.

For one because people would notice he was mother-naked. For another, because someone would have called an ambulance.

How had Kyrie not reminded him to get dressed? Or how bad his burns were? His arm was black charbroil broken only by red welts and bubbling skin. He half turned in front the mirror, and indeed the burn extended to the skin of his back on the right side, from his shoulder to his waist. Seeing it made him more conscious of the pain, and he groaned under his breath, then closed his eyes again. The good thing about being a shifter is that he healed very fast. This would pass. He didn't need medical care. Medical care was for full humans.

Conan? he tried. He could feel Conan very close. Probably in the street outside, freaking out at the fight in the parking lot.

The voice that came back was little and resentful. *Tom why? Why in my mind? You said you wouldn't command me ever?*

I need you, Tom said. *I need your help. Sorry for talking to you like this, but I can't otherwise. I'm stuck in the bathroom at The George.*

There was a feeling of hesitation, and in his mind's eye Tom could see the look that Conan gave when he wasn't sure of something, with eyes half closed, and head inclined. Scared, but also defiant. Which is why Tom liked him. After all he'd been through, after the horror of being enslaved to the Great Sky Dragon, Conan remained defiant. He remained himself. He remained human. Even if his mental voice sounded scared as he asked, *Tom? If I don't obey, will you control me?*

Tom wanted to snap. He hurt. He was exhausted. He was shaking with the effort of staying up and mind-talking Conan, but suddenly he felt as though a bright red traffic light had gone on in his mind. This was, he sensed, a point of no return. This far, and no further. Step out this much but no more. This way lies... not dragons. He was okay with dragons. What lay this way was much worse than dragons. He didn't know what, but he felt it would be the end.

He was about to control people's minds, but only in the interest of not having them rip each other apart while ripping the already flimsy cover off the shifters in Goldport.

He was trying to save a lot of idiot dragons. He was trying to save shifter-kind from exposure. Surely.... It was just Conan. Conan had been mind controlled before. It's not like it would break him.

The red light didn't care. It glared at him from his mind. No. This far and no farther, it said.

And Tom felt at the thought, gingerly, like someone probing a bruise. This far and no farther. Because Conan was a friend. His controlling Conan would be different from whatever it was that the Great Sky Dragon had done.

That had been done under the old dispensation, in which Conan's parents had handed their dragon shifter son over to the clan, and had the clan own him. Conan hadn't liked it. He was born in America and didn't believe he should be owned. But he had known it was part of the people he was born to, of what he was born to be.

This would be different. Before he'd become Tom's friend, loyal sidekick, diner helper and a budding Country Western singer, Conan had been all but the slave of the Great Sky Dragon, mind controlled and used mercilessly. But Tom had freed him They were friends. They were equals.

If Tom violated that, it might not break Conan, but it would break their friendship. And Tom would not do that. No. That was a step too far.

He blinked in confusion at Conan's question, but he knew what the answer had to be. Tom would not break their friendship. If Conan refused, Tom would have to make other arrangements. And if that happened, it would be very difficult to make things work. But–

But ... Tom would have to find another way. He could not control Conan, because if he did, he would lose a friend. Worse, he'd become like the Great Sky Dragon.

It wasn't just that he didn't want the Great Sky Dragon's job. His greatest fear was that the job would make him into the Great Sky Bastard. Because form followed function.

No. I will not make you. I'm only talking to you this way because I'm naked and in the bathroom of the diner, and I'm about to do something pretty distasteful to the rest of dragon-kind. But not to you, Conan. You're my friend. You're my battle brother.

He felt a relaxation of Conan's mind, and perhaps a hint of amusement behind it. *All right. What do you need?* Conan asked.

And Tom told him. But give me five minutes. I need to find pants.

For some reason this made Conan give a mental whoop of laughter, even as Tom opened the door of the bathroom a crack and looked out.

To his dismay, there was a clump of people in the hallway. Strangers. In retrospect he realized someone had pounded on the door not so long ago.

But to his sudden, overwhelming relief, Kyrie was standing there, extending him sweatpants and a T-shirt from their plentiful stash of thrift store buys, laundered and kept in the diner for emergencies. The fact she didn't bother with underwear told Tom she didn't expect it to stay on him very long. And she was probably right. He'd be shocked if he didn't have to shift again tonight.

Grateful, but shocked.

"Husband," Kyrie said.

And he smiled, as he took the clothes through the sliver of open door. "Her worth is beyond rubies" he said and closed the door wondering what the customers would think was going on, precisely.

He realized putting the – long sleeved, bless Kyrie – T-shirt on was going to hurt like a mother and that it would stick to the seeping burns all over his back and arm, but it had to be done. Or at least it should, or his injuries would call as much attention to themselves as nudity would have.

"Oh, hell," Rafiel said, looking up at a circle of faces staring down at him.

He was lying in his tiny bedroom, and an impossible number of people were crammed in there, all staring at him.

"It's all to do again, isn't it?" His voice sounded stronger and steadier than he thought it could. He was a little embarrassed at realizing he was completely naked, the only concession to modesty a sheet around his middle, but the sheet had slipped down somewhat and was bundled over his upper thighs.

Of course, the only people present– Had all seen him naked, from his parents, to Bea, to Dr. Nik and Dr. Nik's very amused wife, Alex, who grinned at him and said, "I don't think all of it, no."

He couldn't even say Bea had never seen him naked, because she had, in the aftermath of the mind-rape. And besides, she was a shifter, and she knew what nudity meant and didn't mean, and mostly it didn't mean very much.

The expanse of his skin revealed in the bright LED light from the ceiling, looked amazingly whole, considering the last memory he had of his own body involved viscera spilling out of the body cavity, and a pain worse than almost anything he'd ever felt.

He remembered when that had happened to Tom and that Tom had died, and it had taken him three days to come back from that.

But the skin of his belly showed only a faint tracery, as if very new scars. And the pain wasn't there. Though he was hungry, too, he wasn't the kind of hungry he had experienced after other injuries, when he had felt like he could eat people whole.

Dr. Nik smirked, "Pretty good, isn't it?"

"Yes?" Rafiel said. "I assume you did something?"

"Alex and I have been working on a solution of various vitamins and... It speeds up the shifter regen. And we managed it, so you didn't die. You should be able to shift. And you realize that's important, right? I mean, you remember everything, right?"

Rafiel nodded. "I know," he said. "I have to ... fight for the leadership of the clan. I am the only one who can bring justice and law into shifter world, or at least my part of the shifter world."

"That's not the only reason," Nik said. "I've been having these... In meditation, sometimes, I have seen things. I think something bad is headed our way."

"Yes, I think so. I think that's why Orvan instructed me in the Labyrinth."

This was Alex's turn to smile. "Or perhaps just the metaphysical form of Orvan. He has a tendency to do that. I never managed to figure out whether he knows what he's doing or not."

"I haven't either," Rafiel said. "He said something about an avatar. I take it he instructed you? Or other people too?"

The doctor and his wife nodded.

"I'm hoping what he said was true, and that I can now defeat Harcourt, Rafiel said. "I think he... I think he will be coming for me." He dragged himself up to sitting, shocked it didn't hurt. And he didn't feel weak. "That solution you guys came up with must be miraculous," he said. "Now I need to get dressed. And I think I should go to the diner."

"Kyrie's family already went there," his father rumbled, from near his head. "Are you sure you're well enough? Should we go with you?"

"No, I'll be all right."

"Not alone, you won't," Bea said.

And he knew better than to argue.

****

Kyrie saw her family come in, her parents' faces looking as though sharpened by hours of worry and wondered exactly what they had been going through. "Mom? Dad?" she asked, walking towards them, and wondering how quickly those words had come to seem natural. Her mom smiled, but still looked like... like she was very tired.

"The New Lion is going to be all right, honey," her mom said. "But I'm afraid his challenger for the Krall is going to come here to challenge him. And I think he'll come here too. The New lion. Rafiel."

"Likely," Kyrie said. "Do you want to come to Angela? I'll bring you some food. I think you've done a lot of work today."

Her dad smiled. "I knew there were advantages to having a daughter who owned a diner."

Kyrie led them to the hallway and knocked at the door to the storage area. When no one answered, she unlocked and opened it, half-scared.

Angela was asleep on the floor by the food shelves.

As she came out, leaving her parents with Angela, Rod hurried from the back door. "Hey," he said, to Kyrie, "We're going to stay outside, ready to help. I think your young man is about to do something unadvisable."

Kyrie wondered if Tom had done anything else since this started.
Then Tom rushed past her, pecking her lips as he went.

Tom stood just outside the back door to the diner, which as metaphysical battlegrounds went was pretty strange. But it was his, and it was where he'd stand. He held his hands clenched tight in fists, and reached out, stretching his mind to encompass all the dragons in the vicinity. All of them.

It was difficult. Like lifting something very heavy and holding it suspended above his head. Like... like lifting up everything he could see.

Dragon's minds were heavy, ancient. It was like trying to lift loose sand, like trying to – by force of will – to make rocks float.

He seemed to have to reach out inch by inch, and the whole thing was at risk of slipping and crumbling and being lost forever any second now.

His shoulder hurt like the blazes, and he felt sweat spring out all over his body. It was much, much harder than calling to all shifter animals. Because this wasn't just an order. This was imposing his will over them. Being the master of them all.

Shaking, his throat dry, his body feeling feverish, he sent out the command, "Stop immediately. Cease this foolishness. Go to the parking lot of the Three Luck Dragon and wait there. Find a way to carry with you the wounded and the dead."

There was a feeling of backtalk, a feeling of backs arching, of people about to complain. But then ...

He pushed his will at them, hard, and he saw them give in, bit by bit.

There was a scream from the crowd. From the other side of the street, where, up from the drugstore, there was a vast patch of grass in the median, had dried in the Colorado Summer, and the scant blowing snow of this dry winter hadn't fixed it came a flaming and smoke. When the smell of smoke spread, people screamed in earnest.

And Tom felt, wordless, amusement and support from Conan's mind.

With all the strength he had he shoved at the collective minds of dragons. The effort was such that it brought him to his knees, pushing, pushing,

pushing. His knees hit the asphalt, and it seemed like the cold wind concentrated and blew around him, excoriating him with icy pinpricks.

But little by little, with grunting effort and pain – metaphorically – the boulders flew, high and up and rising, and in a flurry of screams and wings– As the dragons obeyed his command, diving to pick up the fallen, and then away.

Tom opened his eyes. The parking lot was almost empty, the last dragons hurrying away, some of them seeming to carry with them bundles of dead or burnt-to-a-crisp comrades. There were still suspicious bundles of ash on the parking lot, but Tom wasn't going to ask.

He closed his eyes and reached out, for one particular mind, You, he said. You, oh, venerable ancestor, dress and come back here. I wish to have words.

He got back the sense of a raised eyebrow, but no complaint as such. More a mix of amusement and resignation.

And then, with what seemed like the last of his will power, he sent the same message over his mind, with all his power, to a mind equally old and devious, but much more dangerous, much colder, much less used to the current world, *And you, oh, royal ancestress, Queen of the North, I call you here, to my summons.*

He got back a sensation from the Great Sky Bastard that was the equivalent of a joke salute and *Aye, aye.* From the Queen of the North, nothing but frosty offense, and indignant acquiescence. She knew she couldn't fight him, but oh, she wished to.

And Tom realized Kyrie was there, kneeling by him, helping hold him up. Without her arms supporting him, he'd have fallen on his face, such his exhaustion.

"I did it," he said. His voice was raspy and just above a whisper.

"Yes, you did, if by that you mean you stopped this nonsense. But now you need help with that shoulder. Come inside Tom."

Tom hesitated. As she helped him rise, he felt his knees creak and hurt. The asphalt had been cold. And hard as he fell onto it. As he stood up, he realized his feet were bare. How had they forgotten shoes? "I– I might have also summoned the two ancestral dragons."

Kyrie looked somewhere between amused and exasperated. "I figured. Which is why you wanted the corner booth. That's fine. You come inside, we'll see to your shoulder, and then I'll come back to meet them and bring them to you."

"I need shoes."

"We'll find you shoes."

Tom walked into the diner, his T-shirt clinging to his wounded arm and shoulder, his knees hurting from meeting the parking lot with force, feeling exhausted and starving, his mind just on the verge of red-starvation and need.

And like a miracle, there was Jason and Orvan; Jason put a plate of souvlaki piled high with enough to feed three large starving families in front of him, and Orvan slid in with the first aid kit.

"Easy. Use the fork and knife. There are customers watching. Besides, I understand you're about to hold a royal audience of sorts. Kings use silverware," Jason said, shoving a fork and knife, handles first, at Tom.

Tom grabbed them ate while Orvan? Rod? Someone else? Cut away his T-shirt, applied burn cream and bandages.

There were other people. Anthony and Laura? Standing in front of him, so that the customers couldn't see what was going on.

A clean T-shirt was brought back and dropped over his head and pulled down. This one was loose, and anyway, between the cream and the bandages, it didn't hurt too badly. He felt... almost normal.

When the temperature dropped several degrees, and a layer of frost formed on his glass of iced tea, he guessed the Queen of the North had arrived.

10

THE QUEEN OF THE Dragons did not arrive the way that Kyrie expected. She'd expected a dragon of some description, vast wings, and much power.

Instead... Instead, the weirdest thing formed, midair, and Kyrie was grateful that the crowds had dispersed, first going to see the grass fire that Conan had started, and then who knew where. She was fairly sure that Conan had evaded them, led them a merry chase away from the diner, and was probably now somewhere, perhaps catching a ride with Rya, back to the diner. She wondered if it was Tom or Conan who'd had the idea of setting fire. A fire set in Colorado, even in winter, concentrated everyone's attention. It was danger, clear and present.

She was fairly sure Conan would come back to the diner, because he would want to make sure that Tom was all right.

And she, personally, owed him an apology for getting rid of him so shamelessly. Maybe. At least she'd got Angela back and safe. She thought of what the girl had told her in the parking lot and shuddered.

Now, while Kyrie stood alone, in the darkening parking lot, something like a cloud descended from the sky, a protrusion, slightly curved, and frosting over very rapidly. It was like a form of steam, that supercooled, forming a beautiful, arched bridge from the sky to the parking lot of the diner.

"The bridge of frost," Kyrie said, and smiled to herself thinking in how many places that phrase showed, appreciative and amused at the idea. Apparently, it was a real thing. She wondered if Tom would ever be able to produce the nifty effect.

She was even more appreciative and amused as the dainty barbie-like queen, wrapped in white frosty fabric and fur came dancing over the bridge.

Almost at the parking lot, the Queen of the Compass Point stopped and gave a sort of a sideways lurch as she saw Kyrie. "The pisser," she said.

For some reason this made Kyrie laugh. Probably because she was more tired than she'd ever been and had reached the point where everything made her laugh. "It's all right, your majesty. I don't need to piss on your shoes. I have a bathroom nearby." She stepped away and opened the door. "Down the hallway. He's waiting for you in the corner booth."

The queen looked dubious and gave Kyrie a long, long berth as she circled around her and into the hallway.

Right after her, from the parking lot, walking casually, came the Great Sky Dragon, in his mundane persona as a middle-aged restauranteur, in good jeans, and a nice shirt with a leather jacket zipped against the weather. He shook his head at Kyrie as he went by, "Thank you, granddaughter," he said. He turned and breathed on the bridge, which dissipated as though it had always been nothing but vapor. "That woman is all show, isn't she?"

And Kyrie smiled thinking The Great Sky Bastard might be the sanest of the two. And she wished Tom luck with them.

As Kyrie turned to go in, a car drove erratically into the parking lot.

Rafiel leaned back while Bea drove. There was something tight about her face, and he was afraid to talk to her, because he was afraid, she was going to give him his engagement ring back. And the devil of it was, he hadn't even given her a ring yet. They were supposed to go shop for it together... yesterday?

Rafiel had planned a whole day, of taking her around the local jewelry shops, and taking her to lunch, and– Oh, well. He looked at her, out of the corner of his eye. He felt like she was going to give him back the ring he hadn't even given her yet.

"Look," he said, in a soft voice. "I know you didn't sign up to end up married to the lion leader, and I know you might not want to face something like that. There is nothing I can do, Bea. If there were I would turn it all back for you. But it's starting to look like the way to give this up is to die. I don't really have a choice."

She nodded, and he realized that there were tears glistening down her face.

"I'm so sorry, honey," he said. "I never meant to do that to you."

For some reason, it made Bea drive faster and more erratically. She was driving, he thought, as a dragon would fly, sometimes seeming to forget that other cars were actual obstacles in her way, as though she could wish them away or go over them.

He cleared his throat, and hoped this wouldn't cause them to crash, but it had to be said. "I will completely understand if you want to break—"

Bea was pulling into the parking lot of the diner. Rafiel realized he must have lost some time there in the middle, perhaps because his mind had been frozen in terror of Bea's driving. "I— understand," he said. "I don't like it, but I wouldn't marry me if I could avoid—"

She parked the car and pushed the parking break in forcefully with her left foot then turned around.

Rafiel, in shock, was grabbed, with one of her hands on either side of his face, as she pulled him down, so she could plant her lips on his.

They'd kissed before, of course. They had been dating for a while. And Bea was not exactly a shrinking violet, when it came to showing her love for him. But this kiss was not like any of their previous kisses.

She kissed him with all her attention, with a need, a passion he'd never felt in her before. Her palms, on either side of his face felt like they burned him. Her mouth felt like fire against his lips, like she'd shifted to her dragon form without noticing. And he could drown in her green eyes.

After a while, a small eternity, she pulled away and said, "Rafiel Thrall, listen to me: If you ever try to break up with me, I'll find you and burn all four of your legs off, and your tail too for good measure. And you know what that will feel like when you're human again. And never, ever again come that close to dying around me. I thought I'd die if you did."

Confused, blinking, feeling like the slow kid in the class, he said, "But I have to fight—"

"You will. And you will win. And you will suffer no significant injury. That's an order, you lion-creature. You will not get yourself hurt. Because I will not live without you."

Rafiel found himself smiling stupidly, "Aye, aye, my dragon mistress. It shall be as you say."

"Good, and then I want to get married as soon as possible. Next month at the latest. I'll call my parents and tell them. I'll transfer to CUG."

A lion shifter about to face the battle of his lifetime shouldn't feel this bubbly-happy inside, should he?

Rafiel kissed her again, then nodded. "I will fight for our future, my lady."

Before Kyrie could close the door, she saw a huge lion come into the parking lot, and she saw Rafiel tumble out of the car, already shifting.

Inside the car, she could see Bea, turning to watch.

It was all Kyrie could do not to run into the diner. Instead, she walked dignifiedly to where Orvan and Rod stood guard by Tom's booth.

Tom... Tom was Tom, but his face had that long, slithery look he got sometimes when the dragon shifting was very close, more or less on top of him and barely being held at bay by his will power.

She saw the Queen of the Compass and the Great Sky Dragon sitting like errant children, watching him. She had no clue what he was using to subdue them, but she was sure there was something.

Not wanting to disturb him, she sidled up to Orvan and Rod, "I think the fight for the lion clan is about to happen right now in the parking lot."

Tom heard her, somehow, and turned his head, his movement unnatural and dragon-like. "Not in the parking lot," he moaned.

"It's all right," Kyrie said. "It's dark enough. It's snowing. There's no one around. And stranger things have happened in that parking lot."

Tom stared at her a long moment then sighed and mumbled what might be "Whatever."

His eyes were very intense, like the dragon's. But then he nodded and turned back to the Great Sky Bastard and the bitch queen, "And what I tell you, oh, most revered ancestors," he said in a tone like spitting. "Is that the two of you must not only make peace but you must marry, permanently, and make many, many, many babies."

She said something about how she couldn't trust the GSD and he said she was– But even from here, Kyrie could feel Tom's dragon mind holding the two of them, making them bend to his will, like spoons in a strong-man's hands.

After a while, as though the tension snapped, she saw their heads bow.

The Great Sky Dragon stood up first and extended his hand to the frosty queen. "Very well," he said. "I've done worse. Should I locate the Pearl of Heaven and send it to you? It belongs with the Great Sky Dragon."

"No," Tom said, his face suddenly very serious. "I want no part of your job."

The GSD laughed, suddenly, a great evil movie villain laugh that made heads turn to him in the diner. "I think you already have it, grandson," he said. "I will obey no one but the Great Sky Dragon. Remember that."

And then he and the Queen of the North were gone, suddenly, like mist evaporating. And Kyrie had no clue how they had done that.

Tom put his head on the table and shook silently. Kyrie was worried that he was so exhausted he was crying – she didn't remember having seen Tom actually cry like that – and then realized that was laughing. Little guffaws and giggles escaped him.

She came, quietly, and slid into the booth across from him.

He looked up and smiled at her, extending a hand across the booth to meet hers halfway. "Oh, Kyrie, it was the most absurd role I ever played. I ordered the two of them to go off and procreate."

Kyrie grinned back. "I heard. I wonder how Loki will take it."

By the corner of her eye, she saw Aimee Morgan and a small man in a long overcoat come in. She wondered what was going on. Aimee rarely came to the diner.

Rafiel would never be able to describe it. There was the parking lot, and slices of light across it. And a starting snowstorm.

And his enemy, a blond man who turned into a lion, a huge, dark golden lion. Jason Harcourt, he guessed.

The same one that had almost killed Rafiel.

He sprang at Rafiel, with immense confidence, his face frozen in the lion equivalent of a wide grin.

Rafiel braced, heart hammering, the great lion heart deafening his confused thoughts.

He felt the need for blood and biting in his mind; his human thought insisted he must win and bring the shifters the equivalent of a code of Hammurabi, a first law.

His human instincts gibbered with terror, as the lion got nearer. He sensed the dark endlessness of the creature, how long it had been alive, and the horrendous crimes it had committed.

But Rafiel's lion was sure. The lion had found itself. The lion clutched with all his being to his purpose, to his family, to Bea. He would fight for his loves. For his pride. And for law and justice. It was what he was. What he was made for.

Closer, closer the lion came, in movements like moonlight through oiled midnight.

And then ....

And then Rafiel was pinned down, and the lion's mind was speaking to his mind, You're an insignificant insect. Less than a toddler. My henchmen almost took you out. And you dare defy me?

Rafiel felt it. He felt the insignificance of himself, like a blow. He felt how small he was, how he didn't matter, even as the lion prepared to eviscerate him.

No. His mind formed the word. Just that. No. I am not insignificant. I am Rafiel, and I'm fighting for justice.

His back paws lifted, he sprang up and out of the other lion's grip. He stood and roared.

Insect, the other lion's mind said. But it had no sting.

When the enemy extended a paw, Rafiel wasn't there. He had bounced, evaded. He felt a scratch on his forepaw, but it was nothing.

The enemy pounced again, and again Rafiel evaded.

One time, he heard Bea scream, and realized he'd gotten bitten on the flank, but it was nothing. Drops of blood on the parking lot asphalt.

Then the enemy lion leapt.

And Rafiel was there, counter-leaping, upending his foe, teeth in the enemy's throat, paws eviscerating him.

He retained enough human intelligence to remember that he had to sever the head. He had to. And he did.

Blood poured out dark on parking lot, while his lion paw batted the head – rapidly turning into a human head – away so it couldn't rejoin the body, so it couldn't be fixed.

He stood on shaking legs, and from nearby he heard, "Holy shit." In a familiar voice.

He turned, his mouth bloodied, shifting to human without meaning to, to face Cas' pale face.

"Boss," Cas said, in a low tone. "Was it you all the time? Were you the one who killed the guy?"

And Bea came running out of the car, shoving Cas away, extending a pair of sweats to Rafiel, handing him a box of wipes, and a bottle of water.

He rinsed his mouth twice and wiped his face vigorously before he told Cas, "Don't be stupid."

Tom didn't want to be worried, but he kind of was, and it didn't ease his worries when Bea, Cas and Nick came into the diner without Rafiel. His look must have spoken his worry, because Bea smiled, as she slid into the booth next to Kyrie, pushing Kyrie towards the back. Cas slid next to Tom and Nick next to Cas, till Kyrie and Tom were sitting together, and Kyrie leaned on Tom. He felt her warmth and comfort, as well as all the exhaustion of the last... almost twenty-four hours, wasn't it?

"Don't worry," Bea said. "Orvan got a room at the Leather and Lace, and they're smuggling Rafiel in to clean up. He was..."

"Covered in blood," Cas said, and made a face. "Some of it even his, but you should see the other guy. He looked very much like other corpse. I wonder if–"

"Could have been this other lion killed him for supremacy," Kyrie said.

"I suppose," Cas said. "But though there's some lion-protein on the neck, the lab says it was a saber and Rafiel thinks the lion protein was because the lion was so ancient, and some of him remained shifted. At molecular level. This means we still don't know who killed the old lion leader. There is this professor, this art professor...He told us about this tailor... but the man looks harmless and... I'm not sure."

"I am," Aimee Morgan said. Kyrie looked up, and she was standing by the booth, with the small, very embarrassed man. She gestured, "This is Doctor Travis Lee Clark, a professor of art history at Colorado University Goldport. He really had nothing to do with the death. You guys just think that because he collects skulls."

Kyrie blinked at that, but Aimee turned her eyes to Kyrie. "You guys have got to believe me. He's inoffensive. He's just an artist, and he's trying to make a reproduction of a tzompantli as an educational aid."

The professor mumbled something, and Aimee patted him on the shoulder. "But I'm sure it's a wonderful educational aid, when you tell them that if they don't turn in the work on time, you'll put them on the tzompantli. I mean, they might not think so, but I'm sure they do their best work."

He smiled, and rubbed his hands together, in a very.... Kyrie blinked. She was sure the man was an otter. His smile was embarrassed, as he bowed slightly at Kyrie, and now he was patting the front of his chest, in a very otter-like gesture, "I really have only used old skulls found in rivers," he said. "People dead long ago, with no relatives. At least in the tzompantli their skulls are seen, and in a way honored. I'm not doing anything wrong."

Cas cleared his throat, "I'm sure you're violating about a million statutes about ancient human remains and all that, but I don't even care. What were you doing with the luggage and the overcoat that night? And don't give me stuff about minks. I know you didn't tell me the whole story. Do it now. What do you know? Do you know who killed the Lion Leader?"

Travis sighed. His hand went up to pull back his hair which was flopping into his eye. "Look," he said. "I go into the mountains. I dive in the rivers. I have this overcoat, the shoes, and leg warmers." He opened the coat, very briefly flashing them, and causing absolutely no shock in that table full of shifters. "I take the luggage. If I find a skull, I bring it back in it. This outfit is the minimal not to shock anyone, but ... you know."

"You weren't in the mountains," Nick said. "You were right here."

Travis put his head sideways. His hands patted each other, and rubbed like an otter's, probably in a nervous gesture. "There's the creek that goes through a mile away. It goes through Butterpark, the park that was..."

"Yes, yes, made into a park, without removing the early graves that were there."

Travis nodded. "When there's been a heavy rain or snow melt, the river often ends up carrying bones and skulls down. It's an easy thing to find some. I had three skulls in that bag, but I swear none of them were from a lion shifter. Or at least not one who died recently," he added, scrupulously.

"I see," Rafiel said, which was the first time they realized he was standing there. "And you wouldn't happen to know who might have killed him, then? Since no one else was seen with anything that could carry a saber."

"As to that, boss," Nick said. "The old man had a point, you know. Careful police work–"

Rafiel froze Nick with a look. He could feel the power of the lion, and it was interesting. He didn't know what being the Great Sky Dragon felt like to Tom, but being boss lion felt like a ton of badass crammed into his standard size body. Even the wolves reacted to it, though he was sure they were in another clan or clade, or clsomething of some kind.

"What did Mr. Milagros get right?" he asked, in a deceptively polite voice.

"There was a saber in the dumpster."

"The diner dumpster?" Rafiel asked, raising an eyebrow.

"No," Cas said. "The one near the back of the Leather and Lace B & B."

"The derelict," Rafiel said. "The homeless guy who was crouching there!"

"Right," Travis said. "The badger. I thought I'd seen him. But he's one of mine, you know? I should have given him up, but the lion was so evil, and the badger is one of mine." He made a gesture like washing his face with his hands, that was utterly otter-like.

As everyone turned to look at him, he sighed. "Yes, okay, badgers are also under my jurisdiction, and they're almost as bad as the minks, the slinky bastards. That one... he's a tailor. Bespoke work. He's been doing it for three hundred years. Different fashions, I assume. I can give you the address of his shop."

A paper was produced, and Travis wrote out the address, which Rafiel passed to Cas.

"We should go to bed," he said. "All of us. And Cas, Nick, we should go and see this guy in the morning."

Rafiel woke up from a deep and dreamless sleep. He felt... he could reach in his mind and see through the eyes of lions he didn't even know. And there were things. Things he knew, things he feared. Things he could do.

It was all scary, ancient, old. It was stuff that came at him, as though he'd lived it all. Only not quite. He remembered things Enlil had done and been, but not as though he were in Enlil's mind. More like he'd watched them. Which was good, because he suspected no normal mind could share that creature's thoughts without going insane. The things he'd been and done. And to his own family. The children and... mates lying dead behind him because they'd displeased Enlil.

Now Rafiel knew. And he couldn't unknow it.

But his worst fears weren't realized. He wasn't someone else. He was still himself. Still Rafiel. He could turn off the Lion Leader stuff and just be Rafiel. Maybe a slightly more badass Rafiel.

He pushed them all out of his mind and shook his head. He'd not think of them. Not this morning. This morning he was just Rafiel.

Except for one small thing.

He reached in his mind, for a specific mind, a specific flavor and feeling.

He found himself in a mind that felt familiar, as the person blinked, and open her eyes.

KYRIE? he said.

Rafiel? She said, in her mind, with almost no surprise. Through her eyes, he could see Tom on his stomach, his face half turned, asleep. Was he drooling on the pillow?

Kyrie's mind felt amused. Hey, whether my husband drools in his sleep or not is my problem, not yours. May I help you?

It was clear he might be the boss of all lions and great cats, but Kyrie wasn't about to let him boss her.

I just wanted to check. Everything all right? Tom is still Tom?

There was the sense of laugh. Very much still Tom. Still drooling on his pillow.

He withdrew from her mind carefully. Sometimes he was forcibly reminded of the fact that lionesses held power in the prides of lions. And this was one of those times.

He walked out into the kitchen. The house was miraculously restored to before the lion invasion.

"I see everything is cleaned up," he said, as he came into the eating area where his parents and Bea were eating a leisurely breakfast of pancakes, eggs, and bacon.

Bea made him a plate.

"You slept almost twenty-four hours, son," his father said, setting down the Goldport Conspirator, probably the only paper doing well in the internet age. Mostly because it published "news" no one else would even dream of reporting. Right there in the front page there was something about dragons fighting in the parking lot of *The George* and a rogue dragon trying to set fire to the city.

Fortunately, the Conspirator had the same level of credibility as the Enquirer. In fact, their publishing anything meant that it would be disbelieved. Rafiel was almost sure the owner was a shifter and did it on purpose.

Just then his phone rang. It was Nick. "Yo, boss, how's shaking."

Rafiel swallowed a piece of bacon. "Nothing is shaking. I'm having breakfast."

Something like suppressed laugh came back. "That's good, boss. Cas and I have been up since 6 a.m. and we have been checking the antecedents of that tailor."

"Oh?" Rafiel said.

"Oh. There are funny things in his past. It seems like his identity is largely made up, for instance."

"Milagros listening in?"

"And how!"

"So, this guy doesn't seem.... On the up and up and we should investigate him."

"Yeah. I think a visit to him is definitely indicated. Soonest."

"Come to the house. If you're at the station, by the time you get here, I should be done with breakfast, and I can go out with you. I want this over with at noon. I have to go buy my fiancé a ring, and then get us wedding rings too. We're thinking a month is plentiful of an engagement."

"Hot damn, boss," Nick said. "I might as well hurry Ben to the civil registry too. Seems like everyone is getting married."

"Why not? Seems to work," Rafiel said, as he hung up.

He looked at his father across the table, "Dad, what happened to the bodies of the lions?" he asked. "The ones who died here, the one I killed. What happened to them?"

"Ah. Bea... you know having a dragon in the family is very useful, son. We put them out back and she burned them to ashes. They are in the rose garden. We wouldn't want them in the vegetable garden."

Rafiel nodded. Something bothered him about it, but he couldn't say what. He hurried through his breakfast.

Cas and Nick were waiting up front as he came out. The sun was shining. It was a beautiful day. And he still felt like something was wrong, but he couldn't explain it.

No doubt the feeling would make itself clear soon enough.

Tom looked around the diner. He'd have thought it was impossible to survive the excitement of the last few days and come back to perfect routine, but it was noon, and everything was normal. Kyrie was making the round of the tables, doing warmups. And Tom was minding the fryer. He needed to return the tux to the store this afternoon. He probably owed overdue fees. He tried to figure out how overdue the tux was, but he couldn't even figure out how long it had been since his wedding. Let's see, he'd slept twice, and–

The days were a whirlwind of things done, and things to do and–

Thinking about it, he remembered that he had the envelope from the Great Sky Dragon in the pocket of the tux.

The diner was half empty. As Kyrie came to the counter, to put down the coffee carafe, he said, "Hey, hon, can you mind the fryer? I need to figure out what the Great Sky Bastage gave us. I've never opened the envelope. I don't know what's in there."

"Probably a threat," she said, duking under the pass through in the counter and putting down the carafe. "Go. I'll make sure the fryer doesn't explode."

He kissed her the way by. "Don't let it explode on my kid," he said.

The tailor, who went by the improbable name of Henry Harrykins – Rafiel wondered what his name had been originally, then shook his head. All depended on how old he was – lived and worked in an area down by the river.

It was a neighborhood of painted ladies, but miniature ones, like someone had aimed a shrinking ray at the famous San Francisco ones.

What it actually was, was the abodes of the people who had built the great brick mansions in the North end. They'd built these ¾ point homes for themselves, little two- and three-bedroom houses, but with elaborate ginger breading around the doors and windows, and all over the graceful little porches.

They had miniature lawns, so small most people could mow the lawn with a weed whacker, and in these early days of the twenty first century, most of them were both shop and residence to various craftsmen and specialty merchants.

On either side of the tailor were a used mystery bookstore, and a specialty ice cream store. Further down there was an artisanal jewelry shop, which Rafiel should check out for rings, since they did amazing things in silver and precious stones.

The tailor shop was straight ahead. It was called "The well-set stitch" and it looked charming and old.

Rafiel bit his lip. He didn't want the man to be guilty. This was a beautiful morning. He was going ring shopping with Bea this afternoon. The air was crisp and cold, and he wondered if the skating ring downtown was still open. They still had lights at the zoo, and maybe he and Bea should go there tonight. Wait, tonight was New Years, wasn't it? He should probably take Bea out. And maybe his cousin Art could get him tickets to the symphony. They had a special concert on New Year's. Went till midnight. And heck, he was–

"Boss," Cas said.

And he followed the werewolves into the little shop.

It was set up in what used to be a tiny living room. There were massive shelves along the wall, that held bolts of cloth. There was an old, polished oak counter dividing the room. Behind it were three sewing machines, and a man who looked about fifty bending down and stitching at dark grey cloth. Finishing the hem on a pair of pants, it looked like.

He blinked at them, as they came in. His eyes were rimmed in dark circles, and he looked exhausted.

"May I help you?" he said.

"We would like to ask you where you were on the evening of the twenty seventh?" Cas said pleasantly.

The man dropped his work. He stood. He shook.

After a long time, he sighed. "I see," he said. "May I go get my overnight bag?"

Cas and Nick looked at Rafiel. Rafiel sighed. "Yes. But you should know we are shifters. So, if it occurs to you to change into a badger and run, remember we can track you." He waved at his subordinates. "These guys are werewolves. They can track you through the snow. And I will end you if you try to run."

The man shrugged like it didn't matter and nodded. "I won't be running," he said.

He shuffled into the back room, as though suddenly he'd become 20 years older.

Rafiel almost ducked under the counter to go after him, but his eyes were arrested by a black and white photo, framed in gold, on the wall.

It was a woman, in the makeup and style of the early 20th century. She was beautiful. There was a suggestion of Kyrie around her mouth.

He was wondering if this was Enlil's daughter, when he heard the shot.

Tom reached into the tux's pocked and brought out the envelope. It was paper, but it felt like silk, and it was a very deep red.

It was sealed with wax, too, golden wax with a dragon figure on it.

Tom broke the seal and slid the paper from inside the envelope. There were two pieces of paper. One was a note, letterhead with the Three Luck Dragon's header. It said, in a flowing cursive that gave the impression of having been written with a brush: The Great Sky Dragon should never be poor."

The other was a check.

Tom stared at the check. He counted the zeros. He counted them again.

Some undefinable time later, the door to the storeroom opened. Kyrie came in. "Anthony is here and has taken over the fryer. Is anything wrong."

He handed her the check. "I don't think we need to worry about late fees for the tux."

There was a corpse in the back of the tailor's shop, of course, but there was also a letter. Cas and Nick called the corpse in, called for the van.

But they put gloves on and opened the envelope. It was addressed "To the Police"

While Rafiel stood there, his mind spinning on the thing that bothered him, which was becoming clearer by the minute, Cas read the letter, aloud, in a clear voice. It told of an American GI, who happened to be a were-badger, and who had fallen in love with a beautiful girl in Paris just after World War I.

Her name was Eulalie, and she was a singer. Like many American blacks at the time, she'd gone to Paris, and he thought she was just escaping segregation and prejudice.

It wasn't till her father had tracked them down that he found what she was really evading.

And her father had killed her, rather than let her marry a badger shifter. That he was white, and willing never to return home just to marry Eulalie meant nothing. Enlil had been furious his daughter had escaped, and that she was engaged to someone not a lion.

He'd tried to force her to return. She'd resisted, and he'd killed her.

Since then, Henry had lived for only one thing: to kill Enlil.

But it was impossible. Enlil lived in New Orleans, and his Krall was well guarded. A mere badger could never get through.

Until.... Like a gift of the gods, Enlil had shown up in Henry's own Goldport.

Henry had seen him, pacing and fuming at the back of the diner. It had been the work of less than twenty minutes to go home, pick up his old saber, and an even older overcoat.

He'd poured a whole bottle of rum on the coat. The story going around was that there were shifters in the police department, and he didn't want them to smell him out.

He'd beheaded Enlil, and sat, holding Enlil's head under his overcoat, by the dumpster, until it was all done.

Rafiel listened in silence, shaking his head. So many years, devoted to vengeance.

Harry closed by saying he was tired, very tired, and he didn't feel like fighting any of it, not anymore. He didn't want to go to jail, because shifters wouldn't do well in jail. But he had a revolver.

"I think that's it, boss. Except for the head. We don't know what he's done to the head."

They did find it, eventually, though it took a lot of the forensic unit's looking.

He'd cut Enlil's head in tiny pieces with a table saw. And he'd flushed the bits.

"I guess," Cas said, looking shaken and pale, as soon as they could talk away from the forensics people, "It's a way to make sure that a shifter doesn't come back."

"Miss?" It was a little man, with greasy hair, and a somewhat scruffy raincoat.

Kyrie looked up and blinked at him. For one, she'd think given her rather obvious condition, it should be clear she was no "miss."

"Yes?"

"I ... er.... I wonder if there's a way of speaking to the owner."

"I am the owner," she said. She was still trying to work through the fact that not only was she half owner of the diner, but the check – Tom had taken it to the bank immediately – had cleared, which meant they could pay off the diner, and remodel it, and still have money left over.

"No, miss. The... other owner." He leaned forward, and whispered, even though there was no one near them. "You know, the dragon." His eye twitched a bit.

He smelled shifter, but she sensed no danger from him. And besides... What could he do? Blow himself up?

But just in case, she said, "What's under that raincoat."

The man sighed and opened the coat.

He was holding it in a kind of sling, tied around his midbody. It was perfectly round, larger than a tennis ball, glowing and white and soft.

"Oh, shit," a voice said behind Kyrie. She turned around in time to see her husband standing there, poleaxed, staring, eyes wide. "Shit, shit, shit, the pearl of heaven. I didn't want– I really thought–"

The little man in the raincoat smiled. Kyrie didn't know how, but his smile was greasier than a vat of lard dipped in oil. His eyes twitched. "My name is Loki," he said. "I stole it. I thought if I gave it to you, you could get the Queen of the North not to kill me." His eye twitched frantically. "Uh? Uh? Wha' do you say?"

Kyrie had no idea what Tom said, because he was laughing too hard to be understood. From amid it all the word "Gotterdammerung" emerged.

She had no clue what he meant, and he was laughing too hard to explain. After a while she joined him.

"Dad?" Rafiel said.

He came into the garage, where his dad was working on an old Mustang convertible. For as long as Rafiel remembered, his dad had worked on cars. Used to be he kept the family car going, but now he often bought older cars and fixed them. Sometimes he kept them, sometimes he sold them, a hobby he shared with Cas and Nick.

Right then, he had the hood of the car opened, and looked around it. "Yeah?"

Rafiel sat on the steps of the house to the garage. "I think I'm a massive hypocrite."

"I very much doubt that," his dad said. He came from the front of the car, wiping his hands to a rag. "What's eating you?"

"I think ... I mean, we killed all those lions, made them disappear.... And then Bea did the same to Jason Harcourt..."

"Yeah?" His dad looked worried.

"You see, when I was in the labyrinth, learning to defeat the.... To become the lion leader, I figured what I wanted to do was bring law to the shifters... law and justice."

"Sounds about right," his dad said. "That would be something you'd do."

"But... I mean, we went after the shifter badger." He told his dad the whole story.

When he was done, his dad was chewing his lip. "Rafiel. I don't know what you feel guilty about. It's nonsense."

"But–"

"No. The people... shifter lions we killed, we did because they attacked us. They were going to kill us. It was self-defense. Every just code of law allows for self-defense."

"But what about Henry Harrykins. Enlil killed his fiancé. It was–"

"Revenge murder," his father said, decisively. "Years later. If he'd killed Enlil to stop his fiancé, that's one thing, but he didn't. All these hears after the fact, he didn't need to kill Enlil, even if it was good he did. He couldn't have known it was good he did. So, it was murder. A crime. You did right to go after him."

Rafiel sighed. "Put like that, I'd guess you're right. It just feels... I'm sad for him."

"That you're allowed to be. He wasted his life. There was no reason to waste his life because Enlil was a murderer."

"I guess." He was silent a moment, then remembered, "Oh, yeah, Dad, are we going to have to worry about the cars of people who just disappeared?"

His dad smiled. "Nope. I... ah... called some people. They got taken away, and I doubt they exist now, except as midnight auto parts." He lifted his hands in surrender, as Rafiel opened his mouth. "Peace, boy. I know it wasn't right, but what did you expect me to do? It's not like we could take the whole thing to the police without exposing who you guys are. Look, I'm not admitting I called anyone, understand? I'll just say some car thieves are good to know, that's all. Besides, he's a cousin."

And then something else surfaced in Rafiel's mind, something else that was a piece with his dad's ruthless pragmatism.

"Dad, that gun you killed the lion with? Why did you have it? And don't tell me you never practiced shooting lions. That wasn't a first shot."

His dad sighed. He sat beside Rafiel and put an arm over his shoulder. "Look, it all turned out okay, but... When you were thirteen there was no way to know. You were about to enter adolescence, and there are stories...

"I talked to Ian McMurtrie about it, and he said he had a friend in Texas who runs a safari camp. If you remember, I went out for two weeks? That was it. And I bought the gun."

Rafiel blinked. "You'd have shot me."

"Only if you were threatening other people. I figured I brought you into this world, it was my job to take you out if needed."

Rafiel wanted to protest, but just tilted his head, "Put that way..."

"Yeah, turned out it never was needed. You were a perfectly polite lion, and you never threatened anyone that didn't need threatening." He paused a moment. "I'm proud of you son. You're a good man, and a good officer. Now go buy your young lady a ring."

Rafiel got up feeling light as a feather and looked in dismay at the oily handprint on his shirt. "I will, Dad. After I change."

The diner was half empty, midafternoon, just a few regulars having snacks, and studying or reading books.

Kyrie was in the corner booth, laughing and talking with her mother and sisters. Her dad was in a job interview. Now that the Lion Horror was dead, they were slowly processing what it all meant. One thing they'd realized was that they could work wherever they pleased, he'd realized that he might wish to leave the past behind and settle elsewhere.

And they kind of liked the idea of being near their first grandchild.

So, he'd talked to Tedd Robertson, and he had an interview at CUG for a physics teaching position.

Tom startled as the bell rang with the door opening, but it was only his dad, coming in with a big grin.

"Tom," he said, climbing on a seat. "Will you be my best man?"

"I.... what?"

"I'm marrying Sandra. I never thought I'd marry again, but she is just what I need, and she doesn't think I'm old at all, and I think–"

Tom summoned the memory of the Chinese girl at the wedding. "Dad? How old is Sandra?"

"Uh? Twenty, I think?"

"Dad, she's younger than me. People will talk."

"No, they won't. Her mom is fine with it, and her dad is the Great Sky er... Bastard. And he's fine with it too."

Tom bit his tongue hard. He suspected her mom was centuries old, and the bastard... yeah, a thirty-year difference would seem like nothing to them. And besides, what did Tom care? A ridiculously young stepmother was the least of his problems.

He had a sense of something dark and terrible heading for all of them. Orvan was suspiciously absent. And Rod, when he'd been here a few minutes ago had said something about the Others, the star beings...

In the middle of this his dad's voice broke in saying, distinctly "All hot."

"What?" Tom asked, afraid his dad was talking about his new girlfriend.

"You know, I said I'd like an all hot," Edward said, setting the menu aside on the counter. "A baked potato with everything on it."

"Oh." Tom said. "Oh, that we can manage."